This Time Will Be Different

Veilside, 1

Rachel E. Wilder

CONTENTS

Author's Note

This Time Will be Different is a novel that deals with serious themes which may be triggering for some readers. Please heed the content warnings, which can be found ahead of the acknowledgements.

Generative AI was not used at any point in the creation, illustration, or promotion of this novel. The author does not grant permission for anyone to upload this manuscript, or any related materials, into Large Language Models.

Here is a small fact — you are going to die.

The Book Thief, Markus Zusack

THINGS YOU MISS

When I deplane at JFK, the air has that damp-armpit spoiled-cheese summer smell that immediately takes me back to my childhood, to days at camp, to roasting under boiling summer skies as we kicked soccer balls into the torn nets of our goals. I lower my mask and breathe it in briefly before a stewardess politely but firmly tells me to get moving. Our flight was one of the worst I've ever taken—a baby screamed nearly the whole eight hours, someone stunk up the bathroom nearest to my seat, and we had merciless turbulence—but I wish I could get back on the plane. Anything to delay the inevitable.

I will myself to be strong and follow the line of people deeper into the airport, towards baggage.

The corridors are crowded with spirits, rushing for flights they never made it off of, searching for loved ones that never came for them, or watching people like me go by boredly. A particularly corporeal one, leaning against a people mover's rail, catches my gaze and offers a wave. I nod once, tersely.

At customs, I give the officer the wrong passport–both are navy, and I haven't slept–and he seems more amused than anything, so I count it as a success. He welcomes me back home and tells me to enjoy my stay.

More ghosts drape themselves around the baggage claim, one even riding idly on a big pink Samsonite suitcase. The little girl, her edges and form quite fuzzy, smiles. With the sheer amount of people–living and dead–coming through here each day, there must be others with the sight. Do the spirits feel crowded, I wonder, not for the first time, or lonely? They must.

My suitcases are decidedly boring, black and identifiable only by the pink bandanna tied around one of the handles. Two suitcases, a carry on, a backpack; they are all that's left of the life I just left behind.

But a promise is a promise.

Charlie, my childhood best friend, waits just outside security. I'm half expecting the gangly, skinny teenager I last saw, but he's broader, he's clearly been working out, and he has an eyebrow piercing with a bright green ball. Even his outfit is too formal for him, the khakis and button-up. I only see bits of his old self in the sign he holds, which has my name in bright glittery paint with emoji stickers all around it.

I relax just the slightest. He catches my eye and breaks into the widest grin. And when he hugs me around the bags, he still smells the same; Old Spice and cherry vape and laundry.

"I missed you *so* much, Aaron," he says, plunking his chin against my shoulder. "Welcome back to the shitshow. How was the trip?"

"Sucked," I tell him.

He pulls away and appraises me. Unlike him, I haven't changed so much. I'm no longer so gaunt, at least. "There's a Dunkin. Let's refuel. Need some help?"

"Please." We walk for a few beats, and neither of us says much; he whistles, to fill the silence, drawing the stares of passersby.

I shove the hair out of my face. "...You know it's hard to find coffee in Europe? Like, drip coffee?" I start.

He tugs at his collar. "Really?"

"It's all espresso. And Dunkin makes a pretty bad Americano."

He checks his phone. "Glad to know they're consistent even overseas."

Despite the awkwardness, he still remembers how I take my coffee, and won't let me pay even though *he* was the one who had driven down here just to get my sorry ass. After my long night, the Dunkin hits like fucking ichor.

I gesture at his outfit. "Since when have you started dressing like you summer in the Vineyard?"

He wrings his hands, a blush rising in his tan cheeks. "I've been seeing this guy," he admits. "He wanted me to meet his parents for brunch, this morning of course, and it ended up being like, easier just to get here from there."

A spirit in what I think is 80s clothing throws a glare over his shoulder as he passes by.

My brows pull up. "Wow! You never mentioned him."

Charlie's lips twitch into a smile. "He's not online, and we're keeping it sort of... lowkey, you know. It's just kind of started."

And yet he was meeting the parents. "How did it go? You have to tell me all about him."

As he speaks, his eyes fill with light. "His name is Mike. He's in the class I TA, but don't worry, he's our age."

"You... TA a class?"

Charlie's fidgety again. "It's a requirement for my grad degree."

My smile, behind my mask, freezes. "I didn't know, um, that you were in a grad program."

He scratches the back of his neck. "Well, surprise!"

"You could have perhaps shared some of this in the Discord," I say, trying to come off as teasing. "I'm happy for you. Really."

Talking about the guy gets us to his car–which turns out to have once been mine. "How have you kept this thing on the road?" I ask.

My beloved mid-aughts navy Subaru always had things going wrong right before I left. I sold it to Charlie for like $200 because he wouldn't just let me give it to him. It needed a transmission, tires, brakes, and the AC notoriously did not work. But he never had his own car before.

I can see touches of him here too; the Nick Cage air freshener, the tacky fuzzy steering wheel cover, and the car isn't exactly the cleanest, like how I kept it.

"Well, dude, it wasn't exactly easy," he says. "Mike knows a guy. Fixed it right up. I should have a few years left on it, anyway. I call it Theseus, because almost everything has been replaced twice."

Making me doubt the veracity of "it's kind of new." Why lie?

He swallows. "You, uh, don't want it back, right?"

"No, it's yours now."

It still feels weird to climb into the passenger seat, which is all lumpy. He pulls a vape from the cupholder and takes a long hit.

It will take two hours to get to my father's house from here. I didn't think I would have to find ways to fill the silence.

Charlie navigates through some traffic before speaking further. "So... how's your dad?"

My heart squeezes hard in my chest. "Adjusting okay enough. He's in a rehab facility now. I'm going to see him later today with my sister."

That was the call I wasn't exactly wanting to receive, at four in the morning drunk off my roommate's homemade mead, while my other roommate performed her (very bad) first draft of a new one-woman show. Nobody ever *called* from a US number with good news. Not directly. I hadn't exactly been prepared to authorize an emergency bypass; I hadn't even been aware that he'd made me his healthcare proxy. Nor was it great hearing about the stroke he suffered immediately post-surgery. They'd been able to catch it quick enough to mitigate the *worst* of the damage, but he probably won't be able to work again.

I knew it took guts to ask me to come back–my sister is still a kid, and he'll need help navigating this new part of his life. He was even glib about it, when I spoke to him on the phone. ("Just as I said I was going to quit smoking.")

Charlie nods. "Well. Tell him speedy recovery, and all that."

"Will do."

We're able to get into more of a conversational groove after that. Charlie's decided to become a mental health counselor, of all things, and now he works at a halfway house for recovering addicts. Considering when I saw him last he wanted to design video games, I have to ask what made him make the leap.

He keeps his eyes firmly on the road. "It's just that... after all that... after all that happened to *you*... and then Phoebe struggled with drinking for a long time... and I've always wanted to help people, you know. I took an intro to psychology in college, and it just felt right."

I have been back in the States for fewer than two hours and already Dmitri has been mentioned. I don't know what I expected. "...I'm glad you found a calling."

He clears his throat. "You transferring out here, then? To finish up?"

"Oh, I finished my degree. University's only three years over there."

"Oh. Right."

My heart still beats acidly in my ears, and my smartwatch, which I am obliged to wear given my tattered vascular system, alerts me to the increase. I turn my wrist so he can't see.

"...So what are you gonna do now?" he asks. "You staying? Going back?"

"I... I really don't know." I try to smile. "It's been like an hour, Charlie."

"Right. Sorry." He forces a laugh. "Well, we're glad to have you while you're around, at least. It'll be like getting the band back together."

At long last, my childhood home reveals itself to us; a very average blue two-storey on a sliver of property in the middle of Hyde Park. It was once a much smaller home that Dad and my other parent Matt renovated shortly after Matt got pregnant with my younger sister Jenna, and if you look at certain joists you can see the bones of that place. A car I don't recognize–another Subaru, this an old red hatchback–sits parked outside the closed garage; maybe Jenna has gotten one, but I think she would have said so.

And the yard is a mess; the grass long, scraggly, the bushes out front clearly not having been pruned down last winter. Mold has slowly crawled up the vinyl siding. The most glaring omission is the absence on the porch, where Dad and I spent too many hours smoking and shooting the shit.

Charlie helps me bring my bags up to the door and squeezes me tight. "You have a new number yet?"

"...It's on the to-do list." Along with getting the cheapest health insurance I can. No more NHS, after all. I know myself well enough to know that going off meds now would be a terrible idea.

"I'll Discord you, then," he says. "Let me know how it goes this afternoon."

Something stops me from asking him in for another coffee–mostly because I have no idea what our pantry looks like. "Thanks again. I owe you one."

"After how many rides you used to give me, I think we're even," he says. "See you around." He salutes, gets back in the car, and rumbles away.

It occurs to me just a second after he leaves that I don't have a key anymore–I left it behind–and that perhaps nobody would be home. And of course the spare we used to hide in a fake rock by the steps is missing. I go over to the front window that always manages to creep open a bit, fumble the screen off, stick my fingers under the jam and push. It moves with a nasty and very loud *creak* and I look around quickly, hoping none of the neighbors call the cops on me for breaking into my own house. I see a spirit, a young boy, watching idly from the next driveway. He's new. I didn't see him before.

I wrench the window open wide enough to squeeze my body through and land, crumpled and dusty and swearing, into our old dining room.

The air in here smells stale; I don't think the central AC is on. The old faux-mahogany table and the china cabinet with some grandmother's dishes none of us ever use are still there, and they are dusty, but in a normal just-haven't-gotten-to-it-yet way. I cross to the left, to the kitchen with its bright cherry cabinets and stainless steel appliances, the recessed lighting under the cabinets left on for the wary snacker, and pour myself a cup of tap water. There's a pot soaking with something very burnt at the bottom, and in the dish drain, a few bowls and cups and plates, which is strange only because we have a dishwasher.

I haven't even been able to bring my luggage in yet when I hear the yowling, throaty cat gurgle, and the soft tinkle of a bell. A scraggly, scrawny tabby very carefully goes down the stairs, howling all the while. I know this cat. We do not have a cat.

Seconds later, he's at the top of the stairs, holding a baseball bat.

My face crinkles with surprise. "...Matt?" I ask. "What are you doing here?"

My parents famously did not have an easy divorce. Matt abruptly transitioned nearly ten years ago, which would have been fine except he *also* decided he had enough of us and left with this same cat in the middle of the night, dropping a relatively prosperous career as a CPA to become a long-distance trucker. Only time and a judicious amount of therapy made me see it with a little more clarity, and it absolutely gutted Dad.

I haven't seen him, physically, since. He's been more regularly in touch since I almost died a few years ago, but "regularly in touch" meant a monthly email. His shorn auburn hair is the same as my sister's, with my eyes and even the same coppery scruff I get. The scatter of freckles across his nose, something Jenna and I have avoided, reminds me too loudly of being cradled in his arms as a small child.

"Your father asked me," he says. "I'm between places, and he needed someone to look after the house before you got here, and your sister." He shrugs, wringing his hand around the handle of the bat. "My old name is still on some of the accounts. He wanted me around..."

"In case he bit it," I finish.

That's just like my father. The anxiety he so generously gave me made him a super over-preparer. He has folders with lists of steps to take for very specific situations, like a hurricane, or martial law or, well, him dropping dead. That's how I found out I was eligible for dual citizenship through Gran and Grandad; the passport was an interesting relic until the moment it became my escape key. (*In case of a government coup or overthrow* that emerged soon after January 6.)

Matt sets the bat down and comes down the stairs. At least the cat has stopped screaming, and now she's weaving happily between my legs. I guess she remembers my smell or something.

"You look good," he says. "Spitting image of him. Jesus."

I have heard this so much it no longer has any impact. Same curly dark brown hair, same weedy, rail-thin Scottish stock. But Dad wears his hair brutally short and I like it long, and I got Matt's gray, far apart eyes while his are the shade of a coffee stain. Matt reaches forward to touch me, but decides against it.

"Um, thanks. Where's Jenna?"

"Still at school?" he says, raising an eyebrow. "She'll be back around three."

"Ah. Right. I forgot that was a thing." Exhaustion is starting to set in. I have no idea how I'll make it through to dusk. Chronic insomnia does not account for jet lag. "I should get—my stuff, and is there an extra key—"

"Probably where Alan keeps all the copies," he says. "I'll go look." And he so *casually* goes into my father's office off the garage.

I bring in the bags and hike them, one by one, upstairs to my old room.

Most of the things I remember have been taken down and packed away, leaving blots on the blue walls slightly darker than the paint around it. The double-bed, below a pair of windows, is naked, a folded set of sheets set on top waiting for me. And to the right, my L-shaped drawing desk, barren of computers or supplies or drawings, with the whiteboard-corkboard, blank, above it. I trace my fingers against it, lightly. There was a point when artistry consumed me. I still draw, still paint, in the same way that anyone needs medication; but I miss the desire I used to feel. Before... well.

I go to open the closet on the left, and my eyes catch the reddish flecks near the armoire.

I ease onto my knees and touch the scar on my right palm. I've subjected the stains to any remedy I could think of, bleaching the beige carpet around it to a bone-white but leaving traces of blood behind, still.

I force myself to my feet, my vision blackening around the edges for a minute, and go across the hall to the guest room. That would be fine enough for me, except Matt's shit is *everywhere*. A few dusty boxes surround the unmade bed, and to the right by the window is an open suitcase spilling his clothes. He must be going through his old stuff.

I resign myself to sleep on the couch if the whispers get too loud. Back in my tomb, I plant one of my suitcases firmly on the stain and start unpacking, because what I really need right now is a shower and then a smoke.

The bathroom I used to share with Jenna is just how I left it, except now there's definitely more face products in the clear bins above the toilet. Makeup? Since when has my eternal jock sister been into *makeup?* I pick up the lipstick sitting on top. I wish I could forget that I know the brands. Even the color–cherry blossom–reminds me too much of Amanda, another person left behind.

I lean against the sink, feeling the dismal *thud* of my heart in my ears. It's not a matter of *I can't do this,* but I *have* to do this and I feel choked. I breathe slowly and catch my bloodshot, jetlagged gaze before splashing some water on my face.Something red flashes at the corner of my eye.

"Hi," says the spirit.

I jolt up and crack my head against the bottom of the medicine cabinet. It's just the little boy from before, his head sticking out of the shower wall.

"Did I scare you real good?" he asks. "I've been practicing." He laughs.

I exhale and remind myself this is a dead child. "You did, alright," I say. "Though I gotta say, bud, it's kinda rude to barge in on people in the bathroom."

He drifts all the way out and stands in the middle of the bathtub. Seeing him closer, I recognize him as the Grahams' boy, Teddy. Dad always thought it was tacky they named their kid after a snack food.

He must be a young spirit, to still be able to talk.

"Do you remember me?" I ask him. "I'm your neighbor."

"Mommy called you a headcase," he says helpfully.

I rub the back of my head where I whacked it. "I'm mostly better now. Is your... is your mother looking for you?"

He shakes his head. "She can't see me."

Despite former irritation, a shiver rolls over me. What must it be like to wake up dead in your childhood home, wanting nothing more than to love the family that still lives there, and yet they can't even see you. He probably saw them grieving him. "...I'm sorry."

"I'm happy to see you, though. Will you play with me?"

"Maybe later, Teddy. I have to go see my dad. He's sick."

He nods somberly. "I saw the ambulance."

"I have to get ready now. I'll see you later, okay?"

He smiles and phases through the window. I watch him somersault as he drifts down to the ground. I'll have to ask Jenna what happened to him.

When I'm through with my shower, my blood pressure irritated from the warm water, the whole house smells like garlic. I find Matt hunched over a pot of something, stirring. "I hope you're hungry," he says. "I made garlic bread, and the soup is almost hot enough." A couple of cans of Campbell's tomato soup lay artfully propped up against each other.

I realize I'm starving, and a second later actually feel faint. The last thing I ate was the shitty pain au chocolat that was our "breakfast" on the plane, and before that, not much else. I lurch over to the kitchen table, trying not to pass out.

Matt serves the soup in chipped blue bowls and brings over the bread on a plate. "You alright there?"

I force my eyes up. "I'm just fi–"

Chronic illness, at least mine, anyway, tends to have impeccably comedic timing.

I come to what must be seconds later. He's waving my face with a paper plate, his other arm under me. I am much too close to him. Somehow he, too, smells the same, despite the more masculine products he's been using. Some lizard part of my brain identifies him as *mom.*

I sit up and try to put some space between us.

"Easy. You sick?" he asks. "So much shit on those planes. I hope you wore a mask–"

"It's nothing contagious," I assure him, but my voice sounds wobbly and I'm also not sure I won't throw up. "Just this... thing I have. POTS."

"...Is that a party drug?"

"Postural Orthostatic Tachycardia Syndrome," I say, hauling myself up to a chair. "My blood doesn't work right." An oversimplification at best.

He whistles. "How long have you been dealing with *that?*"

"Since whenever the last time I had fucking COVID." COVID, that fever dream, that emperor of all. Even the isolation was bearable, at least, until the [accident] and I started seeing more and more and more spirits as they sickened and died. And I couldn't help any of them.

That was when people started actually talking about what it meant to see spirits, when the shame, the stigma, became more obvious, though it's possible I never noticed when I was still blind to them.

There's so much earnestness in his eyes when he asks, "is there anything I can do?"

Like he's the first person I'd go to for help. "Not particularly. Let's just eat."

I feel a little better once there's some soup in my belly. Once again, the minutes stretch on long. I can only imagine how Jenna's felt these past few weeks. She's deaf; does Matt even remember ASL to communicate with her? Has she simply been too overwhelmed to tell me about him being here?

He taps his fingertips against the table. "How was Scotland?"

There's so much I miss already: my roommates, my friends, the odd hookup, the evenings spent at the pub and at the university's studios and in dank, smoky student housing talking about ideas we didn't fully understand, convinced we would take the world by storm. The fact of the matter is that since we've all finished our degrees, we would've parted ways anyway as people got jobs and moved. We become footnotes in each other's lives. "I liked it there."

This place, this house, feels too *much* like home.

"What did you study?"

"Digital media management."

"Not art?"

"It wasn't practical, and that university didn't have a very strong program, anyway."

"Not practical." He scoffs a little. "Your father really got to you."

A headache blooms behind my eyes. "He wanted me set up for success. I still draw."

"Don't let *anyone* talk you into giving that up."

Not like I would. My next swallow is bitter. "Why should I take advice from you?"

He turns red, then pale. "No. That's fair."

Before things can escalate further, the familiar screech of bus brakes, a sound so baked into my mind I barely register it, cuts through the neighborhood. Seconds later, Jenna opens the door.

In my mind she is perpetually twelve, lithe and strong. Jenna always knows who she is and what she wants out of life. How she avoided the battleaxe of our parents' mental illnesses, I have no idea. I imagine her always in her soccer uniform, one knee bruised and bloody, her auburn hair smoothed back into a braid at the top of her skull.

Of course I've seen her face in photos since, and whenever she can steal time to videochat, but I'm still somehow taken aback by the very girly woman who just came through the door.

My suspicions of tension are confirmed when she grimaces at Matt, but she sees me, and just like Charlie, breaks out into a smile. Her teeth, newly sans braces, are movie perfect.

I stand just in time for her to pull me into her arms and feel the crush of her hug. She's tried to curl her hair; it hangs wavy and lank against her blouse. Jenna was probably the hardest thing for me to leave behind.

She pulls away and blinks the mist out of her eyes. "Hey, stranger," she says.

"Hey. How are you holding up?" The signs, at least, came easily.

She shakes her head once.

"I came as quickly as I could."

"I know." She clears her throat and adds, in English, "I'll put my stuff away, and then we can head out." She turns away before she can lipread Matt's response and retreats upstairs.

THE PROXIES

Wee have to take Dad's car, a gold Honda SUV that's seen better days, to the facility. Matt declines going with us even though I didn't ask. By then it's been long enough for me to deeply need a smoke, but Jenna's a bit morals police when it comes to smoking. Not to mention, the habit played a huge role in our father's current situation, so stopping to buy cigarettes would be a pretty dick move. So I resign myself to suffer in silence, but the fact that the car smells like it–as well as peppermint and paper–is not helping.

"How has it *really* been?" I ask her, struggling to sign one handedly.

"Ugh, horrible," she says in English. "He keeps wanting to *clear the air* with me. Like I'm just going to sit down for family bonding time."

"Maybe he really wants to make amends." That's generous of me.

"*Or* he wants access to his and dad's money."

I don't want to tell her that there's not much of that money left. Matt had been a shrewd investor, sure, which was why we lived a relatively comfortable middle-class life even though Dad worked mostly pro-bono. Our college funds–which could only really cover full tuition and board at a SUNY–were really all that was left outside of life insurance policies, and mine was already spent on all the hospital and outpatient work when I was losing my mind three years ago. Part of the reason I ended up abroad: university is *much* cheaper overseas. Would you rather pay £9,000 per year or over $25,000? "Sounds like he has prints on at least some of the accounts. He technically was the one that earned it."

She rolls her eyes and looks out the window. "He wants to come to my graduation. Can you believe it?"

At this rate, I'll be the only family member in attendance. That's only a week from now. "No, that is definitely taking it too far."

"So I've mostly been pretending it's hard to understand him," she says, "and lying about how much homework I have. Which is really none."

"It *is* weird to me that Dad *wanted* him here."

"He's not exactly in his right mind," Jenna points out. "He... he doesn't look good. I just want you to be prepared."

My heart skips, causing my watch to alert me. "I thought the prognosis was good?"

"It *is*, but..." She sighs, scrubbing hard at the back of her neck. "He looks old and sick. Because he is."

At least I don't have very long to stew in the dread. The rehab is some half hour away in Poughkeepsie, and while it seems outdated, the facilities are nice enough, though deeply reminiscent of a cheap hotel with the sad industrial grade carpeting and ugly wall sconces. Here and there are spirits, too; worn tired women and men with walkers and canes and casts who barely look up at me. I even see a doctor spirit trying to help one of them. The doctor offers me a tired smile.

We're given nametags and led down to his room.

The orderly knocks once. "Alan, your kids are here to see you."

I'm not sure what I'm expecting–him wasting away in a hospital bed with all the wires and tubes–but he's dressed normally, and is sitting in a reclining chair by the room's window, which overlooks a courtyard. My eyes catch the walker near the bed, the cane perched near where he's sitting. A cup of coffee sits, still steaming, on a small table next to his chair.

He really does look like crap. Clean, put together, but with that drawn, pinched and puffy look of extreme and sudden illness. New grays have sprouted in his hair. And of course, the drooping of the left side of his face, made more noticeable when he tries to smile at me. "Glad you made it in." His speech is slurred, but understandable.

"Hey, Dad." I feel rooted to the ground. The carpet drags at me as I go over and lean down to hug him; his left hand trembles when he puts his arms around me. "How are you feeling?"

"Oh, just dandy," he says. "I think the worst part of it is the nicotine withdrawal. They gave me a patch, but still..."

I raise an eyebrow. "Worse than having your chest cracked open?"

He shrugs, lopsided. "I am still pretty doped up. Right, Jenna?"

She nods and perches on the foot of the bed, swinging her feet idly.

I turn my head just slightly so she can't see my lips. "I wish I could have come sooner."

"You wouldn't have missed much," he tells me. "It would've done you no good to hold bedside vigil." He struggles with the last syllable. "Finishing your education was more important."

"I did," I whisper. "Like I promised."

Another half smile. He gestures with his good hand at the other chair in the room, one of those plastic uncomfortable ones. "Sit."

I put the chair halfway between him and Jenna, so I can interpret the conversation. "What have the doctors been saying?"

He frowns, squinting, his eyes distant. "It, uh, it's still not very clear to me," he says. "I can't really remember–"

"He'll be able to live a mostly normal life, just with some help," Jenna says. "The important thing is to finish physical therapy, then find a good cardiologist and neurologist. And to take things *easy*. No drinking. No drugs. No partying."

"Well, that foils my plans," he deadpans. "They won't even let me talk to our firm's paralegal about transitioning my caseload–"

"She's smart, I'm sure she can figure it out," Jenna says. "You're supposed to be resting."

"And *I am so bored*." He pulls the blanket draped on his lap up a little. Seeing how difficult the simple movement is makes me flinch. At least he's mentally with it. At least he's still Dad. "Seriously, Aaron, I need you to go to the library. Their reading material is abysmal, and do you really expect me to watch cable?"

My lips pull up. "Sure. Whatever you want."

He nods to my sister. "Jenna, can you go get us some coffees? My wallet's in the first dresser drawer."

It is, blatantly, a ploy for him to speak to me privately. She stares at the still-full coffee on the table for a moment, but ultimately obeys.

"How are you really?" I ask.

He looks down. "Everything's so... difficult. And I'm in quite a lot of pain, still." He tries to shut his book, but it flops off his lap. I pick it up, keeping my face neutral, but I can feel how hot my cheeks are. "I'm probably not going to be able to work. They've already sent a social worker to talk to me about applying for disability or retiring."

"Well, one thing at a time." I bite my lip. "Why is *Matt* at our house?"

"Because there are affairs to settle."

"Jenna thinks he's after money."

He folds his good hand over the shaky one. "Well, he's on the mortgage, for one, so yes, he is entitled to half of whatever the house sells for. His divorce lawyer made sure of that. It was one of my concessions to keep full custody of you two."

My stomach flops. "You're going to sell the house?"

"My mind might be swiss cheese right now, but I've had so much time to *think*." He tries to spread his hands. "You've been out of the house, and Jenna will be soon. It makes the most sense to downsize, especially because I can't maintain a property anymore. I'm... I'm going to need your help, Aaron. To go through everything, clean it up, help me with the paperwork. I've already asked too much of your sister and I don't fully trust Matt." He clears his throat. "And of course, I'm sure whatever portion ends up with you will be helpful."

"But you're not *dead*, or dying–"

"I don't have much longer, Aaron. Ten years or so. Cardiac functioning never returns once you lose it."

I can't stop the ragged little noise that leaves me.

"You and Jenna are on almost all the accounts. I just need you to sign some papers–"

"Why didn't you tell me I'm your proxy?"

At this, his brows furrow in confusion.

"They called me. When you had the heart attack. To authorize surgery." My chest aches. "Because the prognosis didn't seem good and they needed someone to consent for you."

He squints, again. "Sweetheart, correct me if I'm wrong, but I *do* remember placing the papers before you. You signed them yourself. It was just a formality when I was having my will prepared. I didn't..." He coughs, and winces as it pulls at his broken bones. "I didn't think it would come into play so soon."

"I don't... remember that." There's just a gap there, an itch, in my memory.

"Well, you know, you were getting all ready to leave the country. I get there were other things on your mind." He pauses, his right hand reaching for a nonexistent pen. "You have power of attorney. Whether or not Jenna wants a role when she turns eighteen is up to the two of you."

I lean against my knees and pull my hands through my hair.

"I know this is a lot to put on you, especially since you just graduated," he says, gently.

My eyes are burning. The pain I haven't let myself feel is crushing in. "It just makes it feel like you're *dying*."

"Well, I am. Not today, but not so very long from now. They told me I could pursue a transplant." He pauses here, lost for a minute finding the next sentence. "I don't want to. People need it more than me."

"Just... stop, okay? Don't you deserve it too?" I ask, alarmed at the emotion in my voice even though I've transcended pain into numbness. The bliss of shock is familiar to me.

"Aaron," he says softly. "I love you and your sister very much. These are my wishes."

I refuse to cry, but my ribs shudder anyway under the strain.

"I'm going to be just fine," he says softly. "Once all these pieces are cleaned up, it'll be easier. You can go pursue–whatever you want to pursue."

Of course I can't. So many conversations we haven't had, so many things I haven't let go–

"I know you were building a life there. I won't keep you."

A tear squeezes out of my eye anyway. I wipe at it, stubbornly.

"And none of this is happening today," he says. "*You* tell me how you've been, Aaron. Things have been so muddled since the surgery, I don't even know what you've been up to."

"Well, this, mostly."

"I wish we could've been there. Your graduation, I mean."

University finishes in June–just a few days ago–, but the ceremonies are usually later in July. I shake my head. "None of my friends were going anyway. They don't want to support the establishment, and all that."

He laughs at this. "More power to them."

Jenna returns from her overlong coffee break bearing a flimsy tray of some of the worst coffee I've ever tasted. Dad tries to lighten the mood, but I can tell he's exhausted now. After a while, one of the orderlies comes and kicks us out because he has an appointment with the PT. He seems even worse when he stands–his left leg can barely bear weight, and he has to shuffle to walk.

My concern must be shown on my face.

"I'm only getting better," he tells me.

WHINE AND SPIRITS

It must be the jet lag that lets me sleep as well as I do. When I wake up, I'm disoriented because my bed is too big and facing the wrong direction, and I remember I'm not in the shitty flat on Chambers Street, I'm home. My head is positively pounding from the withdrawal at this point.

Jenna's already off to school by the time I drag myself out of bed, and Matt's off doing God-knows-what. I go into Dad's office, sure he must have some laying around, even if I hate Marlboros. It's not like he can have them anyway. I find a mostly full pack in the top desk drawer with a lighter. Matt or Jenna must've come in to clean; the curtains are open, bringing light into the small, dark space. Case folders sit neatly on the top of the desk, with one of those calendar things under it all, showing his previously-packed schedule. A cardigan is draped across the back of the office chair.

I know where the will is, where all the papers are, but I can't bring myself to go through the file cabinets.

What I do instead is go outside and smoke, but my headache only eases marginally. I need to get on some insurance today; I only have a few weeks of meds from back home. I figure I'll do that *after* breakfast, and when I see how barren the pantry and fridge are, that becomes *after* grocery shopping.

My headache itches as I wander the aisles, spirits draped restlessly about the store, trying to pick up products. One asks me if I can reach the top shelf for her for an item I know no longer exists. The older spirits are just sad, thin imitations of what was once alive, looping the same activities endlessly. I tell her they're out of stock. She attempts to ask the next person who comes near, but they can't see her. Her form flickers and waffles in the fluorescent lighting, a soft pink-violet.

The pain sharpens to a spike behind my eye. Migraines aren't normally one of my symptoms, but nothing about POTS would surprise me anymore, especially given all the travel and the stress. It pulses as I try to reach for a jar of pasta sauce, and I grip my head.

"You alright, man?" some college kid, blond and burly in his sweats, asks me.

"Headache. I'm fine," I say.

"Horseshit," the spirit says.

Woodenly, I turn. My blood has become ice, and my watch cautions me to perhaps sit down.

I see him. There, between the aisles, his squat, boxy frame, his bright red dyed hair, that square, boyish face marred and half blown off.

"Bateson," he says. "Been a minute."

"You sure you're good, dude?" the jock asks. "You look like you've seen a... *oh.*"

I'm normally good at hiding that I can see them. *Any other* spirit wouldn't bother me.

Of course. *Of course.*

The ice pick behind my eye jabs once, twice, and suddenly my body is a confusing thing to navigate. I crumple, giving way to a sort of not-hereness, and the pressure all around me increases as the boy comes forward.

"Hey!" the frat dude cries. "Someone call for help!"

The boy crouches over me, smiles, a droplet of blood dripping from his eye socket onto my face. "You've kept me waiting long enough."

I want to scream, try to scream, but the next thing I'm aware of is that I'm on my side, I've pissed myself, my mouth is full of bile, and an employee is next to me assuring me they've sent for help. The frat boy holds my hand.

"What the *fuck*," I manage. I try to look for the spirit, but the pain in my head has reached critical mass.

"We think you had a seizure," the employee says. "Stay calm. Is there someone I can call for you?"

"You can't... take me to the hospital." I'm soaked in sweat, and it's sticky against the linoleum floor. "I don't have–insurance, I can't–"

"I'm afraid it's store policy. Can I call someone for you?"

I can't think straight. The pain is permeating my muscles, too. "My... my dad..."

"Okay. Okay, we'll call your dad. Can you tell me the number?"

Some part of me that's perpetually five recites the house's landline number. Nobody's even home to answer it, but I can't even try to think of any other number, not Jenna's not Charlie's not even Matt's, because I'm crumpled into what must be another seizure.

Until I get to the hospital, there are only bits I'm aware of. I don't know if I'm having more seizures, or if I just keep fainting, but always the pain worsens, and I tell them, I try to tell them. The frat guy must've outed me because I hear one EMT? Nurse? Whisper "Ghosts." "I'll tell them we need Leah."

I feel like I'm burning, like I'm on fire. The tranquilizer they give me keeps me from moving so much but doesn't touch the razor edges in my stomach, my head. There's a needle in my hand and I can only catch things in gasps.

"Aaron?" A voice says. A pretty middle-aged blonde woman in scrubs comes into my room. I actually have a room, not just one of the bays. Having the sight isn't contagious. "I'm Leah. I'm a medium."

Her face won't come into focus.

"I can help you, okay? I know it hurts. I know it's scary." She has something in her hand–a bottle with a dropper, not unlike those for essential oils. "Wow, your pressure is high. No wonder you got sick. How have you been managing?"

"Managing?" I force out.

"Are you seeing anyone? For your condition?"

"My–my psych–"

She shakes her head. "A spiritual professional."

"I don't need a–"

"It's alright. You're safe here." She holds up the bottle. "This will help. I'm going to apply it to your wrists, okay?"

"I don't *need* any woo-woo bullshit–" She puts on a glove and takes some glittery looking stuff into her palm.

She spreads it gently against my pulseline, and I have half a second to notice that it smells like springtime before the pain turns in on itself and dispels. It's such a heavy, sudden release, so dizzying, almost orgasmic. I never noticed that the absence of pain could be pleasure.

"What did you do to me?" I ask. I feel lightweight, like I've been carrying this massive burden and only just set it down.

"I evened your pressure," she says. "Nobody told you how?"

I shake my head. "I don't... talk about it."

"Probably for the best." She sets the bottle down on my tray table. "You need to do it periodically. Otherwise... well. This happens."

"So it's like a prescription," I say. "Like a cream?"

She turns pink. "I can't prescribe it, legally, because the FDA won't touch us with a ten foot pole. But I can tell you where to find more."

"Will it stop me seeing them?"

"It does temporarily in some people. But it always comes back. Again, nobody will do the research."

The meds are making me sleepy. I have so much I need to ask her. I've never talked to another one that I know is like me.

"How long have you had the sight?" she asks.

"Four-four years."

"Four *years?*" Her eyes widen. "How have you made it so far?"

"Don't know."

"I am so glad you were brought in, then. Here... I'll leave my card and the medicine under this cup, okay? Get in touch with me..."

I'm drifting, unable to fight the pull of the meds.

"And for the love of God, *please* don't let this go."

***

I wake, disoriented and starving, when it's dark out. The gown they changed me into is sticky with sweat, and my muscles ache fiercely, but at least the headache is gone. I wonder if it's all a dream, at least until my eyes catch the upside-down cup on my tray table.

I pull the table closer to me. The medicine is still there, and the medium's card. There's no list of ingredients on this bottle, nothing other than "CREAM TONER" in a generic font. I open the bottle, smell again that springtime, briefly feel that wave of relief.

It is wholly possible that was a dream. How had a few dabs of some oil "fixed" me? It probably hasn't, though I do feel much better, at least until I start crunching the numbers as to how much this will cost me.

A doctor comes and doesn't meet my eyes the whole time he speaks to me. They want to do a battery of tests to find the cause of the seizure. I try to tell him I am unemployed and uninsured so there is no way I'm consenting to any of this. He says something vague about finding a case manager to talk to me about "financial options."

I really, *really* miss the NHS right about now.

Shortly after the doctor leaves, Matt walks into my room and sits in the bedside chair without asking. "How are you feeling?"

"Why are you here?" I ask.

"The hospital called the house. I came as soon as I got the message. I know you meant Alan, but..." He shrugs. "You probably shouldn't be alone right now anyway. They said you had cluster seizures."

"Yeah, allegedly. I have no idea why." I want to believe that it was just a dream, that what Leah said is new wave bullshit. "I can't–afford the tests. I got off Dad's insurance when I left the country."

"I got it," he says. "Don't worry. You should get it checked out."

"I can't let you pay my bills."

"And you can? You haven't even had a chance to *think* about looking for work." He squares his shoulders. "Let me do this for you. I owe you. I can probably get you on my company's insurance. Won't you need meds?"

I can't pretend the offer isn't tempting. Still, him swooping in like this, brushing past all the trouble he created, rankles. "...Yes."

"Then I'll make some calls. Hopefully they don't make a fuss." He pauses, and I can tell he wants me to thank him. When I'm silent, he clears his throat. "What's that?" He gestures to the bottle, still on the tray table. My clothes have been given back, but they're filthy and in a plastic bag, so I haven't squirrelled it away.

My pulse quickens, and I thank God my nurse muted the monitor. I fake a wry laugh. "Someone was going around giving free samples for their pyramid scheme. It was easier to just take it to make her go away."

He snatches the card, and for a second, I panic. I have no idea how Matt feels about the whole thing, and haven't cared enough in the past to ask. "Therapist and wellness coach? Yeah, real professional of you, pal." He goes to throw it, and the medicine, out.

"Wait–" If she really *is* right, it sounds like I need it.

He raises his eyebrows.

"It smells nice. It's free."

"Alright, fine, if you want it so bad."

Eventually they do come and take me for the bazillion tests. I have to be wheeled around, which is embarrassing enough, except most of the medical professionals will barely look at me. This is why I never tell anybody about the ghosts, they get all grossed out.

Spirits flood the hospital in droves, worse than the airport. I see old people wandering, confused, phasing through each other. More than one person asks where their partner/friend/parent is. Some of them scream, or try to; I see their mouths open and faces contorted, but they make no sound.

When it started to become more of a thing–not just from COVID, but from any number of climate-related natural disasters and mass shootings–politicians and the media of course blamed it on any-thing that furthered their agendas. Vaccines. Us queers. Environmen-tal phenomena. Northern lights. 5G cell towers. Curses from Native American burial sites that have been disturbed. So they said, the libs are exaggerating because if there really are dead people walking around, surely we would know? In the end, nobody has a concrete answer, if you want a cure you could go fuck yourself, don't expect to be believed, and of course we don't want to help your sweet granny's spirit fade or transition or whatever really happens when you die. If you see ghosts, don't show off and shut up. There are so many *alive* oppressed people that need help. How can we help the dead?

There's not one term everyone uses. Mediums. Psychics. The sighted. Freaks, headcases, fakers. A few years ago some activist group tried to advocate for the rights of "Bestowed Americans" and were harassed so badly their foundation went belly-up. So everyone said: they were trivializing *real* issues like racism and sexism and homophobia. Never mind that these issues often went hand-in-hand.

After a few very annoying hours where I am scanned, poked, and prodded, they believe it was a fluke and tell me to get double-checked by a neurologist. I find it hard to believe I just happened to seize out of nowhere, but there's nothing in the bloodwork or the CT scan or the EEG or the lumbar puncture that indicates anything physically wrong with me.

Matt takes me home and buys us McDonald's for lunch. As I have subsided for the past few days on a single bowl of soup and pain au chocolat (the hospital mysteriously did not bring me more than water, even after it was evident I wouldn't need surgery), it's just about the best thing I've ever eaten.

"Did you tell Jenna?" I ask. She has to have noted my absence.

"I tried to, but I don't think she understood," he says. "You would think that language would have stuck with me better. I learned it for her."

"Maybe if you'd tried to talk to her more you'd remember."

He squeezes the steering wheel. "I didn't leave because I didn't love you."

"You gave us up for half of the house's worth," I say. "Dad told me."

Matt huffs. "In what world will a judge grant custody to a–" he refers to himself as a slur only he can say, "--trucker with almost *no* money over a lawyer?"

"I don't think he would lie about that sort of thing."

"Maybe that's what he has to believe is true," he says. "It would've been too hard to fight, and you were almost too old, and I was... tired. I was tired of living for other people. I needed to find *me*. If I didn't leave I would've done something stupid."

Part of me wants to melt. I ran, too, at the first chance. But the other half of me is thirteen and leaving sandwiches at Dad's bedside because he's too depressed to eat. I'm cleaning the house, cooking all the meals, paying our past-due bills. I'm braiding Jenna's hair and holding her when she asks where mommy is. "It didn't have to be this way."

Irritation is a razor in his voice. "Then what do I have to do to convince you I regret it?"

"I don't know!" I burst out. "My dad is *dying* and my brain exploded yesterday, so I'm *sorry* if I can't tell you how to make us feel better."

He grits his teeth and doesn't say anything further.

***

Back at the house, I dump my dirty clothes in the wash. I want nothing more than to sink into my bed. My muscles are sore as fuck and I'm just so done with Matt for making this about him. I'm not paying attention when I open my bedroom door. Not really.

I'm then forced to remember what I saw immediately before the seizure. Mostly because he waits for me, sitting primly on my bed.

His face splits into a crooked-toothed grin. "Hi, honey. I'm home."

PERSONA NON GRATA

H ave you ever had the wind knocked out of you–maybe a fall from a tree, or from your bunk bed, or a too-high jump from a diving board? The way your ribs contract, lungs not accustomed to being empty, leaving you gasping and fragile and oh-so-aware you're made of meat?

Air surges sharply against my chapped lips. The scar on my thigh burns.

"What?" he asks. "Not happy to see me?"

Us, there in the cold, bleeding, my eyes on your corpse, the minute I saw your spirit unspool from your body, hesitant, untethered, like a newborn baby deer, your bewildered gaze as you drifted away–

I turn and try to run, slamming crudely against the hallway, too breathless to scream. Down the stairs, almost falling. Outside, the damp June grass, dizzy, and all it takes is one misstep to fall into our pool (passing through the old gate unaware), cold water pushing me down, and I *see* him as he follows, effortlessly, his remaining eye sharp and eager and—

I breach the surface, gulping a few breaths, chlorine streaking into my eyes.

"You can't keep running away," he spits. "Not anymore." He grins. "Not anymore. Who would have thought that *ghosts* could get region locked?" I hate that I know that laugh, sharp and cruel like battered tin.

He is abruptly pelted in the face with a ghostly ball.

Teddy hangs a few feet above us, the ball back in his hand. "You're mean and I don't like you," he cries, hurling another ball. "Leave my friend alone!"

I've seen spirits holding approximations of things. I've never seen them pass anything to each other. "Teddy?" I whisper.

Dmitri swears. "Fucking kid, this is none of your business!"

Teddy sticks out his tongue and throws again. The balls thump against Dmitri in a sound too much like a playground.

He huffs. "Just quit it, will you?"

Teddy seems to just be getting started. Cold, wet, bewildered, I watch Dmitri get fucking bodied by a seven-year-old. The sight is so bizarre that it allows my panic to retreat some.

Finally Dmitri manages to seize one of the balls and throw it back at Teddy. Spiritual kickballs drift around the yard like tumbleweeds for a moment before dissipating, foglike, in the light.

"You are not going to ruin this for me," Dmitri hisses. "This is *my* territory. You have no right to be here." His voice has become harsh, musty, and the air chokes with ozone; a shadow of that headache returns. "Buh-bye."

Teddy squeaks faintly and vanishes.

"What did you do to him?" I gasp.

Dmitri scowls. "I just forced him out of my domain. He'll be fine in a few hours." His chest heaves, revealing a wrinkled dress shirt. "So. You going to try to keep running, or what? I've got all day."

"What do you expect me to do?" I ask, trying to keep my voice down.

"Are you fucking kidding me?" he shrieks. "I told you. I fucking told you." He surges towards me, and I stumble back. "You made me a promise."

All the jagged shards of memory I have from that day, and yet, nothing. "I didn't promise you *anything.*"

"You did. You know you did." His face is just inches from mine, and there he waits. I force myself to hold my ground. It's not like he can hurt me any more.

As Dmitri stares at me, the anger slowly drains from his face, replaced with... despair? "You... you don't remember, do you? When we were—when you..." He hugs himself, breathing faster. "Oh, this is bad. This is *really* bad."

"What are you–"

"First you're in the hospital, now you're in the pool?" Jenna asks, her voice carrying across the lawn. She must have just gotten back from school. "Maybe you should take it easy."

Sure enough, when I look back, he's gone. All he's left behind is the smell of mildew and something sharper, more powdery.

Jenna cocks her head. "Are you alright?"

"No. No, I don't think so."

She helps me out of the deep end and over to one of the beach chairs by the pool. My heart is trying to claw its way out of my chest, and without my watch, I numbly go to take my pulse. The ache is back and worsening. "Do you need a doctor... again?"

I shake my head, wet curls flapping limply against my cheeks. "POTS thing. I'll be fine."

Dmitri Dmitri Dmitri floods my mind, memories scouring the inside of my throat. I knew this would happen, and yet am still taken aback. What promise was he alluding to?

"I'll get some water," she says. "And, uh, a towel."

I can't do this. I can't deal with Dad *and* him. I'm just going to have to go home. That's all. Make up some lie about some missing thing for my degree. I can't be here and seeing him, not again, I'll explode.

I told myself I wouldn't let myself feel this way again. Not about him. The therapy, the stupid tattoo, the time *away* were supposed to decenter his power. Suddenly I'm seventeen all over again, nursing a bruise I wished I didn't have.

The medicine. The medium said it temporarily banished spirits in some people. I need to know more.

HOLISTIC AND INSPIRED WELLNESS

After a very awkward dinner–pizza from the closest place to the house that is just as mid as I remember–Jenna goes to finish my aborted shopping trip and get the car. I wanted to go with her, to get out of this house, but she told me to just *rest* and she looked so tired that I listened.

In my room, I keep glancing over my shoulder. Using our landline, I dial Leah's number with shaking fingers. All the cigarettes I stress-smoked this afternoon aren't helping.

"Leah speaking, how can I help you?"

I almost hang up. "My name is Aaron. I met you at the um, hospital?"

"Oh! How are you doing?"

"Much better. I was wondering if I could–if I could talk to you. About it. More."

"Of course. Could you come down tomorrow? I'll have a little time in the afternoon."

It seems like I have been here a very short and a very long time. Most of my stuff remains packed, aside from my laptop, a change or two of clothes, and meds.

What promise have I supposedly made to Dmitri? Is it just another one of his lies? I really hope Leah can help make it stop, because otherwise, I'm really not sure I can bear it.

Before meeting Leah at her shop, I first have to go to T-mobile to get a US e-sim. Seeing the 845 area code, and knowing now that I can be reached easily about Dad, is a small comfort. After that, I bring him some pasta I made and some library books, then make my way to the address on Leah's card–a shop called Pathfinder Holistic Wellness. It's nestled in another office building with a Jackson Hewitt tax preparing office and an orthodontist, and is in just the right part of Poughkeepsie to make it a pain to find a parking spot. Inside, the building smells of industrial soap and each plain door has the name of the business in a bland font. It reminds me of my old psych's office building.

Inside it's a different story. Some kind of oil or perfume fills the place with florals I can't identify. The shop is small, less than a thousand square feet, and painted a dark shade of navy, with a bright cream palazzo floor. I don't see any employees behind the wooden cash wrap, just an arched doorway with a beaded curtain.

More of these generic products line the shelves and a few small display tables, each with brown-tinted glass and deep gray labels, but unlike other wellness shops, there's not much information on any of the products I pick up. Nothing describes itself as hydrating or moisturizing or soothing. Nothing says it supports the immune system or beauty or that it detoxifies. Just the name of the product, and the capacity of the jar.

The clattering of a bead curtain startles me, and someone says, "Hi, welcome, let me know how I can help y–"

We stare at each other. Then stare some more.

Of course it's her. Here. Now. Chagrin washes over me and I set down the jar of night cream I was looking at.

Amanda is somehow more beautiful than I remember, her thick black hair curled around her regal face, eyes glittering like micah, her velvety red lips (cherry blossom) pulling up in–almost amusement? "Aaron," she says softly. When she speaks, the light catches the eyelash-thin silvery scar cutting through her upper lip, which she incurred from a fall while biking. I feel like I can't breathe. "I... I didn't realize you were back in town."

My hands have gone tingly. "I-I didn't know you were still here either."

It would be one thing if this were literally any other type of store. Because she knows. I know she knows, I can tell by the way she's looking at me, head slightly cocked.

"I work here," she says.

"You look good," I blurt.

She tucks a stray curl behind her ear. "Um, thanks. You do too."

"All that rain does wonders for the complexion," I say, feeling like a complete idiot.

Her face is definitely pink under her foundation. "I bet."

We were friends, before Dmitri, bonding over a shared love of crafts and navigating confusing bisexuality. Once I was single, and then after the accident, we... we were almost something, finally caving into a years-deep tension during a friend group trip to Ohio when we of course ended up sharing the same hotel room. But Dmitri was around too much, and I was just too broken, and it never went anywhere before I went away to school.

We tried to be friends after I left. Kept it going for quite a while, too. It started to hurt too much, the missing her, the wanting her in my arms. She stopped saying she would visit. Then the calls, the texts, the DMs, slowly dried up, and after a while I saw her on her Instagram with a new girl, arms around each other unambiguously. She moved on like I told her to. That didn't stop it from hurting.

Doesn't.

"I'm here to see Leah?" I say. "I have an appointment?"

She goes to the point of sale, and consults something. "Oh. Sure. Yeah, she's in the other room. Follow me."

I follow Amanda through the beaded curtain, unable to look away from the swish of her skirt on her hip. We go down a narrow, dark hall with a door on each side. Amanda knocks on one to the right. "Your 3:30's here."

"Thank you," comes the response.

Amanda jerks open the knob. Her nails, her once impeccable nails, are now bitten to the quick. Odd. "I'm up front if you need any help."

"Sure. Thanks."

She nods once, her smile skittery and fake, and quickly retreats to her desk.

I'm still processing all that as I take in Leah's office. If anything, it reminds me of the inside of my old therapist's office, with two plush but formal Danish modern brown chairs, a desk with a computer. The deep blue color scheme continues in here, but I see more touches of sage and purple in the art and curtains. A small brass cart holds a Keurig and electric kettle, with handmade mugs.

"Thanks for coming," Leah says. In the light of day, her sharp features are clearer, and she looks just slightly down the bridge of her nose. "That must've been hard."

"I didn't know places like this existed."

She stands, shuts the door behind her, and turns on a white noise machine. "There are more than you think. Which reminds me how incredible it is that you're, well, sane."

"That's debatable," I say.

She gestures for me to sit. "Tea? Coffee?"

"Uh, sure." I can't un-see Amanda. Here of all places.

She blinks. "Which one?"

"...Tea."

She hands me a heavy teal mug with a moon painted on it. Herbal, medicinal steam billows from it, but I like it. She pours her own cup and sits in the adjoining chair. "You really never met another?"

"I'm sure I *have,* I just didn't know," I say. "Nobody... nobody in my life really knows." Except the girl at the counter. "I chalk up anything to mental health issues. Which I have too, to be fair."

"...Psychotic episodes?"

I frown. "A few. Did they tell you at the hospital?"

She shakes her head. "I had them too when *I* didn't know how to manage it."

"Who are you?" I ask.

"I'm a licensed, credentialed mental health specialist–a social work-er," she says, gesturing behind her to a framed certificate. "I just also... happen to have the same condition. None of my peers are willing to fully engage with the reality. They think slapping an antipsych into your chart will fix everything. But it never did, did it?"

"No," I whisper.

"I only know what I've gathered from clients and other people I've talked to, and what nebulous, non-peer reviewed crap I can find online." She leans back and crosses her legs.

"You said you evened my pressures?"

"That's just what I call it. I don't know how to quantify it. I just know that, after a time, after I see and interact with enough spirits, I feel, well, pressure, and that pressure needs to be released. Just like a breath. Or when you need to pee." She grins. "Everyone at the hospital thinks it's, as you put it, woo-woo bullshit. Doesn't stop them from calling me whenever they see one of us."

I blush. "I'm sorry. I don't think so anymore."

"I'm classified there as an alternative medicine provider. But there's *such* a need. Why else do we have all these seizures happening in younger and younger people? Why do we stigmatize what's right there?" She exhales and looks over her shoulder. "Hello, Marge."

A middle-aged woman with a huge perm pokes her head through the door. It shouldn't feel strange, for both of us to see and also acknowledge what we're seeing.

"Hello dear," Marge says.

"Marge is the local spirit of this building," Leah explains. "One of a couple on the block. She's... a consultant, of sorts."

"Something to do, at least. Your package was delivered. Down in the basement."

"Oh, thank you."

Marge smiles and disappears back through the door.

I sip my tea. "How did you do it? That stuff, what's in it?"

"A few different herbs meant to dispel spirits and negative energy. So I guess it *is* woo-woo bullshit. Sorry, that's fun to say. I don't know *why* exactly it works, but I've tried other mixtures, and they're not as successful."

"...And why is it glittery?"

"So I can legally sell it as a cosmetic product, so it falls outside of the FDA's purview." She smiles and shrugs. "I'm just–I'm *fascinated,* by your case."

"I'm flattered," I deadpan.

"Do you feel okay, physically, otherwise?" She dumps some sugar into her tea and stirs, the spoon clinking loudly. "Anything else that seems unexplainable, or that could provide me with greater context?"

"I have POTS," I say, and explain.

She rubs her chin, smudging some pen ink onto her face. "Interesting. Before or after you realized you had the sight?"

"I'm pretty sure it's just long COVID. That's what my doctor thinks."

"Humor me."

"...After."

"It could just be correlational. But I have anecdotal evidence that people like us have such comorbidities. There's just–"

"No hard evidence anywhere reputable," I say. "Right. So all I have to do is put this stuff on every now and again, and I'll be fine?"

"I would. Yes. Oh, and you don't have to buy from me, I have a list of other suppliers, and we keep a fund if you can't afford it–I wish I could charge nothing, but I have to keep the shop, and my manager."

"I get it." I shift my weight, though the chair is plenty comfortable. "Is there anything more you can do? Like... if I want to stop seeing a particular spirit, is that possible?"

She furrows her brows. "I'm afraid I need more information."

I bite my lip, hard. "The person I saw that caused me to... well." The tea tastes like vinegar in my mouth. "He's found me again, and I... I don't know if I can stand it."

"Oh," she mouths, leaning back.

"Is there a way to stop it? Block him?"

"Maybe? What was your connection, if I might ask?"

"....We were lovers." It's like mercury on my tongue.

Leah flinches. "Oh. That's a pickle. Strangers you see in accidents... that's easier. Was there an emotional connection? Or just physical?"

"...Both." To say the very least.

"We can... try," she says. "And there are people I can ask for advice. But love... that marks you. Scars you."

"Tell me about it," I mutter.

"Is there anything else you can tell me?"

"...We were teenagers."

Leah squeezes the bridge of her nose. "Even better."

For a second, I almost want to tell her about that day, what actually happened and how. Nobody except my surgeon, a few cops, my old psych, and Dad know. She did say she is a mental health professional, and it's more likely she'll believe me than most people. The words won't form in my mouth. I shiver.

"I'll do some asking around," Leah says. "Can he still speak?"

"Boy howdy, can he," I say.

"And is engaging directly an option?"

"Things didn't... end well. Us, or his life."

"Sometimes that is the fastest way," Leah says gently. "But even that won't guarantee he moves on from you. He has to either be weak enough to be dispelled, or willing to let go."

Neither seems likely. "If I could even just make a space he couldn't get into..."

Leah sets down her tea. "You could assert your domain, but as a living person that doesn't necessarily mean anything to him, unless he chooses it."

Just like what he did to Teddy. "I just don't get why he has so much *choice* when he's not even alive." I scowl. "Why should I have to keep–appeasing him, when..."

She waits for me to finish, but I don't. "Maybe we should set up some sessions to talk about this," she suggests. "Do you have a therapist?"

"I've spent years in therapy talking about it."

"But I guess that therapist doesn't know you still see him."

The tingling feeling in my fingers worsens, and I tighten my grip on the mug. "I just want him gone. That's all."

Leah purses her lips. "Alright. Well, if you change your mind, I can help."

As if the day couldn't get any worse, Leah asks Amanda to help me pick out some products that will supposedly help. Leah disappears to take a call before I can protest. At least Amanda's making eye contact, though I wish she wouldn't.

"So... banishment, right? We have a couple things that people have had success with." She brings me over towards the back corner and picks up a squat tub labeled SUGAR SCRUB. "This goes on doorways or windows. It might draw ants, though."

"Ants are the least of my problems."

She hands the jar to me, careful that our skin doesn't touch. She's wearing the claddagh ring I gave her after my first trip to Scotland, when I got my citizenship papers. The way she wears it, heart pointed in, indicates she's not single. I can't help but dwell on why she kept it–it isn't like it's fine jewelry. The room feels choked with ghosts, with memory.

Amanda picks up another product, something fine and shimmery in a drawstring satin bag. "This goes around the property. It's basically just refined salt and lavender. And..." she hesitates before picking up a narrow votive candle. "If you still feel presence, burn this candle." She swallows, and considers something for a minute. "Is it... is it him?"

I decide I'm going to lie. That it's Teddy, an annoying kid who keeps playing pranks on me. But instead I say, "yeah."

Her brows pull up, and together, and she comes a little closer. She's still wearing the same perfume, white tea and jasmine that her mother sends her from Mexico. I've seen her apply it, not unlike my Leah concoction, touching it to her wrists and throat. "I'm sorry."

"Well, what can you do?" I laugh a little, but it turns into a cough. "You don't... you don't also–"

"No," she admits. "No, I can't see any of them."

"Then how'd you–why'd you end up here?"

"Because I graduated and needed a job. And I... I always believed, you know, that you–people like you, I mean–are telling the truth. I wanted to help. And even if I wanted to leave..." She shrugs. "The job market's pretty terrible. You... working?"

"I just came back a few days ago."

"Right, your sister must be finishing high school." She gestures me over to the cash wrap and rings up my few things. I expect to be scalped; but altogether it's under thirty dollars.

There's no reason to further unload on her. "Yeah. And my dad needs help with stuff. He wants to sell the house."

She smooths a perfect curl. "So you'll be around for a little while?"

"Yeah. I think so."

"Maybe we could get some coffee and catch up."

My guts clench, and a bright, almost violent hope rises in my chest. I remind myself about the girlfriend and the ring position. "Yeah, if you want to, totally. That'd be great."

She smiles, more real this time, and I want to melt. My watch alerts me to the increase in heart rate. Amanda's eyes catch it, and she blushes. "Who knows. Maybe we can get everyone together. It's been ages."

"You guys don't hang out anymore? Did something happen?"

She slumps a little. "Well–I was sort of—" A store phone rings, piercing in the comparative silence. "I have to get that. It must be the supplier call I'm waiting for. DM me, okay?"

This should not be a priority, and I should not feel like my head is in the clouds. She wants to see me, she wants to catch up. Maybe what I saw online is wrong and she's not seeing anyone–

But I'm not going to be in the States indefinitely, I don't think, and there are other problems. Like the reason I bought this shit in the first place.

THE SHRINE/AN ARGUMENT

Thankfully, no one is home when I get back, and I can perform my silly little rituals in peace. Jenna's out with friends–the senior year bonfire–and I could care less where Matt is. The cat, Rascal, screams at me when I get back inside, leads me to the pantry, and doesn't stop screaming until I feed her a can of tuna.

I crouch down and pet her, feeling the crinkly bones and fur of a very old cat. "Must be nice to be home, huh bud," I remark. "I don't remember you being so noisy."

She audibly gulps the fish down and slow-blinks at me. Cat sated, I take the alleged sugar scrub up to my room and start liberally applying it to the doorframes and windows, feeling crazy all the while. The stuff is gritty, and smells more like herbs than sugar, but at least it applies in a mostly invisible layer. Salt lines are as old as folklore; no wonder Leah started there.

When my room is protected, I move then to Jenna's room for the same thing. Once bright pink walls are now a spring green, her twin bed has been replaced by a queen, and the desk is lopped with textbooks yet to be returned; AP Bio, advanced English literature, psychology. Still more books spill across the dresser, along with unfolded clothes, and a soccer ball sits wantonly below the only window. I protect the space quickly, not wanting to disturb her things. Gone is the *Liv and Maddie* merch, the *Little House on the Prairie* series. Books about necromancers are now apparently more her speed.

Just as I come home, she'll be leaving, off on early admission at Boston University. And it'll be her birthday to boot—I have to plan her party. That itchy ache is back when I blink. Hurriedly I move to protect the rest of the exposed windowsills and doorways, feeling foolish, praying this will work. I don't know what I'll do if it doesn't.

***

As I have a smoke, trying to figure out what teenage girls are into these days, my roommate Kiki texts me. Thankfully her talent for painting murals outweighs her attempts at one-woman theatre, and she sends me a picture of one just completed, an abstract swirl of colors that has replaced a very ugly painting of a pizza. *How's your da?*

Dark gray clouds across the horizon threaten rain, but at least the breeze is nice and cool. All the stress has made my POTS flare up, and now I'm sweating like crazy. *Stable, but he's been better.*

Weird not to have you at drinks the other night. Do you know when you'll be back? The lad we subletted your room to is certainly a creature, I'd rather not deal with him much longer.

I'm not sure yet.

Well, keep me posted x, Nate and Eoin send their love, sad you'll miss the world premiere of my show

"I'm not," I murmur.

The trees rattle restlessly, leaves dancing in the oncoming storm. I'm about to google "graduation party ideas girl" when I see him at the edge of the salt circle I poured. He stares down at it, and I very nearly feel relieved that it works, and then he shrugs and steps over it.

Maybe it's because Leah brought my attention to it, maybe it's because he's doing something taboo, or even just because of the storm, but the pressure squeezes my limbs and gnaws on the headache. Dmitri doesn't appear to struggle, though he moves slowly, as though through water.

"I thought I told you," he says, revealing the silver wire holding his jaw shut, "no more running away."

I try to tell myself that the fingers of sweat crawling down my back are just from POTS. I recall what my old psych told me about trauma responses. "You've done enough to me. Leave me alone."

"You don't think I would if I could?" he snaps. "It's bad enough I was in the dark while you gallivanted your way through *Europe*." He spits the last word. "You know what happens when you bind yourself to a person and place and they leave? It's not good, Bateson. How would you like to be trapped in nonexistence–for three years? So excuse me if I'm not the nicest."

"This is not my fault," I say to him. "If not for you, if not for that day, none of this would have happened. You don't get to gaslight me anymore."

Dmitri straightens and furrows his brows. "What do you remember of that day?"

A harsh laugh escapes me. "I remember you fucking shot me."

"Think, Aaron. Really think. Try to remember."

His spirit unspooling from his body his spirit unspooling from his body

"Was it raining? Did it snow? What were you doing before?"

It was snowing. They said that's part of why I didn't also pass. The hypothermia slowed the blood loss. "I don't owe it to you."

He puts his hands on his hips. "Big historical event that day, too. Isn't that just an unsubtle detail?"

I stand. "No. You don't get to play with my head anymore."

"I am not trying to!" he yells. "I'm trying to get you to see the damn truth! You don't remember."

I hate that it's getting to me, slow trickles of doubt. "You want to see the papers from the hospital? The police report? The fucking weather from that day?"

He cocks his head. "Yes, actually. Look up the weather for me."

"Will you leave me alone for the night if I do?"

"Maybe."

I grab my phone and google "weather January 6 2021 hyde park ny", oh so ready to prove my point, to prove him and his bullshit wrong, I am not the soft little boy he so effortlessly manipulated, and–

My heart drops.

Because it did not snow that day. It was warm for the time of year. Balmy, almost. And clear.

"What's it say, then, if you know everything?" he asks. He's close enough that, were he tangible, I could hit him. The pressure is now crushing. My limbs are full of adrenaline, but I can't breathe.

I drop to my knees, no longer able to hold myself up.

"Try to remember," he whispers. "Try. Please."

"I did what you said. Now go." I've never heard my voice sound like this, so raw and low.

He holds up his hands, as if facing arrest, and disappears.

I sink down on the porch, pressing my cheek into the cool, smooth wood. My heart rate continues to increase, my vision seesawing wildly. What poetic justice it would be if I also die of a heart attack right now.

Salt. Salt will help.

It takes me ages to stand, even longer to drag myself to the kitchen, but I find a Morton canister of salt in the pantry and dump a handful into my palm. Eating it straight like this makes my tongue burn, but at least I will no longer feel like I'm literally about to die in a few minutes. The crushing force is bad enough. How the fuck am I supposed to get upstairs?

Sitting won't really help, but doing anything other than attempting to hold my body together with salt and a prayer seems impossible. I'm still sitting in the pantry cradling my salt canister when Jenna comes home and finds me.

"Hey," I say. "Fun bonfire, huh?"

"Do I want to know?"

"Probably not."

She helps me up. Her face is flushed pink, her pupils are a little dilated, and I get a not-quite whiff of weed.

"Oh, so I can't have a cigarette, but you can smoke weed," I remark.

"Shut up," she signs tersely. "I had one–one hit off a pen, and I didn't like it. Everyone else in the car was smoking."

"Damn, I don't remember my bonfire being that crazy." Having graduated in 2020, the bonfire was one of the only senior events that felt somewhat normal.

"Like you didn't party all the time when you hung out with Charlie and Phoebe and all them. I saw you pull up all hours of the night and I didn't say shit."

"I'm not gonna tell Dad. I'm no narc."

She smiles, watery, and hugs me. Then, "you smell like onions."

OH, THE PLACES YOU PROBABLY WON'T GO

Dmitri leaves me alone for the next few days, so I try to process that whole interaction. Of course it would make sense for me to misremember *details* about that day–severe trauma will do that–but the whole thing with the snow freaks me out. I want to ask someone else to verify that day's weather for me, but how to do so without seeming batshit insane? I don't want to further burden Jenna right now. Maybe I should schedule a session with Leah. Especially because the remedies don't seem to have much of an effect on Dmitri at all.

It doesn't help that it has now become brutally hot outside with approximately a thousand percent humidity. I flare so badly that I have to take constant breaks while Jenna and I get the house ready for her birthday-graduation party. She and her friends are going to hang out around the pool. I tell her I don't care if they party so long as nobody throws up on the couch.

Jenna smiles too largely and laughs too long, and I just know she's upset that Dad won't be able to be at the graduation. It'll just be too hot outside. I try to tell her there are plenty of other old or unwell family members watching the livestream.

"At least you're not graduating from your car," I remind her, because I had. Strange times and all that. "I'll be there. We'll take a ton of pictures."

That morning, it's a very sappy, sitcommy moment, I have to admit, seeing her in the pee-yellow gown that the FDR High School girls have to wear, a rainbow of colored cords from her extracurriculars around her neck. She comes down the stairs fighting a smile. "Yellow's really not my color."

"You look beautiful," I tell her. I offer her my arm.

Matt emerges, then, and I see he, too, has dressed up. Instead of the usual t-shirt and basketball short combo he's been wearing, he has on actual pressed pants and a dress shirt. "Jenna," he calls.

I touch her shoulder and indicate he wants her attention. The joy fades from her face.

"Congratulations, honey," he tells her. "I'm... I'm proud of you. I hope you don't mind that I watch the stream from the overflow seating."

I feel her tense under the rough polyester.

"We should go. I can't be late," Jenna whispers.

She remains silent as I drive her to the drop-off point, her hands tucked between her knees. I realize, belatedly, that I have not grabbed any salt, and it is far too late to go home with all this traffic.

"If he tries to bother us during pictures I may actually end up on the news," I mutter.

"Just let it go," she signs. "I can't stop him from watching. I'll just–I just want to be with my friends."

"Well, good news." I try to keep my voice cheerful and pull up to the curb. "I'll see you on the other side."

She regains some of her light, flashes me an "I love you" sign, and disappears into the horde of yellow- and green- clad graduates.

After attempting to find the shadiest seat in the bleachers I can, to no avail, I resolve myself to stoically roasting in the heat. I will simply not allow my illness to affect me today, which works for about half of the first speaker's speech, when I start to feel faint, the blood pooling mercilessly in my calves. I squeeze the metal seating hard, hoping the pain will ground me enough to keep me conscious. Some mom notices I'm wilting and kindly offers some wet paper towel.

I haven't been back to this school since I've seen spirits, and I see them now, all the teeming teens. Some have their own caps and gowns, graduating in a ceremony they never got to have. Others play football, run the track. Near me, one cheers for her living sibling as their name is announced.

The emotion, the *pressure*, is almost unbearable, but it's all so euphoric, too, and I can't help but cry quietly until her name is called. I see her looking for me as she crosses the stage, and I can only hope that my "applause" signs can be seen from within the sea of bodies.

As I take pictures, my eyes fall on the speck of black and red amid the sea of yellow, green, and summer pastels. All of the noise, the cheering, fades to a dull hum. Dmitri leans against the edge of the bleachers, watching my sister vacate the stage, the expression on his face almost... wistful?

Fury mingles with all of the joy, settling a sour pit in my stomach. This is about *Jenna,* not our stupid bullshit. For the rest of the ceremony, though, there he lingers. He doesn't seem interested in coming to find me. Why come, if not to torment me?

I find my sister's cap among the crowd and focus on it during the recessional. Most people are eager to see their graduate, and they dash down the stairs. I wait until the crowd abates, anticipating confrontation, but when I look back, he's gone.

It takes me some time to find Jenna, and she's posing for some mom of some friend. At least she seems happy, though I can see that she, like many people here, is sweating her butt off. After a few more photos, each with a slightly different combination of friends, I'm finally able to give her a huge hug. By then, it's getting harder and harder to keep my promise and *not be sick*, to be pleasant and chatty with teachers my sister had, to catch up with other teachers who recognize me, to stay standing when blood won't circulate properly. FDR has no air conditioning, and it is so horribly crowded. I have to bail twice, hiding in the unisex bathroom behind the auditorium until I feel less like I'm about to pass out. My head is positively pounding. I should've taken the spirit medicine with me. Or *something*.

After my second reprieve, I head back to Jenna, to the cookies and juice the school provides. People are slowly starting to clear out, and some graduates empty lockers, their gowns open or draped over locker doors. Out of the corner of my eye I see Matt starting towards her, only a few paces away, and I grasp his shoulder.

"No," I say. "Don't ruin this for her."

His eyes are bloodshot. "It'll just be a minute–I just want to congratulate her–"

"You already did. Leave it. You don't get to have this."

He looks over his shoulder again at her, the longing clear. Yet he acquiesces. "You're right."

"Go home, Matt."

Without another word, he turns and slips through the throng. Jenna texted me where her locker is, and I make my way, stepping over the odd lost flower or tassel. Not only is this place clustered with spirits, but memory after unrelenting memory vies for my attention.

Art class with Phoebe before she graduated, painting huge bowls of fruit and laughing over the teacher's terrible taste in music. Biology with the very kooky Mrs. Keil, her room decorated in cow print, Amanda and I scribbling notes to each other at our shared desk– and of course hour after endless hour spent with Dmitri in the AV suite, "helping" him edit his projects, his right hand on the mouse, his left on my knee, or in my hair, his lips against my cheek. We were going to change the world, him and I–

I'm going to be sick. I pretend it's because of the heat, the POTS. At least the men's room is empty so I don't have to lie to anyone.

UNDER PRESSURE

That evening, a dozen teenagers flood my house. Most of them are Jenna's Deaf friends, who went to different schools or were homeschooled. The few who don't know much ASL wander about in a haze, whipping out their phones to talk via text. I feel like I should've made the party more impressive, more generous. More balloons, or something, but Jenna's eyes lit up when I gave her flowers, and Dad even was able to send her a gift via Amazon. The kids seemed content with the pizza and the wings and the cake (homemade, devil's food, her favorite). I leave them be for the most part, content to watch their antics from my bedroom window, my wrists now smelling strongly of thyme.

Were we like that? I have to wonder. They seem so... young, so eager and earnest, deliriously unstable as someone takes out a bottle of Yellowtail moscato.

"Moscato gave me the worst hangovers," he says. Dmitri is perched on the roof under my window, one leg tucked under him. "What about the good stuff?"

I shut the window, but he phases in easily, sugar scrub be damned. "Why did you come today?"

"I wanted to see it."

"That wasn't for you to see," I snap. "Isn't this your domain, or whatever?"

He leans forward. "*You're* my domain," he says. "Where you go, I go, buttercup, unless you get too far away from where we were bound."

I can't allow him to throw me. "I'm not fighting you. The last thing I need is someone to hear me screaming."

"Then let's not fight." He crosses his legs and floats, drifting easily. "We don't always have to scream at each other." His scent, the must of basements, lingers with the oil in a nauseating way. "Haven't you gotten it yet? Put it together?" He spots the medicine on my bedside table and picks it up, spawning a ghostly version of it. "All your rituals and potions... it's funny, not gonna lie. That poor kid has been trying to hang out with you for days."

I turn. "Teddy?"

Dmitri nods. "Worked like a charm for him. He thinks you hate him."

My stomach sinks. I don't want to believe it's true. "Then why doesn't it affect you?"

"Because *you're* my domain," he said slowly, overenunciating every word.

I look at my scarred palm.

He puts his chin in his hands. "You get it? *You* promised me. You owe me. Therefore, I can stay all Box Ghost as long as it takes. Trouble is... well, you don't remember. Which is a pickle for both of us."

"Can't you just tell me?"

He brushes his hand through his slicked-back funeral hair, mussing the gel. "If I only could. *Believe me.*"

The air feels like it crackles. Is it supposed to storm today? The sky is clear and brimming with stars.

"Real scary," Dmitri says.

I begin pacing. "I'm so tired of *appeasing* you," I say. "Two years was enough."

"You think I didn't get sick of *your* bullshit either?" Dmitri asks.

"No. Don't start that. I'm not going to let you manipulate me into–"

"Into what?" The smell of must increases. "It's bad enough you didn't just *let me fucking die.*"

Someone screams. I whip my head around and see one of the teenagers peering through the cracked door. One of the hearing girls, Jessica, with her tan skin and wavy plaits. "I-I heard yelling," she says. "I wanted to make sure–"

Dmitri settles back down on two feet. "She sees me. Don't you, sweetheart?"

She rubs her upper arms, her breath coming hard and fast. "I'm sorry. I'm just– I'm just drunk. I'm sorry." Her eyes are too clear for her to be drunk.

"It's okay," I say, then, to him, "is there any way you can... like... look less freaky?"

Jessica relaxes. "You... too?"

Dmitri snaps, replacing his gaping eye socket with a bright blue hydrangea. "You're all good."

I sigh. "Yes, me too."

She straightens up. "I've never... I haven't... it's only been a few... *months.* How do I stop it?"

I shut my eyes. I offer my hand, and when she takes it, squeeze gently. "You don't," I say.

***

I send Jessica on her merry way with Leah's information and a little of my supplies. I guess I must seem like enough of a grownup, because she spilled her whole story (bus accident, on the way to soccer's sectionals, driver had a heart attack). Everyone else on the bus denied seeing it happen, but Jessica knew better and tried to keep talking about it. It's part of the reason she transferred to FDR for her last semester, despite that being a terrible time to do it. She also got debilitating headaches that she attributed to a lasting concussion from the accident. I tell her she can reach out to me whenever, but that my sister didn't know about my condition, and I would like to keep it that way.

"Asking a minor not to tell people she's talking to you. Nice," Dmitri drawled.

I roll my eyes.

"Jenna really doesn't know? But... she knows what happened to you, doesn't she?"

I light a cigarette and lean back out the window. Dmitri fabricates one of his own. "She just knows I got hurt, and you died. Maybe she thinks I was unconscious. She's dealt with enough."

He takes an overlong drag. The fake smoke, pink, hits my bedroom ceiling. "Maybe she does know, or at least suspect. Didn't she find you during one of your... episodes?"

My watch registers the shock. "I never told you about that. How did you know?"

Dmitri blinks. Then, "I don't know, it just seemed to... come to me. Felt natural."

"When you saw it. What did you see?"

He cows slightly at my tone. "I saw her through the door, and she was all pale, and she saw we were hurt and–"

"*We?*"

"I think I, um, saw your memory. I didn't mean to, I swear, I–"

"Get out of my head!" So much for staying quiet. I wonder what the rest of the hearing guests must think. "You can't have this. You can't *also* have this." I sink onto my bed and curl into a ball.

"Look on the bright side!" he wheedles. "Maybe I can help you remember–"

"*Get out of me.*"

He grunts like he's been punched, and disappears.

Before I can even start to freak out in earnest, Matt's barging in. He sees me curled up, on the brink. "I've been hearing screaming. I had to pass it off to one of the kids that it's a horror movie. What is *wrong*?"

My chest heaves. Dad would understand. Dad would know what to do. "I-I had a nightmare," I lie. It sounds exactly as fake as I think. "I'm sorry. I thought I saw something."

He pauses. Licks his chapped lips. "Honey..."

"Do *not* call me that."

"Do you see spirits?" The way he says it, like someone might say *are you an addict,* gives me pause. "Did one scare you?"

"No," I assert.

"It's okay if you do, I just–"

"I don't. It was a nightmare." At the ripe hour of nine PM.

"Okay, just..." He gestures. "Keep it down."

I force a nervous laugh. "Why would you even think that?"

"Well, it sounded like you were having a conversation with some-one. And I thought–"

I immediately compound my previous lie. "I could've been on the phone." Stupid, that would've been a better excuse.

At this, Matt just looks exasperated. "Maybe I haven't *lived* with you for a while, but Aaron, I know when you're lying."

"Why do you even–*care*?"

"I *care* when you're being harassed by that little shit."

Still, I play dumb, though I'm reeling. "Jessica?"

He's had enough. "Are you gonna make me fucking say it? The shit I've seen on the road, did you think I *wouldn't*?"

I let go of my knees. "When did you... realize about me?"

His shoulders sag. "After he died... I wondered. And when your father told me you've been having episodes..."

My eyes are burning, and my chest starts to spasm.

Matt starts towards me. "Hey. Hey, it's alright."

"Please go."

"Honey..."

"*Please.*"

Matt drops his gaze. "Okay." He shuts my door, leaving me, as I wanted, in silence.

NOT A DATE

After another sleepless night, and a few rides around town for the teenagers who got too drunk to drive, morning finally comes. Jenna (mildly hungover and hiding it badly) and I go see our father–she even puts her gown and cords back on, so he can see. His smile, even halved, makes it worth it.

I have to face the music: Dmitri has somehow bound himself to me, and he can't move on until I remember that promise. He *also* apparently can selectively see my memory, and who knows what else. I scrub myself almost raw in the shower, but the dirty feeling remains.

Well. If he can see inside my head, he'll see *exactly* what he did to me.

I make another appointment with Leah. If he really *is* bound to me, and she can see him, maybe she can help me. He was so eager to talk yesterday that I'm surprised he's not on my ass today. At least I'll be able to catch my breath. How many other people are dealing with this? I'm not the only one who experienced such a deep and dramatic loss.

Maybe there are people with spirits bound to them who don't even know, who can't see.

Leah is able to squeeze me in before the shop closes at noon on Saturday. She listens to the whole story with that same uncomfortable fascination. "Why didn't I think of that!" she says when I'm finished.

"Do you know anyone else with this problem?"

She shakes her head. "It's *incredibly* rare. You would have had to have a brush with death yourself, at the same time, *and* had that complex bond..." She trails off. "What is it you "forgot" to mention?"

I take a deep breath. "He killed himself and shot me when I tried to stop him. I was legally dead for two minutes." No matter how many times I say or think it, no matter how dispassionate the words are, it still aches.

Leah presses her hands together and is still for a moment. "That would have been pertinent information to have."

"Yeah, well, it *was* sort of the worst day of my life. Definitely very easy to talk about."

She takes a long drink from her mug. "This changes everything. Of course the remedies don't work–they're for human-spirit interaction, not *spirit*-spirit interaction. Can you make physical contact with him? Have you tried?"

"I really don't want to."

"No–I get that. Sorry."

"Why couldn't he reach me abroad, even if I'm his domain?" I ask, then explain where I've been.

"Well–spirits *are* sort of "region locked," as he puts it. Whatever force holds them here–their lingering energies can only go so far away from where they died. But his energy couldn't fade entirely, because it's still attached to you." She flinches.

The horror wants to set in, but I don't let it. I don't want to feel sympathy for him when he ruined my life.

"Perhaps," Leah continues, picking up a pen and twirling it, "maybe, as a temporary measure, you can banish him... from you."

I blink. "I think I did. Yesterday, I mean."

"Obviously... not a great solution, in the long run, but it should grant some relief." In the light, the pen glints. She scribbles something on a canary-yellow legal pad, so like that of my old psych. "I know this is a... touchy, subject, but... perhaps you might... consider working towards a resolution, if your bond is that deep."

"A resolution?" I sputter. "He abused me and tried to kill me."

She holds up her hands. "Not to forgive. That's not what I meant to imply at all." She takes a breath. "I do feel, long term, you are going to have to work together. I'm sorry."

I lean back in my chair. That's what I'm afraid of.

"Maybe... when the banishment ends, you bring him here," she says. "I can be a mediator."

I scoff. "Like marriage counseling?"

"Might not be a bad idea."

"Yeah, I'm sure he'll be thrilled."

She won't take a fee this time, either, but does admit I can't keep getting freebies. More than anything I want a cigarette. As I'm fumbling for the pack, to light up outside, I catch sight of Amanda at the cash wrap, typing something.

It still feels like a jump scare, if a jump scare could be nice. Especially because she's wearing this beautiful blue sundress with white edging, and her hair is lying just right on her collarbone. "You work Saturdays too?" I ask dryly.

"I have two and a half jobs," she says. "2025, am I right?" Amanda clears her throat. "I saw about the graduation online. Tell Jenna I said congrats."

"Yeah, I will. Thanks." I stuff my cigarettes back in my pocket. "She's going to Boston in a few weeks. University. Full ride."

"That's amazing! You must be so proud."

"I think it'll be good, so long as the accommodations office has their shit on lock." Even the high school hasn't been consistent regarding accessibility options. Jenna's friends just started habitually giving her their notes after a while.

She types something else. Then, "I have a few hours now. Are you busy?"

"...Busy?"

"For coffee?" She tilts her head slightly. "I could really use some caffeine after the morning we had... unless you no longer want to?"

"No, I really do!" If I knew this was how today would end up, I'd have worn something nicer. I'm in a rumpled T-shirt Kiki designed and jeans that were old before I found them in an Edinburgh charity shop. "It would be nice. Coffee."

I forgot about this, about how she was like the sun; you couldn't help but look.

She gathers her purse and we head out; she locks up behind us. "There's a place right up the block. Nice vibes, not too many Vassar kids around. I know how much of a pain parking here is." Is that a once-over, or is she just looking back at me? "You can smoke, if you want. I saw you reaching."

I offer her the pack, and she actually accepts, and there's this very pretentious breath-stealing moment when I light it for her. Her hands, her lips, too close. "You said it was a bad morning?"

"Leah has crisis cases just like any other therapist. The parent showed up. It got... kind of ugly." She flinches. "That's really all I can say without jeopardizing their privacy."

"So you're part salesgirl, part medical receptionist?"

"I prefer reception manager, but yes." She takes a drag, then flinches. "I thought you hated Marlboros."

"I do. These were kind of an emergency acquisition."

"How you can tell any difference in flavor is beyond me."

"Well, I'm a filthy smoker. Can't bring myself to vape. It freaks me out, like, nobody knows what's in them."

"Versus the hundreds of carcinogens in cigarettes?"

"You didn't have to take one."

"I know." She laughs.

Today's not so boiling hot, but it is very humid, and threatening rain, and that rancid cheese smell is back. At least the streets aren't busy. Poughkeepsie's a mixed bag: one street is all gentrified, with uber expensive sandwiches and yoga studios; and the next, someone will ask you for money, you shouldn't leave your car unlocked, and there's guaranteed an exposed needle around somewhere.

This cafe is somewhere in between. It's got simple laminate tables and wooden chairs, and many of the surfaces are overloaded with greenery–ferns, devil's ivy, spider plants. The whitewashed walls have local community notices, mostly in Spanish. "Good sandwiches," Amanda remarks. "Mostly everything is good."

So it is perhaps one of the last real local places. A few people see us coming in and smile at Amanda, offering greetings in Spanish.

I used to be fluent in Spanish–immigration lawyer dad, took it in school, and so on–but my three years in a very English speaking country definitely show. I follow Amanda to the front counter. A plump older lady strikes up a conversation with Amanda, also in

Spanish, complimenting her dress and asking after someone named Greta. Amanda orders "the usual," and I say the same. We're presented with espressos in pristine white cups and homemade muffins, and we go find seats in the back.

Even the spirits here seem relaxed, clustered around the counter, reaching for drinks they cannot have. Some chat idly, others try to join who cannot speak. There's even someone trying to cook behind the counter. One notices me watching and glances back warily.

Amanda holds up her cup. "Cheers."

"Slainte."

The coffee takes me back to a simpler time, when we thought we could almost be together. The espresso is rich, deep, and has a subtle sweetness to it. It would win Dale Cooper's approval.

"I love coming here on my lunches," Amanda says. "Hanging out, seeing how everyone's doing. We went to school with the owner's son–Josh Blanco, you remember?"

A quiet band kid type who always had his face buried in a book. "Yeah. Nice guy."

She shifts her weight and her leg brushes mine for just a second, a quick, accidental kiss of skin. We go to speak at the same time. "Do you miss–"

"How's your girlfriend?"

Her eyes widen in surprise. "Oh... well..."

I stare at my muffin. "Sorry. That's none of my business."

Amanda shakes her head. Her eyes glitter with amusement. "No. Not my girlfriend. Was my *something*, I guess. She cheated on me, said it was because she was poly, but when I pointed out she never asked for my consent..." She makes a "poof" gesture. "What made you think–"

"Your ring," I say.

She looks at it. The silver hands cupping the heart are clean but scratched in places, and one of the two clear crystals on the left hand's wrist is missing. The stone is allegedly spinel, according to the jeweler, but small enough it could just be a red cubic zirconia. "What about it?"

"The positions have... meaning." I'm so embarrassed I'm actually nauseous.

"Oh–*oh*. You even told me that. I, ah, forgot."

"I'm surprised you kept it."

Amanda breaks a piece off the muffin and eats it. "It was a gift. It wasn't like we... ended poorly. We didn't really... *begin*."

"...No. I guess we didn't."

I wonder if the pressure I feel is just from spirits.

She drinks down the last dregs of her espresso. "So are you? Seeing anyone?"

"Other than a million ghosts?"

She laughs once, then covers her mouth.

"No. I'm not. Couple contenders in university. Nothing... serious."

Amanda leans forward, knotting her hands. "I have to admit, it's hard to imagine *you* just hooking up with randos."

She has to be flirting. Before I can consciously make the decision, I lean in too, my fingers almost touching hers. "Something about that shock you?"

She turns bright pink and looks around quickly. "No, I mean, of course not. Do whatever you want. Um. So how was... everything?"

I consider the non-answer I gave Matt. "I'm glad I went," I say. "I felt like I found this different version of me nobody immediately associates with... well. I had some cool roommates, and we even traveled when we found the money. I helped paint murals." Ceiling fans stir the air above us lazily, wafting the smell of baking pastries and hot sandwiches around the space.

"Murals?"

"My roommate Kiki is a painter, and sometimes she needed help. It's a lot of fun. Feels almost like a legacy."

"Maybe you could show me sometime. Pictures, I mean." She shakes her head slightly, tossing her sculpted curls. "You were always bent over a tablet, working on comics, I figured that's what you would do."

I smile. "I haven't tried one of those in a while. It felt too... *earnest,* if that makes sense." I take a bite of the muffin, pleasantly surprised at the orange flavor. "Artists cashing in on their mental illness are a dime a dozen."

"Too vulnerable?"

I tried so hard to have something so profound to say about all I've been through. But none of the traumas or the psychotic episodes made me stronger or a better person. All it did was air too much dirty laundry and fill my inboxes with hate. I made the website where I hosted them private, but I can't bring myself to stop paying for the yearly domain renewal. "Maybe."

"So what will you do now?"

"Try to find some part time gig. I'm really here to... help my dad." Her reflection forms through the crema on the glossy surface of the coffee. "He's... he's not well. He had a heart attack, so a surgery, and a stroke..." I speak quickly. "That's not your problem. Sorry. He's going to be alright, but he needs me to help with stuff."

She takes my hand, and I'm disoriented, the brush of her smooth skin against mine reminding me of those brief precious days. "I always liked your dad. I'll pray for him." Too quickly, she lets go.

"...Thank you. It was all the stress, you know, and he smoked like a chimney." I clear my throat, feeling a few crumbs stick. "What have you been up to? I mean I saw some things on the Discord, and Instagram..." Our friend group Discord server also used to pop off all the time. Those messages, too, have slowed to maybe a few a week. We're all so "busy."

Amanda looks away, out the window. "I was sick for a while," she says.

"...Sick?"

She flicks her hand up to her mouth, as if to bite her nails, but stops herself. "I didn't stop–reaching out because I didn't want to talk." Her voice is scratchy. "It was all so fast, and so embarrassing, and I ended up... just not telling anyone other than my mom and aunt." She lives, or used to at least, with her aunt.

I can sympathize with that. I don't tell anyone about POTS until I invariably pass out in front of them. "Are you okay now?"

She nods, her face pinkening below makeup. "I had... I had cancer. Ovarian, stage 3, good prognosis, but I still had to, like, do the whole process. That threw a real wrench into finishing school."

"Holy shit." I should've known, somehow. I should have been able to support her. All along I thought we stopped talking because the distance naturally grew. The pictures of her slightly too thin with a pixie cut, when she always had long hair (captioned with something to the essence of "I felt like a change"), suddenly make a lot more sense. "I'm glad you're okay. Thanks for telling me."

She shrugs. "That's kind of how I drifted away from everyone, and now we all have our own lives. I can't exactly waltz back in and be like, "Sorry I ghosted you, I was too busy dying.""

"I mean, you could tell them. We would have supported you, Amanda. You wouldn't have had to do it alone."

She considers something for a long moment, her lips slightly pursed. A child spirit runs up to our table, inaudibly says something, and bounds off. "You did it alone. I found out how you were coping through—comics."

Shit. "That's different—I didn't want to burden—"

"It's the same, Aaron, it's the same thing. I didn't want to burden anyone with my chemo or radiation. You didn't want to burden anyone with the trauma or the—you know." She frowns. "If we were such good friends, why did we keep that secret?"

"I don't know," I whisper.

She smoothes her hair back. "Sorry, this wasn't meant to—be a confrontation."

"No, I'm glad you said something. You're right." Doesn't it at some point just become lying? Even if the intention was pure? "We should try to get together. You, me, Charlie, Phoebe. I haven't heard much from Ann, but I think they're around."

She's still a bit flustered; she's twisting a strand of her hair back and forth, which I know she does when she's nervous. "I think that would be nice."

"And I want to... really be friends." I bite the bullet. "I missed you. I didn't realize how much until—"

She softens. "Yeah. I missed you too."

"SOME BORING LOGISTIC THINGS"

My whole way home, I turn facets of our conversation over and over. We could have stayed in touch this *entire* time. I can't fault her for wanting privacy during such an intense period of physical distress. Like she said, I did the same thing, even if my trials were different. If we just matured, admitted how much everything sucked, maybe things would've ended differently for her and I.

Is it bad to wish they still would? Long-buried feelings lurk under my skin. I have to either keep suppressing them, or give in entirely. And it isn't exactly prudent to do either of those things when I have to deal with Dmitri. That, and Dad, and prepping Jenna for college, should be where the brunt of my focus lies. But even just that afternoon sitting across from her... she's even more beautiful than before, even more Amanda, and I am wholly not above my nature.

I buy a pack of actually palatable cigarettes and smoke for a few minutes on the porch, willing my eyes to glaze over. How long will the banishment last? Where does Dmitri go when he's banished?

Is that not a hellish nonexistence? Apparently I put him through three years of that.

No. I can't go there. I can't somehow make him the victim in all this. Not after—everything. My hand strays to the deep, pitted scar on my right thigh. Even covered, you can see the irregularity in the muscle if you know where to look.

I glance up, over at the yard, and see Teddy at the edge of the salt line mooning me. God knows what Dmitri said to him. I stub out the cigarette and go towards him, averting my eyes. "Sounds like I owe someone an apology, if they would just put their pants on," I say, after making sure nobody will see me talking to myself.

Teddy does, but pouts. "You said you would play with me. Why can't I see you?"

It's hard to find the salt line. Rain, wind, and perhaps animals could have disturbed it. "Show me where the line is. It doesn't work anyway—not how it was meant to."

He points to a spot by my feet and I smudge it as best I can. Teddy hesitantly steps over it into the yard and glares up at me, his ghostly eyes watering slightly.

"It wasn't meant to keep you out," I tell him. "Just that big meanie. The one you helped me with. I didn't think. I'm sorry."

"I just want someone to play with. I'm so..." He hiccups, that sniff little kids make when they get really worked up.

"Lonely?" I offer. "It must be really hard, living at home."

"I wish they would believe *I'm here.*"

"Not everyone is open to seeing spirits. But you're right. It's not fair." I kneel down so we're more on eye level. "How about I come play with you tomorrow? Or..." What on earth did seven-year-olds do for fun? "Can you interact with phones?"

He shakes his head. "I can watch what's on one though."

"Maybe you can help me learn *Fortnite*."

He actually jumps up and down. "Yes!"

I stand. "I have some boring grownup stuff to do now. If you see the big meanie, let me know." Before I walk away, though, I decide to ask, "when he banished you... what happened? What was it like?"

Teddy knots his hands. "Real... empty," he says. "I felt like I couldn't breathe... but also like I was asleep... and also like I was falling. I thought I would go poof."

"What do you mean?"

"Stop being here."

I bite the inside of my cheek. "Is that something you can choose to do?"

He shrugs. "I don't wanna yet, anyway."

I nod, and turn to leave, but he adds,

"Sometimes I see this... shiny thing." Teddy lifts his gaze to the sky, shading his spectral eyes. "Always there waiting for me. Calling me back."

"Does it seem nice? Or mean?"

He shakes his head. "It's hard to explain."

"Maybe you can think about it a little more and tell me," I say.

He wrinkles his nose. "Don't want no homework."

I have to stop myself from sighing. "Alright. No homework."

It occurs to me I could *ask* Dmitri what his experience has been like, but then I'll have to trust his information is reliable–and who knows about that. Many of the other spirits I see around, if they're even able to engage with the living, can't speak. Maybe I can get them to write? But not all of them can create facsimiles of objects like Teddy and Dmitri. There's that verbal spirit at Leah's, Marge. The "consultant." Well, I could sure use a consult.

"Aaron?" Teddy calls.

I look back.

"...Can you put on Mr. Beast for me?"

***

That afternoon, Jenna and I unearth the first set of boxes and totes from our attic. It's too hot up there for me to do the work, so she does most of the bringing down. The contents are meticulously labeled, courtesy of Dad, and seem to be things they use often–winter clothes, packed to save closet space, sports equipment from Jenna's various endeavors, legal files Dad can't shred but can't get rid of, either. Jenna knows she's responsible for dealing with her own stuff, and the legal files can get sent to Dad's firm for the paralegal to deal with. We find a few things worth selling: a printer new in the box, a very ugly antique lamp, some of those drink dispensers you can use at parties (which would have been handy a few days ago).

I'm grateful that we haven't gotten to the older stuff yet, the stuff more likely to trigger painful nostalgia, but seeing the sheer amount of shit up here to sort through, it's going to be a long uphill battle. If we can get through a few boxes per day, it'll really only take a few weeks. And by then, Jenna will be gone, off at college.

Dusty, sweaty, our sell/donate/trash sections of the garage established, she helps me make chicken cutlets and scalloped potatoes for dinner.

I haven't cooked, not properly, in what feels like ages. Before this there was the haze of my own final exams, and a flurry of events where food was usually provided. And admittedly our flat slipped into a bad habit of grabbing a quick bite at the pub. I used to flirt with the idea of being a chef, but then I watched approximately one episode of *Hell's Kitchen* and knew in my heart I would not survive.

I guess I have Matt to thank for being a good cook; he was our primary meal preparer until he left, and then I scrambled to learn to feed us. There's an order to cooking, a symmetry, objective ways to fix what you've fucked up. Not like art. Never art.

"How have you been doing, food-wise?" I ask her once the chicken is breaded and frying. "The pantries took a hit."

"Dad and I split it up, before he got sick," she says. She's wearing one of my old National Art Honor Society shirts, and a streak of dust is on her cheek. "Followed your recipes. We managed. Since..." A shrug. "The history on my UberEats account is between me and God."

"...So Matt isn't exactly looking after you."

Jenna crosses her arms for a moment. "He has left some stuff out for me, but... I don't know. It's uncomfortable having him here."

"Do you know where he went today?"

"Don't know, don't care."

I flip a chicken breast with a fork, inadvertently causing some of the oil to spatter. My hand catches a little of the fallout. "All I wanted at uni was a propane stove, and I'm not even used to them anymore."

I do indeed burn some of the chicken, but the potatoes are fine, and we have a nice quiet dinner on the back porch. I'll miss this, when she's not here. When Matt and I are the only creatures in this house.

"I've been meaning to ask–what happened to the Grahams' boy?" I ask.

Her expression becomes a bit crestfallen. "So you heard about that. He drowned at Vanderbilt last summer. Apparently he wandered off into the cove, and fell into the river, and by the time his parents noticed..." She shakes her head. "It was so sad. We went to the wake. What made you think of it?"

At least he didn't drown in our uncovered pool. "I didn't see any toys in the yard like there used to be."

"The mom went a bit nutty. Not like... you know, but Dad found her in a bathing suit, crying, in the middle of a snowstorm."

Teddy must have seen all that. Frozen at perpetually seven, how much does he understand? I don't think his mother would believe me if I tell her I can see him. And it's not like I can give anyone the "gift." Maybe it would be worth the embarrassment to tell her anyway. She already thinks I'm crazy.

***

By the time I wake up this morning, Matt's car is back in the driveway. I find him making scrambled eggs in the old cast-iron pan.

"Where were you?" I ask.

"I drove over to the closest branch of my company—over in PA. I wanted to see if they had any contracts available, and besides, I had to get you on my insurance before the start of the new month." He gestures, not turning, towards some papers on the table. "Took some finnegaling, and not everywhere takes it, but it's definitely better than nothing."

I didn't expect him to actually come through. "Oh... thanks."

"Some woman is going to see if she can get it to retroactively cover your hospital visit. She'll call the house." He dumps the eggs onto a plate and pulls toast from the toaster. "I see you and Jenna are starting to clean out the attic. I'll handle my own things. Just set them aside. Most of it's junk, anyway." His women's clothing. "I wonder if he sold any of my jewelry."

Matt's jewelry box still sits on Dad's dresser, collecting dust. I poked inside a few years ago, curious if Matt had taken anything. Most of it is simple, plain pieces, but there are a few diamonds and gold necklaces that must be worth something, and a few pieces handed down from *his* mother and grandmother. And, of course, his wedding and engagement rings. Dad used to sleep with them on his bedside table. "He wouldn't do that."

He digs into his toast, crumbs scattering into his beard. "There are pearls in there that were your great-grandmother's. Could you give them to Jenna for me? I don't think she'll take them if I do it."

"Uh... sure."

"I called a plumber to look at the downstairs bathroom. Should be coming by today around two. Will you be around?" He's already almost through with his eggs. I wonder if all truckers eat this fast.

"I can be–"

"Great. Well, Alan wanted to speak with me before his morning therapy, so I'll see you later." He sets the dish in the sink. I must be making some kind of face, because he adds, "what?"

"I'm surprised you're leaving again."

"Well, neither you nor your sister seem much interested in conversation. As you said, I don't get to have that." Very matter-of-fact. He picks up a baseball cap, puts it on, and leaves.

I scowl.

***

A few more days pass in this manner; all the while, Dmitri is conspicuously and blissfully absent.

My old psych is months from retirement, but he somehow accepts Matt's insurance and is willing to book me in. It's a miracle because I am rapidly running out of psych meds, and withdrawing from them is a special kind of hell. I've been taking the pills for nearly ten years now, my regime ever growing in complexity. Starting first with innocent SSRIs, then the mood stabilizers, the drug enhancing Rexulti, and of course, the sleeping pills I'm told to take if I haven't slept in three or more days, because it seems all my episodes were triggered by lack of sleep. And clonzepam, the red-button pill to take during severe anxiety attacks, which makes me feel like I'm a million miles away swatting through wet laundry. Xanax used to be better. But I am not allowed to take Xanax anymore.

I wonder if it's a pipe dream to hope that, with the medicine with Leah, I will feel more stable. She *seems* to say yes, but I trust my psych Fitzl more than I trust her. As logically as she speaks, some of this still feels like, well, woo-woo bullshit.

Fitzl lives down in Wappingers, a forty-minute drive, but I don't particularly mind making it today. The mindless strip of Route 9, with all of its red lights and plazas, feels downright novel to me. It does not feel like home. His office is in his home–there was a point where it was in an actual practice, but he started slowly transitioning patients to colleagues of his as he got older.

It's strange to reflect on the fact that he has saved my life dozens of times. Any doctor or EMT that resuscitates you in emergencies, or even strangers giving CPR on the street, those guys are lauded as "heroes." But psychs, deftly navigating the healthcare dumpster fire, are often overlooked. If you're lucky enough to be able to get one in the first place.

Part of me feels like the same scared teenager I used to be, rolling up to his office in Dad's car. And when I go up the stone steps and open the front door, the old brick house yawning over me, the smell is so the same–ginger tea and patchouli and basil and dust. The mud room has been converted into a makeshift reception, 60s and 70s classic band posters cluttering the wall around the certificates and accolades and calendars. The receptionist is new, but takes my info. I pay my small copay. It isn't like I came from the UK with much money, just a small pittance from a few jobs I worked with Kiki and the pale remains of my student loans, and I fear to look at my checking account. More reason to get back into the green stuff immediately.

How to even get a job at the grocery store when my resume consists almost entirely of odd jobs? No retail experience, a foreign degree, and should I be lucky enough to get hired, unholy demon triplet illnesses requiring accommodation–I'm not exactly an attractive prospective employee. I can probably subsist on house money for a while if I'm frugal. Maybe disability once that's gone–if I'm lucky. One thing at a time.

A spirit lingers around Fitzl's house. It must be very old; its form is very indistinct, and it cannot speak, and it seems to have difficulty propelling itself around the space. I just see the warm slash of its mouth and its eyes.

I wonder if I will be like that someday. "Hello," I say to it.

It blinks, holding out a wavery palm, and I offer mine, but of course we cannot touch.

Fitzl's actual office holds two mid-century modern replicas, each worn and shabby, with claw marks from his oriental shorthair cats. One of the walls primarily consists of double-doors open to a squat yard with a garden full of wildflowers. To my left, one of the walls is studded with ivy, a single devil's ivy plant manipulated across the wall in lattices and curlicues. To the right are more classic psych-y stuff;

brown wooden bookshelves full of texts, and file cabinets with patient information. He doesn't have a computer, at least not in this room.

Fitzl is lithe and flexible from fifty years of yoga, with silver hair and a long, contemplative face. He shakes my hand and we briefly chat–how was uni/great how is retirement/coming along just fine. But because every minute is precious, he gets down to business. Dextromethorphan and bupropion/yes Rexulti/yes clonzepam/yes. Seroquel has been in and out of the rotation for years–depends on how recently I had a psychotic episode–but he declines to prescribe it today. I am "stable." I am doing "flawlessly well."

Despite the fact that I see ghosts and my heart and blood hate me.

"Wonder if you should tell him," Dmitri whispers in my ear. I *smell* him–the must of basements and morgues and sharp gunpowder.

I can't look. Don't dare. My heart stutters, and my watch flashes at the increase. A cold, vinegary sweat seeps into my t-shirt.

Fitzl frowns. "Are you alright, Aaron?"

Fitzl doesn't know about me. I don't know his stance on it, if he believes it. He seems like enough of a hippie to be okay with it, but can he even help me?

Dmitri drifts through the space with ease, his rumpled funeral suit in all its glory, and nests somewhere behind Fitzl. "That was a good trick, I admit. Almost clever."

There's not much of the session left to muster through, but Dmitri's stony gaze pierces into me. I don't want the deep intricacies of my psyche laid bare in front of him, not like this, not in my old safe space. Sticky, fizzy panic scratches along my limbs.

"There is no safe space," Dmitri says. "There never will be."

"Do you think someone can repress memories?" I ask Fitzl. "Or change them?"

Fitzl taps the tips of his fingers together, a cracked Bic pen perched between two knuckles. At his billable rate he surely could afford nicer ones. "Well, certainly," he says. "While actually repressing memories is not quite supported by scientific evidence, dissociating during a trauma, or willingly distorting your own memory, might cause discrepancies. We've worked through this. I can provide you some of the notes from your file, if you'd like."

So Dmitri was just gaslighting me. Again. And as usual, I fell for it. "Why is it you ask?"

I exhale. "It's just hard, being home, you know?" I say instead. "All these pieces keep coming back to me that felt missing, and I was... doubting."

"That's very understandable, all things considered. My caseload is quite small now, but perhaps you might like to explore that further?"

It'll do no good if Dmitri can snoop into everything anyway. I shake my head. "I think I'll be alright."

I make another appointment some six months off for renewals, but he cautions me to begin the search for another provider, if I stay local. Dmitri hangs onto every word, tracing the ivy leaves with spectral palms. He chases me out the door back into Dad's Honda and sits like a prince in the passenger seat.

"Where to next?" Dmitri asks. "Any errands to run? Looks like you need gas. ... And more cigarettes. Hey, you know those will kill you, right?"

I cut my eyes towards him. His form is fuzzier than normal, now that I'm not so freaked, and paler. Would subsequent banishings make him weaker? Would it eventually force him away from me? *Leave me,* I hiss. "Just go."

He clings to the passenger door handle, as if being dangled, his face contorted. "You can't keep doing this."

"Watch me."

He drifts off into nowhere, into smoke, and that sharp piercing between my eyes returns.

CAT AND MOUSE

So it goes, for the next week or so—he appears, makes some cutting remark; I banish him. Every time, that oppressive crush of force seems to get a little worse, and before I know it, the little TONER bottle is empty. He crowds the air, the insides of my head. He threatens to retread the moments of that horrible day, as if I haven't done it dozens, hundreds of times in my dreams. As if I don't know every beat, every stone, every sick lick of pain.

The headaches worsen. I convince myself that it's because I've switched from one from one manufacturer of psych medication to another; even if the med is the same, the difference in chemical makeup *can* cause unintended side effects. I am not here for Dmitri, I remind myself, trying to avoid his gaze.

Even when Dmitri's nowhere to be found, already that hot, sharp ache is forming behind my eyes, and a staticy sensation dances along my skin. What I really need is to go down and buy more of that stuff from Leah. Part of me wonders if this is psychosomatic. I really hope it is. The last thing I need is to be addicted to something else.

So I take the L and drive down to Poughkeepsie, figuring I'll drop off more books for Dad while I'm there. His recovery is very slow but at least seems measurable, though it's clear he won't be able to be independent for quite some time. I knew on some level I was returning home to be a caregiver, but now it's staring me in the face.

Late-afternoon sunlight plays upon the brown dashboard of the Honda, illuminating dust motes. Historical old buildings, with their stone facades and ionic columns, are right next to crumbling 60s office buildings and shuttered convenience stores. Gentrifiers are slowly "cleaning up" Poughkeepsie, and I notice several new townhouse developments as I struggle to find a parking spot. I try to remind myself to be calm if Amanda's there, just to have normal chit-chat about whatever, but my anxiety is unwarranted because Leah's at the front desk counting the till.

She straightens, brushing a stray lock of hair back into its bun. The hair immediately slides out of place. "Hi, Aaron. How are you holding up?"

I pull the empty bottle out of my pocket. "I need a restock. You recycle?"

Leah raises her eyebrows. "Already?"

I shift my weight. "Is that a problem?"

"No, but it is... unusual."

"I did give some to a girl I met who needed it."

Leah crosses her arms. "Has it become that much of... a hassle?" She glances around briefly, as if looking for Dmitri. "We should really consider–"

"I just need a refill, I'm meeting someone," I say quickly. "Amanda's not in today?"

"She had something she needed to take care of," Leah says warily. "You friends?"

"We know each other, yeah. We go way back." Turning back towards the wall of products, I notice the shelves are much emptier than they were even a few days before.

"My courier flaked," she says. "I couldn't get my hands on the ingredients, so I'm running a little low. I just haven't had the *time* to go pick them up."

And indeed, the small section labelled "toner" is barren of products. I honestly did not think the business was doing that well. "Oh... well... I mean, I'm not working right now, or anything, I could go get it for you."

She raises an eyebrow. "Are you sure? That's quite a big favor..."

I squirm. "We're both going to need it at some point."

She stares at me. "But for four years you were fine."

"Yeah, well, you know how it is."

Leah plunks the till back into the register drawer. "Right, well. The distro is a bit farther upstate. I'll have Amanda contact you."

While I'm in the area, I go to see my father. Down at the rehab facility, Dad seems to be in good spirits. He was able to read the books I brought last time, and even was able to tell me what he thought about them. But his skin tone is still decidedly gray, and he's even thinner.

"You doing okay?" I ask. "You look tired."

"I *am* tired," he says. "It's... tough. Things are tough."

When he doesn't much elaborate, I say, "Well, you know, it's probably going to take some time. It hasn't been all that long since you got sick..."

He frowns. "How... how long has it been?"

I try not to let the surprise register on my face. "You had the heart attack about a month ago. I've been back nearly two weeks."

"Oh... I thought..." He trails off, his dark eyes unfocused. "Never mind what I thought."

Suddenly I'm doubting myself. But no, a quick glance at his chart on the wall confirms the date. "It's okay, you must have a lot on your mind. I'm sure being here is pretty mind numbing."

He looks over his shoulder. Squints. I do too, instinctively, and I see an older man's spirit, pot-belly and all. He says something to us inaudibly and walks through to the other side of the room.

"What an odd gentleman," Dad says. "How rude."

My heart's in my throat, though I try to play dumb. "Dad. What are you talking about?"

"The... the gentleman who... just came by? Did you not—"

A very hard choice stares me in the face. I can either admit I saw him too, or tell Dad he might be seeing spirits. But *how* had Dad suddenly started seeing spirits? Was it because of his own near-death experience?

He looks very pale, the veins in his eyes bright and protruding. "Can you get the doctor for me, sweetie?"

"Of course, I just think you're–"

"Now? My chest hurts..."

I obey without thinking, my steps twitching and clumsy from anxiety. If it happens again–if he–I grasp the arm of the first person in scrubs I see, and they dash off immediately.

I find myself huddled in the waiting room of the closest ER, a sweat-sodden mask on my face. Bright fluorescents frame the narrow bay, which is lined with a dozen plastic chairs, with more in the center facing each other. Sterile, bleached air punches through the space, but it hardly affects me; dysautonomia loves stress. A few other assorted people are here, and always, the spirits, some sitting with newspapers in their old-fashioned outfits. One even puffs a cigar.

The worst by far are the baby spirits, often cradled by parents or siblings. I wonder, sometimes, if they must adopt one another, or if they've connected otherwise. I can't think about it too hard without feeling sick.

Under me, the plastic seat is very hard, and the edge has grooves worn and torn into it. Tracing it with shaking fingers, I try to force myself to have the thought, to have the realization; he may very well die right now.

No. The doctors didn't say anything. They didn't say he had another heart attack. It could just be a facility policy to transport—why didn't they let me go with him? I'm proxy, they *need* me.

I need to tell Jenna, even Matt, what's happening, but I am in an endless void of alternatingly icy and acidic panic. Angry red blotches sprout across my forearms. Calm. I need to be rational, be calm. Want, need, a smoke, but if I get up surely they'll be looking for me. As each second mercilessly passes, I chew on the inside of my cheek instead.

"He's going to be fine," Dmitri says. He's appeared next to me, and this time, he's even more washed out, the hole of his eye blurrier. "I just walked past. It's angina, not a heart attack."

I meet his eyes before I can stop myself.

"He didn't notice me. They have him tranqed, or something." He reaches over to the table between two chairs and grasps a magazine, making a copy he can read. The text fades from whatever tabloid to "lorem ipsum" before dissipating entirely.

A slow force, a pressure, exudes from him. It creeps down my left forearm.

"I'm guessing he saw someone pass at the facility, and just can't remember," he continues. "Happens to the best of us. But the tough thing is—are you going to come clean?"

I shouldn't engage—I have no way of ridding myself of the film he leaves on me. "They'll put him on psych meds if I don't. I'm sure that wouldn't be good for his heart." I whisper through my mask, but I wonder if I'm audible to others.

"Not much is," he says. "You've put me into a real jam, Aaron, I've got to say. You're only going to make it worse for yourself."

"I can't *deal* with you now."

"Well, when *will* you?" he growls. "I'm not exactly happy with this situation either. You put me in hell for three years, and you're putting me in hell again and again *now*. Haven't you ever thought that maybe that makes us even?"

My jaw is clamped vice-tight. "Unbelievable."

"You know you're just hurting yourself, right, doing this?"

Composed. I must be composed or people are going to think I'm losing it. "You are *not* the victim, here, okay?"

He scowls, revealing the silver wire holding his jaw shut. "You want to get yourself killed? Fine. Go ahead. Then *maybe* we'll finally get somewhere."

I turn to retort, but he's gone.

***

What seems like hours later, a doctor confirms what Dmitri's said, and they let me go see Dad. He looks sad and pale in his half of the small ER bay.

"I didn't want you to see this," he murmurs.

"How are you feeling?"

"I–I'm not sure. I think they gave me something to be calm."

Barbiturates on a patient with a weak heart. Fantastic. I pull up one of those stubbornly uncomfortable chairs. "They told me they'll be taking you back soon."

He looks away from me, up at the ceiling. "I'll be the talk of the town, for sure." He struggles over the alliteration. "Those people? *Terrible* gossips."

"Must need something to pass the time." Now that I know he's okay, the worst of the reddish splotches on my arms are fading. His eyes linger on them.

"I know this has been hard on you," he says.

"I'm used to it."

"Have you been talking to your friends? You shouldn't–"

"Dad. Don't worry about me."

Sheepish, he tucks his good hand over the shaky one.

I brace myself. "Before you... got taken here. You were telling me you saw someone walk through your room. Do you remember that?"

Dad squints, his left eye following belatedly. "Not quite."

"I was wondering if you were... maybe... seeing ghosts?"

He's still and silent. "I'm not *dying*."

"...Those things are often irrelevant." This is harder than coming out, Jesus. "I just don't want them to put you on any meds you might not need. Especially now. I'm... I'm pretty sure you weren't hallucinating."

"The doctors... did tell me my mind would play tricks on me as I healed," he murmurs. "I'm sure that's all it is. No need to alarm them."

I swallow. "Will you tell me? If you see... more things that don't seem quite real? More people who might not be... alive?"

"Of course." He tries to laugh it off, but winces from the pain. "If only I could remember."

ROAD TRIP

Dad is stable enough to return to the rehab facility, so Jenna and I visit him as soon as he's able to accept visitors. Even "just" palpitations, this early in the healing process, could feel serious. From his chair near the window, he keeps staring into the middle distance.

"Things going well with the house?" he asks me.

Jenna crosses her legs. She has bright patches of sunburn on her exposed shoulders. "Steady as she goes."

"And the realtor? Have you met with–"

"Not yet." My knees are jiggling. "There are a couple more things I wanted to have fixed before they do the appraisal. I'll take care of it."

He squints at me, again. I've heard people can lose eyesight in the affected side during strokes. "You doing okay, honey?"

"Don't worry about me. It's just been hot, you know." I shrug.

The conversation turns to Jenna, who's been packing to get ready to go to Boston University. Dad hoped to be well enough to at least ride over to the dorm and say goodbye to her, though at this rate I doubt it. Heart surgery patients, when driving, needed to stop and stand at least every hour. I shrug my shoulders, as if trying to remove a physical weight. I still have to take her over to Walmart, to get her the twin XL sheets and the toiletries and the cleaning supplies and whatever the hell else college freshmen needed—what did I even have to buy when I first got my uni flat? I can't remember...

I fade back into the conversation. Jenna bobs her head towards Dad, urging me to interpret, because she's not used to reading his new face yet.

"I wish I could be there, honey," Dad says to her. "I just... I don't think..."

She crosses the room to hug him. "I'll be there four years. I'm sure you can see my dorm whenever you feel up to it."

It isn't long before he sends her on another pointless coffee run.

Whoever shaved, or helped him shave, his face has missed a spot of scruff on his affected side. "You look pale. Have you been sleeping?"

"Enough," I say.

"Not smoking too much?"

Depends how he classifies "too much." I am not chain smoking like him. But a half pack a day feels like an awful lot. "Trying not to."

"I know this is a lot of pressure to put on you—"

"It's fine, Dad, I knew what I was in for. Don't worry about me."

"I could probably see if Marianne could use some extra cash, I'm sure she could help you—" The paralegal.

"She's in over her head right now as it is. I'm *fine. I'm fine.*"

His raised right brow says otherwise. "I don't want you to jeopardize your health either." He slurs over "jeopardize."

I wonder when the pressure around me started to feel ever-present. A bubble of nausea twists around and within my stomach, and I swallow hard to rid the excess saliva in my mouth.

"Is it really just the heat?" he asks.

I exhale. "There... there is something going on, but it's managed. I'm working on it." Pulling the damp t-shirt from my back, I clear my throat. "Have you seen anything else since? Like that... hallucination?"

Dad shakes his head. "I don't think so. Nothing seems out of the ordinary. I'm just looking forward to coming home. And then... I'll figure out where to go next."

"I'll help you. You probably shouldn't live alone yet anyway."

"I can't ask you to do that." He sighs.

"It's not exactly going to be easy for me to get a job," I point out. "A lot can change in the next few weeks, anyway–you could feel back to yourself in no time."

A spot of darkness comes into his eyes. "We'll have to see."

Jenna knocks and then opens the door a moment later.

When she and I leave, the weather has shifted and changed, hot stinging droplets of rain falling from a slate gray sky. From the hot pavement, steam rises in slow waltz. The windows of the Honda immediately glaze over with condensation. We drive back, passing through the mid-day summer traffic.

"What didn't Dad want me to know?" Jenna asks. She crosses one leg over another, revealing one of those temporary tattoos just above her knee, flaky and peeling.

"He just wanted to make sure I was okay," I tell her.

"You do kind of look like shit," she points out.

"Gee, thanks, Jenna," I sign.

"But—seriously, though, did you ever go to that doctor?" Meaning the neurologist the hospital referred me to.

I haven't had insurance long, and besides, my brain isn't actually the issue. At least not right now. "The waiting list is like a year long. I'll be fine."

She frowns. "The last thing I need is you falling apart when I go away."

"I'm not *falling apart*." I sigh. I want a smoke, my right hand twitching towards the console where I've hidden my cigarettes. I'm sure she wouldn't appreciate that. "It's gonna be... weird, with you gone, for sure."

"Yeah, but you'll still be around for a while, right? Boston's not *that* far."

"Sue me for *trying* to say I'll miss you."

She smirks.

Later in the afternoon, as we're bringing down boxes labeled "COLLEGE TEXTBOOKS" which threaten to break my back, I get a DM on Discord from Amanda.

Hey, I texted you a few times but didn't hear back. You still good to help with a delivery? Leah said you were interested.

I glance at my phone. *I've had a new number since I got back. It's 845–*

She immediately texts it. *I should've totally thought of that.*

No worries. But yeah. When are you wanting to go?

Tomorrow morning? Around 7? We've got to go up through Oneonta, and I'd rather get it done sooner than later. Do you think you can drive? Leah will pay for gas. It's just easier than trying to get everything into my teeny car.

Sure, that works.

She sends up a thumbs-up emoji and ends the conversation there.

***

In the morning, clean, presentable, I meet her down at her apartment. It looks like the weather may not be on our side–the sky is that same simmering bruise color from the day before–but I can drive in the rain. Amanda still lives with her aunt, though her aunt lives most of the week with a boyfriend down in the city. Something about not officially living together until they get married.

Like me, her outfit is utilitarian: yoga pants and a branded T-shirt, her hair in one long braid instead of its usual curls. She brandishes a deep purple credit card. "She's giving us $200 for gas and snacks."

"Gas'll be like, $40, tops."

Amanda shrugs, slipping into the passenger seat. "She doesn't need to know that. Besides, you're not actually on payroll, so just buy something, would you?"

We buy a small feast of buttered rolls, cheap iced coffee, trail mix, and one pack of American Spirits to split between the two of us. And then we hit the road.

For the first twenty minutes or so, she pretends to fuss with her GPS. Her nails are still raw-looking and today her fingers are naked. She puts on some music at last. How on earth we're going to make the next three hours feel anything but awkward is beyond me. It doesn't help that this feels too much like times past, like that day we left on the road trip to Ohio, the light glancing on her collarbone, whispers over a motel room pillow.

"So where is this place?" I ask her.

"It's a small herb farm not far from the college," she says. "They also source containers for us."

I up the AC, which still smells like tobacco, but she takes it in stoically. "She does know we have herb farms down here, right?"

Amanda tosses her hands up. "Believe me, it's a whole thing. Something about the intention of the people growing them. It usually isn't that much of a pain."

From the sky, a few fat rain droplets patter onto the windshield. "So... how did you take an interest in all this?"

Her face colors, and she squirms in the passenger seat.

"Amanda, this is hardly the most embarrassing thing we've shared with each other."

"I *know* that, I just..." She takes one of the American Spirits, lights up. "When I was going through chemo, and in and out of the hospital, and all that... I started to take death a lot more seriously." Another long drag. "There was this girl, Gina, who had her treatments at the same time I did. Same kind of cancer, only she was stage IV, and it was all in her bones, only you'd never know. Beautiful girl. Gorgeous red hair..." She mimics waves by her shoulders.

"Oh..."

"One day we're both sitting for chemo and she starts having a hot flash, and she reaches up and takes off her hair. I hadn't realized it was a wig, and of course I was pretty vain, I wanted to know where I could get one when my hair inevitably all fell out too."

"I don't think that's vain," I say, but I can't help but see the girl peeling the wig off in my mind's eye.

Amanda shrugs. "We... struck up a friendship. Neither of us really involved the other people in our lives, so we were... lonely." She picks up the end of her braid and twists it around her fingers. "I go in one morning to start my drip, and she's just gone. A nurse said she had some fluid in her lungs, and, well... there wasn't a whole lot more they could do for her." She takes a long slug of her coffee. "And they didn't want me visiting, in case the pneumonia was catching."

How horrifying that must be. "I'm so sorry."

Amanda tries to smile and shakes her head. "It was a while ago now."

"Still—that's really hard."

"I saw a lot of people come into the ward and never come back," she says. "And I wondered... if I *saw* them, you know, if I could find out how to offer them peace..." She trails off. For a while, I pretend not to notice she keeps "scratching" her eye. "Is he... here?"

I shake my head. "Not right now."

"Had it been... bad?"

"It hasn't been good."

Amanda bites her lip. She glances out of the window, then back at me. "That's why you really left, isn't it?"

I swallow. I pretend it's the smoke that's given me a raw throat. "Yeah."

She reaches across and closes the distance, taking my hand in hers.

"Why else would I have given everything up?" I whisper back. "He was there, in *everything*. I had to learn to be a person after..."

"I know," she says.

On Route 28, rain starts to fall in earnest, making slow drivers the least of our worries. "I hope we don't have a solid schedule we have to stick to," I tell Amanda.

"No. Not quite." She tightens her grip on the passenger door's handle.

White-knuckled, I get us about halfway to the destination before the conditions feel actively hazardous. At top speed, the windshield wipers cannot keep up and the rain has rendered the world outside foggy greenish gray. I find a shoulder to pull off on, and here we wait, condensation blotting the windows. The rain beats a staccato rhythm into the roof of the car.

She leans back in her seat. "What a beautiful day."

Outside my window, the world is a pointillist dream. I trace my finger against the glass and try to remember the last time I created something–not because I had to for class, or for a few quid, but because I genuinely felt the urge to create. I almost do, *almost,* if not for the headache slicking behind my eyes. Popping off my seatbelt, I prop the seat back and pull the cover away from the sunroof so we can watch the water dance.

Amanda also puts her seat down. "What is it like?"

"What's what like?"

"Seeing them."

"You must hear what it's like from other people all the time."

"I haven't heard it from you."

My face warms. "It's almost... scary how quickly you get used to it," I tell her. "They're just... people. Not the freaky ghosts you see in movies or games, where they knock shit over and write messages in blood or possess people. They just... go about their days. At the grocery store. At the bank, schools, airports... anywhere people are, so are spirits. And some of them know they're dead and they can talk back, but most... just don't. They go about their day, ad nauseum, until eventually... what makes them, *them* is gone."

"Passed on?"

"Or dissipated. I really don't know."

She places her hand on her breastbone. "There's this ex-Catholic nun whose Substack I'm subscribed to. She has this whole idea that we're *lingering* more than we're used to because we're supposed to be stewards of God's earth, and earth is dying. He's leaving us here to try to get the living to get with it."

I turn onto my side to look at her. "Do you believe that?"

"I think it's kind of cynical, but there's some wisdom to it," she says. "I think we linger to help one another. Or help ourselves."

"...So what do you think about it making people sick?"

"You get sick because you're not given the space or resources to honor what you see," she says. "It goes all the way back since time immemorial; marginalized group doesn't get care, dies." She flips onto her side, too. The car is full of our breath, and I catch her perfume. "What do you believe?"

"I think eventually we return... somewhere," I say. "I don't know if God made us, or if there's just some form of a lifestream we come from, or if we're just animals and the electromagnetic field is what makes this all possible. Wave returns to the ocean. Or at least, it's supposed to."

His spirit unspooling from his body his spirit unspooling from his body

I look away from her. This is too close of a space, and I feel the crackle of her touch against my hand. "My neighbor's kid left behind a spirit. He said something interesting. Something about this–shimmery something that always beckons to him, but he's not ready to go to it yet."

"Leah said Marge said something similar, but she saw it more like a veil," Amanda says. "She can peer through the veil briefly, but if she goes all the way through, she feels confident that's it. So why do so many drift off instead of answering the call?"

"Well, for any reason people are scared of dying," I say.

"Do you see it? That shimmering?"

"...No."

She looks at the roof, at the rain whaling against the glass. "Is it bad I *want* to see?" she asks. "When I was really fucked up, right after Gina died, I kept watching all these videos of plane crashes and accidents where I *knew* people died. But nothing worked."

"It has to be in person," I say. "Trust me, *that* part fucking sucks."

"I can only imagine. It didn't even *occur* to me until *after* I saw your comics that you might... I always wondered, but I couldn't exactly ask."

I could touch her hair. Pull a strand free from its braid, curl it around my finger. I could cup the softness of her throat, feel her heartbeat. I could lean against her and listen to her heart, her breath.

Amanda's fingers brush mine. "I feel like... I lost hold of who you were."

"...I was pretty crazy for a while."

"No, I mean, even here right now, you feel so *distant.*"

"I don't want to be. I really don't want to be."

Her hand brushes my cheek. I know this, I know exactly how this feels, she touched me exactly like this when we first kissed. My breath feels too hot in my chest.

We measure each other up, see who has the gall to break the stalemate. I want to be unravelled, to open myself, my mouth is so close to hers–

Someone is knocking on the window. A state trooper in a wet hat. I hurry to roll down the window. "Alright. Party's over. This is a narrow road. Move on."

ROSE HILL

S tock-straight, silent, we get back on the wetter-but-much-more-visible highway. My vision swims black in the corners. I feel my heart battering the inside of my ribs, and my cheeks burn hot.

What the fuck what the fuck what the fuckkk

I have to focus on the task at hand. We have to go north to get the supplies to bring to Leah so I don't have another seizure, or lose my mind. What I want more than that is to find some quiet place where we can—

No.

When we make it to our destination, I'm beyond grateful.

Oneonta is a cute little town, artsy and independent, despite the darkness lingering at the corners–The Yellow Deli and its cult, for instance. The farm is hidden about ten miles away from the SUNY on a gravel path slick from the day's rain. We bump along the uneven road, gritting our teeth, before pulling down a straightaway framed by greens in neat rows. When I think of *herb gardens* I imagine cute little window boxes with those starters you can buy at the store. This is on a whole other level. The plants are *huge*. A tan woman in a kerchief stoops over to inspect the plants for damage from the storm. She raises a sun hat towards us.

I realize, slowly, there are no spirits within this space. I'm so used to seeing them that their absence is nearly uncomfortable.

We park in front of an old farmhouse. Nothing about the place strikes me as particularly commercial–there are no trucks or vans, just an old Chevy on blocks in front of a detached garage. "You sure this is the right place?" I ask Amanda under my breath.

"Yes. I've been here." She gets out of the car.

Beneath my sneakers, the earth is squishy and a peculiar shade of pale brown. We walk up the gravel drive, across a porch with chipped paint, and Amanda knocks on the bright red front door.

A white woman with wildly curly silver hair answers. "Hello, dear," she says to Amanda, in an accent I can't place. "What auspicious weather."

Amanda shrugs. "It made the drive a nightmare. This is Aaron, by the way. He's helping me."

The farmer stares me down. She has these very dark eyes–so dark her pupil is indistinguishable from the iris. "The cards told me about you," she says. "Can I offer you tea?"

It'll be a long three hours back, but Amanda answers before I can decline. "That would be lovely."

The woman gestures us into the small, shallow front room of the farmhouse. Bundles of herbs hang from the exposed wooden beams in varying states of dryness; some look like they belong in bottles at the store, others are nearly fresh, green petals straining against butcher's twine. They fill the cabin with their bright, sharp, and floral smells, making me nearly hungry. Across from the heavy stone fireplace, a black cat sleeps curled on the corduroy couch. The walls are lined with built-in and floating shelves, all of which are lined with votives, and crystals in intricate patterns, and the odd photo or two, as if to reassure us people do indeed live here.

The woman shepherds us to a round wooden table with a silky paisley tablecloth. A bouquet of wildflowers is in an oxidized copper teapot. "Earl grey or oolong?" she asks, a rasp rolling across her tongue.

"Earl grey," I offer, the same time as Amanda says, "oolong."

The farmer laughs. "I'll break the tie in favor of the lady." She disappears into a teeny kitchen with an old-fashioned iron cookstove and trough sink.

"Who is she?" I mouth to Amanda.

"Greta. The co-owner." I recognize the name - someone at Amanda's cafe mentioned her. It's possible there are two Gretas, I guess, but it's an odd coincidence.

A few moments later, Greta emerges with another kitsch teapot on a silver tray with some scones and a pot of jam. "You must be hungry after your long day."

I am. Starved, in fact, those buttered rolls had less sustenance than air. But I also get the sense that I'm eating a boon offered by a witch. I wait until I see Amanda put jam on her scone and bite in before I eat. More milky than buttery, the scones are delicious, and there's a little bit of cardamom scattered within them.

"I'm sorry about the delay," Greta tells us. "The factory where we get our jars—there was an incident with their annealer. A very *strange* incident. Annealers don't typically blow up, you see."

I cup my hands around my mug of tea. The loose leaves bob in their strainer. "No. They don't."

"Is everyone okay?" Amanda asks. "Did they make it out?"

Greta nods. "Some minor burns, but nobody *dead*, thankfully. Though the plant is a total loss."

Amanda clucks her tongue. "I'm sorry."

I look at Greta. "I'm guessing it was ruled an accident."

"But of course." Greta picks up a shortbread cookie and waves it, scattering crumbs onto her silky shawl. "It always is. So we... we had to find somewhere else. No more issues, but... a moderate increase in cost."

Amanda nods. "Leah budgeted for that."

I want to ask what's so special about these containers that we can't buy them, say, from Amazon, but I get the feeling now is not the time to ask.

Greta retrieves a card reader from a desk drawer. Seeing the small, slick white device *here* causes more dissonance. Amanda signs off on the order and gets a receipt, and we go to finish our tea.

"How long have you been involved, dear?" Greta asks me.

"He's just helping," Amanda says, very quickly. "As a favor to me."

Greta laughs a little. "I know you remember the last time I read your cards."

She blushes fiercely and ducks her face into her cup.

Hm. Interesting. "I do have it, though, you know," I tell her. "Four years now."

Greta stares at me, and I do mean *really* stares, her dark eyes shiny in the natural daylight. "You are quite odd, aren't you," she murmurs. "How long have you had the attachment?"

I straighten. "How did you–"

"I can see it." She pinches her fingers and plucks the air around me. "These little... wisps."

I take such a sharp breath, it hurts my throat. "Is there anything you can–"

Greta shakes her head. "No more than you have already been told. Perhaps *listen* to those unlikely forces."

Amanda rubs her upper arms, though the room is quite warm. "It wasn't pretty."

"No, I can see that," she murmurs.

I choke down another mouthful of tea. Being from the bottom of the cup, it's very bitter. "I appreciate the tea, but can we, um, get the packages? We have a long way–"

"Yes. Yes, of course. This way. I'll see if I can get Bill to help you two."

Bill is one of the other farmhands, one of those stereotypical strapping midwestern boys. The boughs of herbs are in old mason jar boxes, wrapped in canvas. Most of the order is the little jar containers meant to hold the products. After we load up, I get in the car, my fingers itching for a smoke. Amanda lingers with Greta for a moment, her expression pinched and downcast. Greta grips her hands and nods in that old, wise, grandmotherly way. Amanda bobs her head too, swipes at her eyes, and climbs back in the car.

"Are you alright?" I ask her.

"Fine–*fine*," she says. "Where are those cigarettes?"

"You're reading my mind."

She lights up with ease, and I navigate towards the main roads. "You would think, given my history, I wouldn't smoke," she says.

"Hey, look at my Dad. I still smoke more than I should." I clear my throat. "So... Greta has some weird vibes, huh?"

Amanda exhales smoke. "Yeah. You could say that."

"What was it she was saying about your cards?"

"Just *drive*, will you?"

I can't help but smirk.

ENDYMION RISING

Later that evening, after we drop off the herbs and jars to Leah's shop, after I accept the car will probably smell like thyme and rosemary in perpetuity, I shower and lay in bed, desperately trying not to think about Amanda. This proves more easily said than done.

She says that I feel *distant*. Which is probably true, but so does she. That was the thing about trauma; it picks away the thin fabric of who you were, weaving a tapestry from the threads left. But I meant it when I said I *didn't want to be distant*. I want to feel that sense of connection, of intimacy, again. All of the should'ves and could'ves are piling up. I could've, should've, reached out to her. Seen if she was okay. Just fucking *said* something about how messed up I was. We had a few days together in Ohio, our skin no longer so unfamiliar. How long has it been since I wanted–

"You're not alone, babes," Dmitri says, from somewhere near my bed.

My hand, halfway towards its destination, snaps back up. "*Jesus.*"

"It could be worse. I didn't have to warn you."

I scowl at him and sit up, disrupting the covers. "How many times have you watched me–"

He holds up a hand. "It's hardly a one-way mirror. Besides, it doesn't seem like... *that* has been on your mind. Until now?" He drifts closer, his empty eye socket good and bloody. "Was that all I needed? A pair of nice titties and–"

I rub my temples. "Maybe it has something to do with you being a maniac, and not whether or not you have boobs."

He points at me. "And there it is. How long do we have to argue about cosmic scales before you *do* something?"

"Have I mentioned that *you tried to kill me?*"

"And have I mentioned *you're keeping my spirit here?*"

A jackknife of pain, so hard and hot that my hands go numb and my head feels suspiciously liquidy, spikes behind my eyes. My watch alerts me to the increase in heart rate, but this is something no salt will fix. It's the sort of agony that demands your full attention. Heat leaks down my face, pattering softly red against the bedspread. A nosebleed. My stomach churns. There's no way I'll make it five feet, much less to the bathroom. I barely make it to the wastepaper bin beside my desk. It's the type of puking that *hurts*.

He crouches besides me, his form fizzing. "I told you this would happen."

I flop down next to my sick, trying to breathe. The last time my head hurt this badly I seized. I don't have to wonder long before I disappear and come back to find my muscles sore and spasming and my pants soiled. I pray to anything listening that Jenna and Matt were somehow oblivious to the attack, the onslaught. My brain still vaguely feels like putty. I strip off my filthy clothes, pull on my robe, and go into the bathroom to shower off the mess.

"Aaron..." Dmitri begins, his eyes on the floor.

"Here, I'm naked, isn't this what you wanted?" I hiss. "Isn't this–"

Hot water/plastic/darkness

When I come to, Jenna's waving a paper fan in front of my face. A loose, wet towel has been draped over my unmentionables. I feel like I can't breathe, the air is too hot, too humid. Did I drown?

I squint into the uncertain light–the bathroom sink's high-beams are on and they burn.

"Can you hear me?" Jenna asks, in English.

"Yes," I say. "I think I... fainted."

"I think you hit your head."

I groan. "No ambulance. Please?"

Her expression is hard to discern. "Aaron..."

"I've fallen tons... I don't want to..."

"You threw up in your room."

The edges of the room are still wheeling around me. "POTS," I manage. "You remember."

She raises an eyebrow.

"I'll be... I'll be fine. Hard day. That's all."

Behind her shoulder, Dmitri lingers. Is that... contempt, on his face?

Jenna waits outside the curtain while I finish my shower, and she walks me back to my bed. She brings me water and a Gatorade with an extra Liquid IV added to it, which only helps marginally, because that's not really the problem. Once she believes I'm asleep, I go to my suitcase in the closet and take out the bottle of clonzepam. Not exactly a painkiller, but better than nothing.

"Aaron..." Dmitri says softly, shortly after it kicks in. "I don't *want* the pain to go on."

And maybe because I'm high, my chest shudders with an unborn sob.

WHO WE WERE

Change happens slowly. Abuse isn't like the TV shows or the movies. The person doesn't wake up one day and start swinging. It creeps, like the proverbial frog in the pot.

We were fifteen when we met, him newly moved to the district to pick up his sophomore year of high school. He marked me that first day, walked up to me in the hot September afternoon, when I was watching Charlie dribbling a basketball in the school parking lot.

"Aren't you just darling," Dmitri said. That was before he started dyeing his hair; his natural shade was a blonde so pale it was practically see-through. His fashion consisted primarily of knock-off Converse, basketball shorts, and black t-shirts.

No boy ever flirted with me before that. I only had a vague notion that I might not be totally heterosexual, a notion blunted by too many SSRIs. All I knew was that I liked the way it felt when he looked at me, when his eyes kissed me up and down.

He said, "what is it exactly that queers do for fun around here?"

And I said, "I don't know, you tell me."

He brought me back to his house–his godforsaken house, the tiny three-bed in Poughkeepsie that was pretty much a biohazard zone–one afternoon when he was sure his parents would be gone for the afternoon. We took the late bus, pink address change slips in hand. We walked past the empty vodka bottles and plates piled high in the kitchen sink. He brought me back to his pocket-sized bedroom off the living room full of crosses. The room could barely hold a twin bed, a desk, and a dresser. He booted his old laptop, pulled out a Logitech controller, and loaded a PS2 emulator.

"Have you ever played *Kingdom Hearts?*" he asked me.

I think that was the most earnest he ever was; he wasn't trying to wow me with some author I'd never heard of or some poet I'd never read, he was just a kid showing me his favorite video game, and the *shine* it brought to his golden-brown eyes lit something deep within me. Before long my trembling hand was tracing the ragged edge of his t-shirt, and he was setting aside the controller and we fumbled towards each other in the center. He tasted like grape soda and boy and potential, his lips soft, full. I'd only ever had the chastest, strangest pecks in middle school. I did not know a kiss could have *weight,* or heat. I did not know *want,* though I felt it deep within my still-forming body, wordless.

He was kisses, he was earnestness. Until he wasn't.

CASSIUS

When I wake the ache is still there, though it's less apocryphal. I feel filthy, sweaty, despite my alleged shower, and I'm naked. As I get up the sheet slides off of my mutilated thigh in the early morning light. I have long taught myself not to feel it, not to feel any of it, the deep pit of my quad muscle, eaten away by gunpowder. And it doesn't physically hurt, mostly, it just pulls, a jagged opposition around the bone.

They tell me I'm lucky; at that range, the gunshot should have *shattered* my femur. All I got was a chip. The doctor said it was fortunate that I drank so much milk as a kid.

I tried to have the scar covered, in Edinburgh, by a wonderful tattoo artist who specialized in such tattooing. They admitted it was so deep they were unsure anything could *cover* the evidence, though it could make it more appealing. After a few sessions of white-knuckling it in their chair, the fronds of a fern formed around the harsh edges of my scar, making it not quite so obvious what *kind* of wound this was.

I still limp when it rains.

I trace the edges of the somewhat numb tissue. He watches, his eyes bright from within my closet.

"How are you feeling?" he asks.

I don't respond. I stroke the pits and grooves of my scar and think of the person I might have been.

"I don't–*want* you to suffer. You *do* know that?" he continues.

I can't engage. Won't engage.

He perches his chin on his hands. "Aaron, I–" He vanishes as I descend the stairs. I see Matt making a bagel in the kitchen.

"Morning," he says to me, gesturing with a half-full coffee pot. "I heard you had a rough day yesterday?"

Jenna wouldn't have said shit. "How?"

"I saw your light on in the middle of the night."

I shake my head. "I've always had trouble sleeping."

He sighs and plucks his bagel from the toaster oven. Everything bagel; the onion and garlic and carby smell makes me feel weak. "You did even when you were a baby," he says softly. "You would... cry and cry and cry, and nothing would soothe you. Milk. Being held. I felt like such a failure. Moms are... supposed to know."

I brush my hand across my face. "Dad said the same. About me not sleeping, I mean."

"I wanted you tested for everything. But they always made it seem like I didn't do enough."

For a second I'm fooled into feeling sorry for him. I'm not sure at what point Matt became aware he wasn't a woman–I never asked–but I'm sure childrearing, and the inherent femininity society assigns to it, has to have been crushing. As a cis-passing, straight-passing, white person, my concerns have always been addressed when I raise them at the doctor's. But a trans guy believing his baby might be sick? He must be wrong, of course. "I'm not sure it would have made much difference," I say.

"Sure it would've. If you slept better, maybe you would..."

I raise an eyebrow. "Not be so cracked in the head?"

He rubs a dusty palm against his shirt. "No, that's not what I mean. I wanted... things to be easier, for you."

The ever present "so why did you leave" almost leaves my mouth. He told me why. It was either escape or suicide. I have no leg to stand on, so to speak; I did the same thing.

"I don't even know you," Matt says, leaning against the counter. "What your life is like. Who you are now, as an adult."

"I'm distant?" I ask, a lump catching in my throat.

"Well, yes. I know that's my doing."

I blink, and blink, and blink, my eyes wanting to water. I know Dmitri is here, just not visible, the wisps of him too evident in every-thing.

"Is it so hard to believe I really want to make things right? It's not about the money–I'll sign over the money, if that's what you really want."

I wonder if I, in my isolation, did what Matt did to me.

He comes forward and takes my hands. "Hey. Hey, honey, it's alright."

I'm not even high anymore, but my chest aches and tears roll like sweat down my cheeks. How much pain can one body store? Too much. Not enough. What happens if Dad dies? I can't take it, I'll...

He eases me over to a chair, gives me a tissue. His hands are differ-ent–callused, bonier, the skin not as soft, but they are recognizable to my five-year-old self.

Emotion wells into a fresh headache. I don't feel well. I'm so tired of feeling sick, from spirits, from POTS. To his credit, Matt lets me cry largely without commentary. And while the spiritual pressure is still all-consuming, some other valve in me has been somewhat released.

"Whatever comes next," he says. "With Jenna, with Alan, I can be as close as you want. I can help you as much as you want. You know that?"

I nod and swipe at blotchy eyes.

Jenna and I spend the rest of the day packing and unpacking—boxes of stuff from the attic, totes for her to take with her to university. We're starting to hit some of the deeper cuts. The clothes we wore as kids, family photos passed down from Gran (acetate faces I do not know), boxes of schoolwork we did and drawings we made, old stuffed animals in vacuum sealed bags, the air crushed out of them.

"Hey, check it out," Jenna says. She opens the bag of plushies with a *whoomf* and pulls out a pink poodle. "It's Missy!" She squeezes it closed to her chest. "She even still smells like kettle corn."

One of our rare family vacations, driving across the midwest to see my estranged aunt Marie, before she went full crazy Trumper and my parents cut her off. Jenna, barely older than a toddler, had eaten an entire bag of caramel corn while our parents bickered up front. Poor Missy took the brunt of the upset stomach.

Jenna sits Missy onto an open box and pulls out a few more plushies, lining them up in a neat row. A tortoise she got for sitting through a hearing test bravely. A tie-dyed bear from Woodstock. A Build-a-Bear cat from some birthday party, bedraggled. Her entire arm is in the bag by the time she gets to the bottom of it, the corpses of our childhood all around us.

She frees a calico cat with an eyepatch hurriedly hand-sewn on.

His right eye fell off ages ago, a result of being dragged everywhere. When it happened I cried and cried because Pirate *couldn't see.* Matt sat me down and helped me sew a triangle of denim over the loose threads, so he could now *be a real proper pirate...*

Jenna, visiting me in the hospital four years ago, placing him besides me on the pillow when she thought I was asleep. A deep bone pain no opioid could touch, Dad gnawing his fingernails because he hadn't smoked in hours but couldn't bear to leave the room. Dmitri's fresh white-hot spirit lingering behind the room's curtain–

I'm not here; I'm there, in that room, in that bed, watching him, as he watches me now.

My breath is hot in my mouth, the familiar vice-grip of panic, and I cup my throat. Every time it happens–every time an old truck backfires, or I watch a movie without researching it first and there are firearms, or a good-old fashioned red-blooded American shoots at a coyote, or even just the odd *loud noise*–it feels like the first.

Jenna's still standing there, holding the stuffie, her eyes wide. I can keep the reality of it from her *most* of the time. "I take it you, um, don't want him?" she says.

"It just surprised me, is all," I sign when I'm something resembling composed. "Let me?" My hands shake as I reach for Pirate. Pirate will not hurt me. Pirate is mostly polyester, and polyester never killed anybody, not immediately, anyway. His fur is pilled from the constant rubbing and his tail hangs on by a few threads. The seam on his back is starting to split, knotwork from some minimum-wage teenager at Build-a-Bear finally giving out. His little heart, red and satin, peeks through the threads. I poke it back down into the white stuffing. "He's... smaller than I remember."

"You got bigger," Jenna points out. "So... donation? Trash?"

I set him down next to Missy. "I'll hold onto him. I need to sew up his back."

Later that evening, Dmitri watches me do exactly that with some brown embroidery thread.

"I didn't get to have stuffed animals," he murmurs. "Maybe when I was a baby, for a few years. They'd make me too soft, Papa said."

I remember this story. He's told it before, the first time I won him one at the Dutchess County Fair; a dog with floppy velour ears and sparkly eyes.

"I drew a face on a pillowcase and stuffed some socks in it," he continues wistfully. "I called her Amber. No idea why. Mama found it one day when she went to change the sheets. That was the first day I was ever really afraid of them."

What must that feel like, small and vulnerable, your grownup standing over you, grasping, hitting?

"I thought about that dog when I was dying." He leans on his fist, a shiver running over his form. "How soft it was. It's... strange, the places your mind goes. You remember, right?"

I shake my head.

"You thought about American Girl dolls," he tells me. "The responder you reached was named *Addy*. Your sister used to read those books all the time. You remembered her being happy, because the Felicity doll looked *just* like her, and Matt had gotten her one for Christmas."

Pirate's heart has slipped back out of the stuffing. I unravel the thread and jam it back in deeper, almost touching the opposite edge of the fabric. What did I wish on his heart for, back then, when they took me to make him? I don't remember–

"You wanted your sister to feel better, because she was sick," he says in a low voice. "Your father took you when she had meningitis, as a way to explain what was happening. You wanted her to be okay *so* badly."

"Stop," I whisper. "Just... stop."

"I can't really help it," he says, crossing the room to hover near me. "The memories run up and down me like currents. I don't seek it out. It comes to me."

I glare at him and force a hot memory back; the first time he gripped my arm just a little *too* hard.

But Dmitri doesn't take the bait. He sinks down onto his haunches on the floor. "That, too," he says. "There's an awful lot of that."

I pull the thread tight–too tight, at first, it snarls the fabric–and tie a knot.

"I'm sorry," he says to me, his one good eye glimmery and piercing. "I'm... I'm *sorry*." Dmitri laughs once, a rattling sound. "You ever think about how hollow that word is? All the words we have to convey how fucked up shit is, and all we're left with is *sorry*."

I can't believe he means it. But I don't think I have ever heard him say those words. Out loud. To anybody. At most it was "my bad."

He wraps his arms around spectral knees. "Maybe this is... my penance. My purgatory. I have to witness what I made; I have to feel it, like you feel goddamn everything. You feel *so* much, all the time, I don't know how you do it."

The needle sinks into my fingertip; not enough to break the skin, but enough to sting. I stick my finger in my mouth.

"Do you believe me?" he asks, almost *begs*. "Do you believe I'm sorry?"

How many times did he call me, text me, message me, saying he *didn't feel like himself, and it won't happen again?* But time again and again–

"I *know* that," he interrupts. "I know. I just–I just want it to stop."

My laugh is almost a bark. "It's never *going* to stop. I'm going to carry this–everything you did–for the *rest* of my life, God forbid I don't also hang around. Is this just what it's going to be–you and me, snapping at each other for eternity?"

"No," he says. "Not if you let me go."

And there it was. The motivation. He's only apologizing so he gets his way.

"That's not true–"

"You think I don't want you gone?" I ask. "Away from me, *out* of me?"

"Then why aren't you *listening* to anything anyone's telling you? Me, Leah, that old kook from the farm–I'm not being hyperbolic when I say *this will kill you*." He huffs.

I stand. Pirate flops to the floor. "Then tell me what to do. Tell me where I need to go, who I need to talk to, anything to get you to just *fuck off*."

His eyes bulge, and he vanishes with a faint *puff*. I didn't even mean to banish him.

"Fucking... fuck," I say. "I hate this shit so much."

INDEPENDENCE DAY

I spend the next few days in a clonazepam-induced blur–not particularly because I *want* to go on a bender, or because I have nothing to do, but because it's Fourth of July. It's not just veterans who get triggered by fireworks. I never had to worry about that much in the UK. There are of course the odd holidays where people feel the need to blow stuff up, like November 5th, but nothing to the scale or magnitude of our friends across the pond. No parties for me; I instead cowered in our unfinished basement, eyes and ears covered, and waited for hell to pass.

I used to love fireworks. Dad used to take me and Jenna–he always found time for that day, somehow–to Cantine Park in Saugerties, the best show around. He'd put me up on his shoulders so I could see better, bright blue red pink gold flowers bursting against a navy sky. The sound would reverberate in my chest, and everyone cheered, and the days tasted like cherry snow cones and popcorn.

That stopped when Matt left. First because of the depression, and then because he was just working too much, and gradually, the holiday just became an excuse for me to hang out with my friends and drink and smoke too much shitty weed. We would curse the nature of our country while being mesmerized by the small blots of color forming on the horizon, some primal part of us finding pride.

When I come out of my stupor, deeply hungover, it's already time to take Jenna away to school. I feel like I've barely seen her much, and she's already gone. I take her to see Dad one last time, and he asks to speak to her alone. Back in the room, her eyes are red, but she's smiling, the unique pleasure-pain of change.

I wish I could enjoy this, could engage or find some form of catharsis; the pressure has become not just intense but actively *unbearable.* I can barely keep anything down and my heart rarely strays below 100 bpm even when I'm sitting still. But he's gone. At least there's that.

Dad is able to stumble around now, slow shuffling steps, and get his hands around knobs. He looks smaller, despite us being the same height, and still has that thin-and-unwell puffiness about him. He keeps assuring us that *he's doing well,* but I'm not so sure. I have to check with the doctors, the cardiologist–

By now that jab of pain behind the eye is familiar. It's become an annoying companion. I feel my face twitch, unable to fully hide it. At least I have POTS as a rock to hide behind.

"Are you going to be okay to drive to Mass all by yourself?" Dad doesn't even try to say the whole state name.

I flew all the way to Edinburgh. Didn't even look back as I passed through security. But yes, the three hour ride to Boston, in this heat and humidity, feels no less daunting. "I'm just in a flare. Happens every summer. I'll be fine." I force a laugh. "She might be on her own to move her stuff, though."

Jenna rolls her eyes.

Dad doesn't totally buy it, but also as a frequent flyer of the "I'm fine" flag, he can't really push much. "If only I were released–two weeks earlier," he says. "I'd have been able to go–"

"You won't be missing much," Jenna lies. "Just stuff in a dorm. I'll be there any time. I'll call you and show you."

I squeeze her hand briefly. "So they're springing you soon, Dad? They didn't mention it to me."

"They just told me–this morning." He fumbles with his bad hand and picks up a notepad, which seems to have a running list of things to keep track of, some crossed off. *10:43am–nurse mentioned release date, pending sign off from dr.* "It'll be nice to be out of here. Home. I'll still have... PT, and all that. They think I can still get most of the motion back into my face and hands."

"That's great!" I still can't get the image out of my head of him doubled over with the palpitations. Despite all evidence that recovery is slow but sure, all I can feel is foreboding.

And nausea, along with a slow burning grind in my stomach. God forbid I try to drink a protein shake for breakfast. There's a bathroom attached to his room, but I hardly want either of them to hear me puking. I resolve to sweat it out. Literally. The smell of rubbing alcohol helps curb the urge–I keep those little prep pads in my wallet the way some people keep condoms–but it would be a very strange thing to dig out and sniff. My old roommates got used to the little quirks forced upon me by my illness (eating straight salt, laying upside-down, sniffing rubbing alcohol), but I kept the brunt of the effects from my family. I don't even fully know why.

"Maybe you need rehab, too," Jenna remarks.

"...It really feels like that some days."

The original plan was to take her to lunch, but I'm too nauseous to eat more. At least we're close enough to Leah's shop for me to stock up again. Jenna will razz me for buying "fancy skincare", but the prospect of *not* feeling like garbage is too tempting to resist. I make my sister wait with the car so I don't technically have to feed a meter. Outside, the weather has started to turn, humidity congealing into mist and threatening rain.

Amanda is not there. I didn't realize how much I wanted to see her until I couldn't. Instead, Leah is at the front desk, a laptop perched next to the POS. Despite the stifling summer, she has on a black turtleneck and a long, deep purple skirt. "Hey! Thanks again for taking care of that for me."

"No problem." I'm already moving towards the products, the shelves no longer so barren, and pluck out two of what I had before.

She hesitates when she rings me up, double-checks there are no other customers. "You shouldn't–*need*–two."

"It's for someone I met. They need it as well." It's an incredibly flimsy lie.

Leah raises an eyebrow. "Maybe we should–set up some time. If it's getting worse, if you're starting to feel more physical effects–"

"My sister is standing with the car, I really have to go. Amanda not here today?"

"...She stepped out to pick up our lunch. Aaron." She tries to meet my eyes, but I feel like I'll lose it if I do. "Don't take any risks. We *can* help you."

I force a laugh. "Do you want the sale, or not?"

Leah sighs. "If you run out so soon, I'll tell her not to sell you any more until you meet with me." She takes my money without further comment. At home, in the sanctity of my room, I dispel the pressure. It's not pleasurable like that first time; it *hurts,* a weird deep crawly nerve pain up and down the backs of my arms, making my vision swim black. But still, relief persists, and the world is no longer so crushing. I flop onto the bed, utterly exhausted, and start doomscrolling on my phone, only to notice a few texts.

I haven't saved her contact; it feels too intimate. But I recognize her phone number. *Leah said you dropped by today. Sorry I missed you.*

My heart skipped. *Was lunch good at least?*

If you consider very mid lo mein good.

I smile. *I would've hung around, but I was in a rush. My sister had to do some errands.*

That's right—she's leaving, isn't she?

I take her in a few days.

Amanda sends a few sparkling heart emojis. *I remember when she was a little kid. Must be weird.* She has no siblings; her dad died before she was born, and her mom was deported some years ago. Part of how we met—Dad worked the case, did his best, but the judge Amanda's mother was assigned was notorious for being harsh. As far as I know, she is doing well down in Oaxaca, working as an office manager for an interior designer; the distance remains ever-present. They are, or used to be, close.

We've also been going through our attic, so there are all these memories, I tell her. *When we were kids. Before Matt left. A lot of it I thought I forgot.*

I can only imagine. Isn't your dad, like, hoarder?

A hoarder with a label maker.

She laugh reacts to the message. *You used to be, too. Is your closet still organized by color?*

I glance over to my open closet, the folding doors left open, a pile each for clean and dirty. *I barely have enough stuff for that.* I found clothes from my nineteen-year-old self among the detritus. It isn't like my style's changed, if you could even call it that. T-shirts. Flannels, soft cotton button-ups in pink, orange, pale blue. The problem is that most of it no longer fits.

From the accident up until after I left, it was hard for me to eat. Partially due to the meds–new and increasing doses of SSRIs, a mood stabilizer, an antipsych–but partially due to some *mental* block that made everything taste like paste, no matter how meticulously seasoned it was. One doctor proposed mild brain damage, because severe blood loss can do that. Fitzl was certain it was the meds, because some make food taste like pennies. Coupled with the fact that I've *always* had a bizarro metabolism, and the appetite-suppressing effects of nicotine, I was nowhere near a healthy weight. I don't know if I'd consider it an outright eating disorder, because it wasn't exactly *deliberate*. Especially because once I got to the UK, the fog lifted and I could eat again.

I wonder, now, if it's also a symptom of the sight, attachment. I'll have to ask Leah.

Even my single suit, unworn since junior prom, is too small in the shoulders.

You still sew? I ask her.

On and off, yeah. She makes some of her own skirts and dresses, partially from thrifted fabrics, partially from old garments. Polyester, she said, makes her skin crawl. I remember the feel of those dresses, the cotton and satin and wool, hints of lace under my fingertips. *I took up crocheting when I was in treatment. Easier to manage. I must have made one million scarves before I finally learned how to do the more fun stuff.*

I imagine her sitting there, in one of those big recliners they use for IV meds, pale, head covered with a hat or a scarf, her hands busily working a hook. *What else did you make?*

One of my on-again off-again hustles is to make stuffies–amiguru-mi–because they're quick. She sends me a few photos of a tortoise, a penguin, a duck, in soft soothing colors. Their eyes aren't those big plastic ones, but all different kinds of buttons: denim, mother-of-pearl, starfish, smooth red balls. *Sometimes I give them to the kids at Mid Hudson, when it's safe to.*

Why wouldn't it be safe?

A lot of them are on immunosuppressants. I have to put them all in bags, then they have to wait a certain amount of days and douse them in Lysol.

I melt. Of course that's exactly what she would do. *I'm sure you made a lot of them happy.*

The little dots of her typing start and disappear a few times. *I want to hope they all made it, but...*

In my mind's eye, I imagine a little girl's spirit drifting through those white halls, gripping the leg of one of Amanda's toys. *If it's any comfort, little kid spirits tend to be better at holding items from life. So you might still be providing one comfort.*

That's... weirdly peaceful.

I could take a look one day, if you want.

No. I'd almost rather not know. Thanks, though.

I don't know what to read into that, if she was uncomfortable. *Which is your favorite to make?*

Turtles, when I'm not in the mood for fancy patterns. Birds are fun–more realistic ones, with wings. She sends a few more photos. A parakeet, with small wooden legs, its head cocked slightly to the side. I can almost see it in motion. What array of twists and stitches did it take to accomplish that?

Those are gorgeous!

Thanks, I like to think so. She adds a cat-with-heart-eyes emoji. *Have you been working on anything lately?*

I bite my lip. My drawing tablet was in fact still in my suitcase, which itself is still planted on the old stain. Forget paper. *Not... really.*

You've been busy. A moment passes, then, *Leah said you might be helping us more?*

Sounds like she needs to see how much she can spare, but yeah. I could use the money. Before I can hit send, though, I hear Jenna yelling, the sound reverberating upstairs. Without a single thought I dash down towards her, my body protesting badly. It seems Jenna and Matt are in the middle of some fight; he's perched at the kitchen table, his shoulders slumped, and she's over by the kitchen counter, her feet planted straight, and her face a bright red.

"Just *stop* it," Jenna snaps, in English. "Just stop *trying.*"

I hold up both hands. "What's going on down here?"

Her chest heaves. "He won't *leave me alone.* I said *no.*"

Oh Jesus. I stand halfway between them. "Okay. You said no." I look towards him, seeing an equally flushed face. "What happened? Why are we yelling?"

"I'm just *sick* of it," Jenna continues. "The way he–keeps trying to pretend things are normal. You don't *get* me. You don't *get* to have me." Her eyes are full of tears, but they don't fall.

Jenna doesn't *get* angry.

I meet her gaze. "Are you okay?" I ask, only in ASL. "What did he do?"

She's shaking so badly that it takes her a moment to be able to sign back. "I found my baby clothes. I went to bring them out into the garage and he *saw* me, and he just started reminiscing about what kind of *baby* I was, and how hard it was when I lost my hearing, and how he's so glad he gets to see me grown up–"

"I get it," I sign. "Why don't you go take a nice swim? Cool down?"

She huffs and pushes past me upstairs.

I take a deep breath. I knew I was going to have to have this conversation sooner or later.

"Is she okay?" Matt asks. "I couldn't quite understand what you were saying…"

I pour myself a cup of water and drink the whole thing down. "She took it really hard. When you left." I plant my hands on the edge of the sink. "She asked where you went. Every day. For weeks. "Where's mommy?"" Maybe if I pretend this is a monologue–a performance–it will feel easier. "What was I supposed to tell her?"

Matt makes a *whumpf* sound like he's been punched. "I thought–Alan would have–"

"He was *heartbroken,* Matt. For months he could barely *eat.*"

He drops his hands and gaze into his lap. "…Really?"

"Oh, yeah." I can feel how hot my face is, but I won't break down again. "He loved you so much."

"…Then he had a strange way of showing it."

I clench one fist hard enough for the nails to dig into my palm. The pain is grounding. "You know who ended up picking up the slack, right?"

He doesn't say anything. Won't look at me. He looks like a beaten puppy.

"I was thirteen," I whisper. "And I did the best I could."

For a second, only the soft hissing of the central AC and the hum of the refrigerator break the silence.

"Would you rather me die?" Matt asks in a very small voice.

"You could've called. Written. Come to see us. Anything but–what happened."

"I told you why I didn't fight for custody–"

"No, that part is completely clear," I tell him. "It just seems like the only times we heard from you involved death or money."

"And I *told* you the money doesn't matter–"

"Then why are you here?"

Jenna stomps down the stairs in a swimsuit, a towel wrapped around her protectively.She must be going around the house to avoid looking at him. I don't blame her.

"Maybe I want to do better," he says. "Maybe I want to *be* better. Maybe I want to say sorry."

Sometimes even holding up my body is too much. I look down at the sink's drain, the steel. "So many words for all the fucked up shit, and we only have "sorry.""

"...I know."

"You were never going to be able to swoop in and save the day."

"Apparently that's your job." There's no malice in his tone, no anger. In fact, he sounds completely defeated.

"Yeah. It fucking is."

He stands. "Is that all this is, then? What could I do to make it up to you?"

I'm starting to crack. I know myself well enough by now to categorize the symptoms, the effects, enough. Blood pressure through the roof. A watch that advises me to *stop exerting myself*. A pinching layer of sweat around the crown of my head. A jaw that feels like it could snap. As much as I try to stop from raising my voice, some petulance falls out anyway. "The fact that you're *still putting the work on me* by even *asking* that–"

He nods once, twice, brushes away tears, or sweat, or both. "Then maybe I should go."

"Maybe you should. I don't fucking know."

Without another word, he ghosts back upstairs. I need a cigarette and I need to calm down. I'm almost through another pack. If I keep going at this rate I'm going to end up just like my father–

I force the front door open and see Jenna, still in her towel, sitting on the wicker couch on the porch. The corner of the towel is knotted in her palms. I sit on the opposite end and light up.

"Can I have one?" she asks, timid.

I raise my eyebrows. "That bad?"

"I know I said I would never, but I don't–" I can practically see her pulse in her throat.

It goes against all big brother instincts, but I offer the pack to her. "Just the one. Can't have you being like me."

She fumbles to get it lit, but to her credit, doesn't cough. She makes a face. "This tastes good to you?"

"...You get used to it."

"My friends said the same thing about beer, and it still tastes just as icky as always," she murmurs, then, "you won't tell Dad I said that?"

I mime zipping my lips and throwing away the key. "Look at you, Miss Perfect. Hitting the penjamin and drinking and *smoking*."

She shrugs. "I was overdue for a rebellious phase."

BOSTON

The next morning, Matt's car is gone. He's left stuff in the guest room, and the bathroom, and of course he left the cat and all her things. I am positive he wouldn't have left forever without her. He hadn't the first time.

So of course now I have to feed Rascal and scoop her absolutely monstrous shits out of the litterbox he put by the closet. She watches me do it and meows, hollowly. Rascal has mostly kept to Matt's side, sleeping in and around his things. Getting up and down the stairs is too hard for her. Considering that she is old enough in the US to drink, I can't help but pity her. "I'll leave the AC on for you, old scrunkly," I tell her, scratching behind the ears. Her fur is soft and oddly greasy.

At least my "flare" is over, and I feel mostly physically okay, and the morning I take Jenna to Boston is one of the coolest in weeks. I make her her favorite breakfast–waffles with cinnamon and honey, bacon, fried eggs–but she struggles to eat.

"Are you nervous?" I ask.

"Well–maybe a little," she admits. "I've emailed with my roommate a little, but I... I've never lived anywhere but *here*. And this place might be gone by the summer."

"No, I understand."

"And I'm so used to how my school handled the whole Deaf thing... what if there aren't any people who sign, or that I can talk to?"

"There's got to be a Deaf community in Boston. The city's huge."

She takes a sip of her coffee (French vanilla creamer, three sugars, barely coffee). "...What if they don't like me?"

I laugh. I can't help it. She stomps on my foot. "They're going to love you."

We finish packing the Honda. It's squished with stuff–bedding and her clothes and her school supplies and of course her sporting goods. It'll be weird not seeing those cleats by the door.

I notice Jenna holds Missy when she gets into the passenger seat. A last crystalline minute of childhood. "Let's go," she signs. "I have to be checked in by five."

The hours slip by too quickly. I almost hope for traffic, but the roads are mostly clear until we get into Boston. I've only visited the city a few times, briefly for school trips. She gawks at the landmarks, takes a few pictures. We arrive at her dorm a little after noon. Nervous tension hangs on her like hair on soap.

"Ready?" I ask.

"Always." She nods once, twice. "Okay. I'm here."

Her building is old and nearly austere, if it weren't for the chipping bricks. We carry a few armfuls of the lightest things and follow signs to a small office. Perhaps one of the benefits of early admission; the place isn't crawling with people, though there are more than enough spirits going about their day. Some even carry what looks to be move-in stuff.

Jenna signs in and we meet her RA, a junior named Melody who has a service dog. Melody brings us to her room on the second floor.

Blank white walls, each lined with a narrow strip of corkboard. Two thin twin beds, the naked mattresses like ice cream sandwiches. Melody explains to Jenna that she can put in a request to get her bed lofted and leaves us be.

I go and open the rickety blinds. At least she has AC; not all of the dorms do. "It's certainly... a blank canvas," I tell her.

"It's... small." She wrinkles her nose. "At least it won't bother me if she snores."

There are a couple of other upperclassmen hanging around, real buff dudes on one of the sports teams, meant to help the incoming athletes move in. They attempt to talk shop with Jenna, but I can already see she's struggling to keep up. I knew this was a part of it, the adjustment–there are growing pains–but it doesn't make it any easier to let her go. *Especially* when I see one of the buff dudes checking her out.

We spend most of the afternoon getting the room ready: setting up the bed, hanging her clothes, sticking up some twinkle lights. She only brought a few decorations, knowing she'll probably acquire more. By the time we've shown the room to Dad, and we meet her roommate (a middle-eastern girl named Eleni with a bright pink streak in her hair, seemed sweet, even learned a little sign over the summer), there's really only time for a quick dinner in the dining hall. There's an evening house meeting at six, I guess to keep friends and family from lingering.

Jenna appraises her grilled chicken. "...I can already tell I'm going to miss your cooking."

And that's that. Just like that.

Jenna walks me to the car (the sad, empty car) and we hug each other tight, tight, for at least a few minutes.

"Text me about your first day," I tell her. "I want to hear every-thing."

She nods. "I will."

"And be *careful.*"

"I will."

"And... eat your veggies?"

She slaps my shoulder. "I probably eat more vegetables than you do."

Okay. This is the minute where I walk away. I can't cry; not yet. Only after she sees me drive away smiling. "I love you, Jenna."

"Love you too."

I get in the car. She flashes another "I love you" sigh before disappearing into the building. A bird in flight.

NOT HAVING A BAJA BLAST

I decide, on my way home, I am going to get drunk tonight. It seems like the right level of reckless. Drinking more than a beer or two gives me awful hangovers; the meds make them hit hard, and I suspect I'm a natural lightweight. When I get gas, I get two twenty-ounce bottles of Mountain Dew Baja Blast and more cigarettes, and stop at a liquor store to get the smallest bottle of vodka they have. A good cathartic drunk cry; that's what I need.

Back home, Matt's car is still missing, and Rascal meows for her evening feed. Exhausted, I make a boy dinner of frozen chicken tenders, tortillas, and some shredded cheese so old I probably should not eat it. I make myself a drink, throw on some trashy reality TV, and try to forget myself. What I underestimate is how perfectly the alcohol disperses into the soda, making it taste like nothing, and only when I'm staring at molding that edges the walls, wondering if it's too late to order a pizza, and *also* finding a random desire to read *Twilight*, that I realize I'm more than a little buzzed.

"This–now *this* is a new one." His voice, in my impaired state of being, sounds almost living. "Aaron Bateson, are you *drunk*?"

"I know you are, but what am I," I stutter.

"God I *wish* I was. I fucking wish. Can I join you?"

"You're gonna anyway, so."

"Fair point." He crosses over to the loveseat, grasping at my mostly-full beverage, but it doesn't make a facsimile for him to pretend to drink. He sighs and flops onto the loveseat, kicking his feet up on the coffee table. "Oh, you're gonna be so fucking sick tomorrow morning. You almost finished that bottle."

"No." I wave at him vaguely, my hand moving as though through water. "No. No bad vibes."

His remaining eye glitters with amusement. "Okay. No bad vibes." He twiddles his thumbs. "So... what do you want to talk about?"

"Did you really hate *Twilight?*"

He blinks. "No. Of course not. How could I? Girl gets a guy who will love her forever, turns rich and beautiful, *and* has a hot werewolf sidepiece? God forbid a woman have a hobby. Do I wish the Mormon undertones weren't so obvious? Of course."

"You always said it wasn't literature." It comes out like "lichera-ture."

"Well, I'm also the asshole who read *Infinite Jest* in fifth grade, so."

"I bet you thought you were Holden Caulfield."

"I did. Boy, did I. But if we're getting meta, my dear, that's more your speed. My little meow meow."

I give him a thumbs down.

"Alright. No endearments."

My head feels warm and tingly. I want to do something stupid.

"I love this energy, but I probably *wouldn't.*"

I fumble for my phone. I could call someone. Charlie? Or maybe Amanda? Is she crocheting right now, working her fingers into worsted wool? Maybe with some wine? I want wine. There's probably some left in the old liquor cabinet in the dining room.

"You should absolutely *not* do that. Relax. Watch some TikTok, or something."

I don't want to relax. I want to fight something.

"Easy, tiger. Easy."

So tell me why I start crying.

"Because you're a mess and chock-*full* of idiot juice." He joins me on the couch; he doesn't make indents in the cushion. "Just let it out, kiddo. You'll feel better. You know what Shrek says, better out than in."

I laugh a little, despite tears. "Why are you being nice to me?"

"You tend to catch more flies with honey than with vinegar. Besides, maybe I just... want to. Maybe I owe you that."

"Why weren't you nicer to me?"

He clasps his hands. "I don't know."

I sniffle and swat at my eyes. "I loved you so much it *hurt*. I thought maybe if I tried hard enough..."

"You could save me?" he offers softly. "Oh, Aaron. You tried hard enough. Too hard. Maybe you should've been saving yourself."

Dizzy, still sobbing, I reach for my drink, almost knock it over.

"We can still end this. You can still let me go."

"I don't know *how*."

"You need to remember the promise you made me that day," he says. He's nearly eye-to-eye with me. "I can't tell you and I can't make you."

The walls are waving. "Was it... was it my spirit, that promised you?"

He gasps. "Yes, Aaron, yes. Keep going."

"But how can I... remember what I said, when I–" A hot, desperate nausea crawls up my throat. I run for the kitchen sink. Baja Blast doesn't taste nearly as nice coming up.

Dmitri lingers by my side, his remaining eye desperate. "You have to. If you want any of this ending, you have to."

"Okay. Okay. Okay." I rinse out my mouth with the faucet and wash away the mess. "Fine."

It takes one million steps for me to get back to the couch, and I crash into uncertain dreams.

THE DROP

At some point in the night, a shrill keening wakes me up. Disoriented, smarting with a fresh, squashy hangover, for a second I'm back with him in that field on that day, until I realize it's the landline.

No good calls come on the landline. Especially not in the middle of the night. Either it's Matt, and something happened, or it's Jenna's school, and *something happened,* or it's Dad's facility and *something else worse* happened.

I lurch, my limbs still sticky with sleep and alcohol, over to the phone and answer. "Hello?"

"Is this Aaron Bateson?" A feminine voice I do not recognize. Never good.

"Yes?"

"I'm calling about your father."

No. Please, God, no. "Which one?" I swallow a mouthful of spit.

"It's about Alan," she says.

I hate when I'm right.

***

I'm not sure exactly how I get to the hospital. Just because I was no longer drunk, that didn't mean I was in any fit state to drive, but waiting on an Uber in this dead zone was not feasible. I got myself there without hurting anyone else or damaging the car, skin slick with sweat, unable to catch a full breath. The front desk person, when I get there, suspects at first that *I'm* the one that needs help.

The ICU is cool and dark, low lighting left on to assist the medical staff. And everywhere noise—the hiss of ventilators and oxygen, steady beeps from monitors, murmuring loved ones. Spirits in similar states of discombobulation. A tech shows me to Dad's room.

Any surgery comes with risk. For my own, they had no idea what anesthesia to use on me—I bled too much. General could've stopped my heart, but local risked me waking up during the delicate artery repair. Dad's bypass created a new artery in his heart. What nobody anticipated was how *slowly* he, after a life of stress, would heal. The tissue began to bleed.

Things must be dire, because a doctor stops me before I can even see him. "Healthcare proxy?" They are just a blurry figure to me.

"...Yes. What's happening?"

"We suspect the bleed triggered another stroke; he's not been responsive." Whoever they are sighs. "We can try to operate again, repair the tissue. Given the neurological impairment... I'm not sure I can in good conscience recommend it. Hence why we contacted you."

"It won't—it won't just heal?" I feel as though I'm standing at the end of a very long, drafty hallway.

"I'm afraid not."

"What do I do?" I whisper. "Everything was–*fine* a few days ago, I don't–"

They touch my shoulder. "That's just the way these things happen, sometimes."

I can't stop gasping. This is a different flavor of panic, sharp and acrid, and I feel inches from my skin. "What's the... other option?"

"You say goodbye. I promise it will be peaceful for him."

I am an actor. I am an actor in a play and this is not real. "M-my sister... she's all the way in Boston–is there time for her to get here?"

"I can't know for sure."

I can't stop shaking. It is so *cold,* and I don't have a sweater. I know what I would choose. But I also know what he would choose, and to go against that would be evil. "He wouldn't want to suffer," I say.

"Is that what you wish?"

No. Of course I don't want any of this. "...Yes."

"We'll need to get your consent in writing, and then someone from hospice will–" They talk at me some more, about who will come, about what will happen, about tubes and wires and electrodes and their removal. When I see him, he's a husk in white, eyes shut.

I pull up a chair and take his less encumbered hand. The flesh is cool to the touch. I force myself to drag out my phone, to text and attempt to video-call Jenna, but of course it's the middle of the night and she does not answer. I try the RA next, then the RA on duty, who finally answers, but they have to get authorization from the asleep resident director to use the master key to open her door and *nobody is acting with any urgency.* By the time she texts back, and I tell her what's going on, he's already started doing something called *agonal breathing.* She shouldn't spend his last minutes on a bus, a train. She calls him so he can hear her voice.

I take his hand into both of mine. "There was this place in Edinburgh that had the most outrageous pasties," I begin. "Not, like, outrageous in the good way. They were pretty awful. Nobody goes to the UK for the food." I attempt to choke down the lump in my throat. "But we would go there because they were always open, and they had this balcony in the back of the building that, if you timed it right, and it somehow wasn't raining, you could see the sunrise. One time–I was going to get another round, and this guy stops me, and he asks about you. You went to law school together, and he–he thought I was you, at first, it was pretty dark. People make that mistake–all the time. Somehow, across the world, you still made that person smile." I can feel myself starting to dissociate. My feet are numb. "I hope I can be half that person."

Jenna starts her own story, but I can't take anything in. His heart still beats, he still breathes, but I see these pinkish-white wisps beginning to form and unravel. The movement is deft, graceful, even, and he sits up in his body, looking around. He sees me.

"Aaron?" he whispers. No longer slurring.

"Hey, Dad."

"I had this... strange dream..." He looks down and sees himself. "Oh dear."

"You're sort of dying," I tell him. I don't know why I didn't expect *this*.

"That's unfortunate," he remarks. "I must be having an out of body experience."

I shake my head. "You're a spirit."

He blinks, running a hand along his head, ruffling spectral hair. "I always... suspected," he admits. "That you were... you would sometimes just fix your eyes in the distance and wave, or nod, I let myself believe–"

"That I was crazy?"

"That you were struggling with a mental imbalance." He sighs and wriggles his legs free. "It is so–strange. I see you, but I also see–" He looks past me. "Something else..."

"Do you want to go towards it?" I ask him.

"Yes..." He takes a deep breath. "I suppose I should let myself properly die first, no? At least we can... at least we can talk."

The tears spill free, and my chest spasms.

He looks sheepish now. "There's no need for that, sweetie, I had a good enough life."

"Maybe you could stay around? For a little while? With me?"

He touches my hand with his spectral one; I can't feel it. "I don't think I can...is there... do you know... what happens after?"

I shake my head. "We think it's peaceful."

"I don't want you to worry. If you follow the instructions–"

"I don't want to talk about that," I say. "I'll figure it out."

He settles more comfortably, crossing his legs. "I remember that place," he says. "With the pies. They were *awful*." He clears his throat. "Will you... will you be okay?"

"I... I think I will," I say. "This is weirdly helping."

"You, and your sister... look after each other." His lip trembles. "I'm... sorry."

"For what?"

"I wasn't the best dad–I wish I could have been *stronger*. I'm so glad that you are. You'll need it."

I scoff.

"It takes a lot to survive what you did. Did you ever... make your peace? Are you happy?"

"No," I tell him. "I... I will be."

"Will you tell your sister you saw me?" he asks.

"If you want me to tell her something, I could," I say.

"I just know she's going to take the world by storm." He laughs a little; his body rasps. "I think that's it..."

"Wait—"

His fingers brush my cheek. "I love you both."

Before I can even say it back, he disappears; not the way Dmitri pops in and out of existence, but slowly, the way fog does under sunlight.

AN ENDING

I've never seen it before, but I am certain he's transitioned into the next phase, gone beyond. Despite my body buzzing with panic and grief, I am... strangely calm. I tell Jenna he went, and he went peacefully. Someday I will tell her about his spirit.

They come and pronounce him dead, offer me hollow condolences. They say I can sit with him as long as I like, but he's already gone. In the cafeteria, the hangover asks for more of my attention, and I eat three bagels without stopping. I feel so... heavy. It takes real effort to go back to the car, *Dad's* car, and to drive away. Tomorrow I have to obey his end-of-life plans. Today I will grieve.

***

It's oddly embarrassing to admit. Trying to muster up the words in a text–to Amanda or Charlie, to Kiki and the gang–makes a weird smile cross my face. I don't want pity. I just want someone to know.

Matt is home—they must have called him. I barely get a foot in the door before he comes over to me from the kitchen. "Is it true?"

"...It happened so fast."

He crushes me in a hug without my consent, but I'm too tired to fight, so I let him. "At least he didn't suffer."

He had, though, for weeks before the sudden decline. I can't bring myself to snap about it. "No. I want to... lay down, I don't feel well..."

Matt nods. He looks misty-eyed too, and I wonder briefly if he really does feel it. "If there's anything I can get you, you let me know. I should... look over the arrangements—"

"He wanted me to handle it," I say. "I will, I just... I need to sleep."

I shower and drop into bed, my bones like stones, and I sleep for the better part of the day. When I wake up, everything seems normal, until I remember. The sense of acceptance I had at the hospital is starting to fade. I lay for a long while, half-curled under my covers, feeling my heart beat, my lungs expand. I thought I knew the weight of grief; this is different, this is less immediately crushing, but still tiny fractures rattle around my chest.

Woodenly, I go downstairs. No Jenna, no Dad, it's just Matt and I in this corpse of a house. I make myself start a pot of coffee, scramble some eggs with extra salt. Every bite tastes like paste, a sad and familiar sensation, but I force it down anyway. My POTS has kicked in, leaving me sweating through pajamas despite the AC. And yet I keep shivering as though to physically rid myself of the pain.

What I need more than anything else is a friend. Not someone I have to keep at arm's length, or protect, just someone to *tell* that this happened. I dig out my dying phone, plug it into a charger Matt must've left out. Midafternoon, I'm sure she's working, I fumble to send a text to Amanda.

I'm not sure how to put this, but my dad died last night.

I don't want her to comfort me. Or maybe I do. That certainly is a heavy load to just put on someone, especially with things between us so tenuous. I go to recall the message, but she's faster and she's already seen it.

And now she's calling me. I almost don't answer. I gulp in a breath, trying to calm myself.

"Are you alright?" she bursts out, her voice full of concern. "I mean–clearly you're not *alright, but...*"

"It's so strange," I admit. "I think I'm in shock. It was like, one minute I was having a few drinks and going to bed, and then a few hours later he–" The pinkish-white wisps of his spirit, emerging softly. Not nearly as violent as Dmitri's had been. "I spoke to him. After it happened. He decided to move on."

She breathes out. "Oh wow."

"And I guess that was helpful? But now I just–"

"Do you want to come down and sit with me? I can't not work, but at least you won't be alone."

I do want that. Desperately. "I have to... take care of some stuff. The arrangements."

"Your poor sister... the minute she leaves..."

I was never a nail biter, but I find myself gnawing on a thumb nail anyway. "It's... yeah. Raw. Very. I should–I should text her, but I also have to call Sweets before they close–"

"Aaron. Breathe."

She's right. I'm well and truly working myself into a panic attack. I breathe in, then out. "Sorry. I should let you go, I'm sure you're busy. Um. Is Leah there? I want to... I think I'm going to need an appointment."

"I can see. Sure."

"Thank you. I'm sorry. Again." I hang up. Cigarettes. A smoke will help. I should quit, quit so I don't end up like him, but I am about three seconds from flying apart. Two. One and a half. Breathe in. Breathe out. I can't afford to tap out with a clonzepam, not right now. I'm a grown up, I can do this, all I have to do is *follow his instructions–*

I stumble into the open office, kneel down, open the bottom file drawer to the left of the desk. The blue welled folder with the string tying it shut. Open it. Okay. There are labeled tabs packed with papers. One offers passwords to all of the necessary online accounts–mortgage, electricity, internet, the various bank accounts, the old health insurance portal. I find a document lying out his wishes–no wake, no funeral, just an urn and a "celebration of life" if we felt it was appropriate. He even bought the damn urn - it was in his closet. With receipts. Wrote his own obituary, sans dates.

I pull the cardigan off the chair and wrap it around myself. I can't get warm, now, I can't *breathe.* All I have to do is call the funeral home to make sure they get his body from the hospital, and then, I guess, *find* the urn and take it over there. Just wrap it up and drive it over. It's just an object right now.

My headache, my little buddy, is back. I climb upstairs and look over the open threshold of the master bedroom. The king bed, the mattress sagging to one side, neatly made, a journal sitting out on the bedside table, vacuum lines in the carpet. Closet door to the left, partially open, clothes missing, some at rehab, I guess. Above the racks were a few boxes; a crank radio for use in emergencies, a few old pairs of shoes, and then a square black box the size of my ribcage. That must be it. I reach with noodle arms, grasp it, bring it down to my level. Someone will have to carry this forever–me, my sister. My grandparents, who I have to call and tell their son is dead.

The headache torques in intensity, and I almost drop the box. The medicine. I *was* at the hospital, probably was touched by other spirits, and of course Dad's, and Dmitri has been around, and I just feel..

I feel...

My tongue is numb in my mouth. Now that I've acknowledged it, the pressure practically crushes me to the floor. I drag myself over to my bedroom, find the bottle in my bedside drawer, dose my wrists, and it *hurts* again this time too, my vision graying at the edges. At least it makes the headache ease.

I can do this. I have to do this.

A NO GOOD VERY BAD TIME

The next days and weeks pass in one unending, hot blur. Everything I must do is either bad (picking up Jenna from the train station so she can see our father's body, collecting his things from the rehab, navigating the very adult world of bills and insurance claims) or worse, like calling Gran and Grandad, or having the other lawyers from Dad's firm show up to offer their condolences, or all the calls and emails and letters from former clients once the obituary dropped. I feel like I'm dropping in and out of my body, the world terribly far away.

I attack my chores with a fervor. Hired a landscaper, sold a bunch of stuff. Matt is still around, still trying to *help me through this,* so I give him some of the admin-y bullshit to handle, like renting a storage unit for the stuff that's being kept, transferring the title of the Honda to my name, and sitting in Social Security to get the survivorship benefits. I keep finding small pockets of money that seem to immediately disappear into expenses, namely, the rehab and hospital copays, with more sure to come.

My friends–old and new, distant and close–all try to get in touch with me, to see how I'm doing, and as much as I try to be normal and respond, to assure them that I will be fine, along with everything else it gets to be too overwhelming.

One early August day, as I scrub out the garage fridge so some guy from Facebook Marketplace can pick it up, I get a notification that I've been added to a group chat, DEAD DADS ANONYMOUS, and it has Charlie, Amanda, and his roommate Nellie in it.

Charlie writes, *Adding our newest member. Cheers and our condolences. In case you forgot: us half-orphans convene once a year to celebrate our dearly departed (sometimes deadbeat) dads. Normally we just meet Father's Day, but frankly buddy, it seems like you could use the support right now.*

...And I'm back within myself and the strangling kelp of my feelings, my eyes watering. *Hi, I'm Aaron, and I'm an alcoholic,* I write back.

Charlie continues, *this is the second-best club nobody wants to join. The council has decided that you are going out to dinner with us, tomorrow, 6pm, to retroactively claim your first dead dads dinner.*

And if I'm busy?

It's only legally trafficking if you cross state lines, he writes.

I brush away faint itchy tears. *I guess I'll leave the doors unlocked.*

***

It isn't until the next day, as I'm trying to get ready for this dinner, that I realize I can't remember when I last showered. I've just been stuffing my hair into bandannas, in the guise of keeping it out of my face as I clean and organize. It's not like I've been close enough to anybody for them to get a whiff. I've been so out of it that I didn't even see how bad the depression has gotten. I no longer have a single clean-ish thing to wear, and when I go to de-goblin myself, there's a pronounced ring of mildew in the tub. On my hands and knees, I scrub, and accidently spray cleaner directly through Teddy's face.

"Hi," he says.

"Oh—hey, buddy. Sorry about that."

Pulling himself up to his full height, he shrugs. "Doesn't matter to me."

I set down the bottle. "I'm sorry I haven't been able to play much, I've had a lot going on."

His face scrunches with apparent confusion. "Oh… I just saw you yesterday."

"Well, I've been around the house."

He shakes his head. "I mean you and me hung out."

I blink. All I did yesterday was clean out the dining room and doomscroll. "Are you sure, bud? I don't remember seeing you."

He looks away, an opaqueness coming into his cheeks—a blush? "Last night? After you went to bed?"

I raise an eyebrow. "Listen, Teddy, you're a cool kid, but I am *not* okay with you being in here when I'm sleeping."

His face puckers, becomes more urgent. "No, I wouldn't, but you were—" He trails off. "I know it was you."

I wonder if Dmitri has been fucking with him. "Like I was sleep-walking?"

He relaxes slightly. "Maybe that was it, yeah."

Great. I don't *doubt* it happened—it's a side effect of Ambien, and I've been taking it to sleep more often lately—but it is unusual for me. "If it happens again, can you try waking me up?"

Teddy pouts and folds his arms. "What if I don't wanna?"

"I mean, I guess I can't technically make you, but I would really appreciate it."

He sits on the lip of the tub. "...I heard Mommy say your dad died."

I clear my throat. "Yeah. He did."

"He's not... here?"

"No. He chose to move on."

Teddy considers this, his eyes on the bathroom floor. "I think about it sometimes," he admits. "But I want to make sure... mommy's okay."

"Maybe I can help you talk to her. Do you think she would believe me?"

"I dunno."

"Well, you just let me know, okay?" An alarm I'd set earlier, to get ready, goes off on my manacle. "I have to get cleaned up. Can we talk later?"

He huffs. "It's always "later.""

"I'm sorry, bud."

He steps out the bathroom window and descends back down to his house.

As I scrub and yank the snarls out of my hair, I think about what Teddy said, about wanting to make sure loved ones were okay before moving on. Mrs. Graham does, or used to, believe I'm unwell, because frankly, I was. There are only so many times you can wander into the yard in the middle of the night in a dissociative fugue before the neighbors start to catch on. But death can change people's minds, or at the very least make them more amenable to things they wouldn't be. It would be wrong not to try. It's not fair to Teddy to suffer, to linger if he truly doesn't want to.

Leah first introduced herself to me as a "medium." She seems more focused on us living folks, but I wonder if she's worked with spirits themselves to move beyond. Someone has to have. All of the movies and books about exorcisms and hauntings, it's hard to believe some semblance of the real thing doesn't exist somewhere.

Clean, hair diffused-dry, I put on a dark button-up and jeans, and I wait. The fruits of my labor are starting to become evident; the mowed lawn, the pruned bushes, the nearly empty dining room. I'm sweeping up one life; what comes next?

I can't make any more decisions until the house is sold. And until I do something about Dmitri. Even drunk, that night is now seared into my gray matter. My spirit promised him something as we lingered waiting for death. Problem is, I can't remember it. Why would I have promised him anything? Is it another ploy, another game? Would I have to bite the bullet (ha ha) and have Leah mediate? Dmitri alluded to at least a partially scrambled account of that day. If I choose to believe he's right, how do I go back and find the "real" version? Surely, in my current state of mind, that wouldn't be good.

Neither are the headaches. Or seizures, for that matter. What if one happens when I'm driving?

The only people left living with any idea of what really happened to me are Fitzl, the surgeon, and two cops. Did Dad keep a record of my statement? Can I call the station and ask? Is it available through FOIL requests? That is, if I can even be considered a reliable narrator.

I lean against my knees and trace the edges of my scar. These are the head games I did not miss. The muddying. He was only kind to me to further his agenda. But at this point I might have no option but to help him.

Why does it always fall on me?

Before my mood can get worse, a dull rumble fills the streets. Charlie's Subaru, smoking slightly, rolls into the driveway. He kills the engine and takes a hit on his vape. Nellie, a cute black girl with pale pink braids, waves from the front window.

"I don't think it's supposed to do that," I tell him, gesturing to the car.

Charlie gets out of the car, appraises the smoke, shrugs, and opens the trunk. In a swift and practiced motion, he pops the hood and dumps some coolant into the radiator. "Problem solved."

I wince and remind myself it is not my problem anymore.

Once the car has had its drink, he crosses up the driveway in a few long strides. Like me, he's wearing black. This is as close to a funeral as I will attend. Charlie folds me into an embrace. The strings keeping me afloat are close to snapping, and I shudder without meaning to. "Don't say "sorry,"" I murmur into his shoulder.

"Me? Never."

In his arms, the layers I've built between myself and reality threaten to clear. I manage to choke down the tears, but only barely.

After a long minute, I force myself to let go. Charlie appraises me closely. "All good?"

"Good enough," I say gruffly.

"I hope you're hungry. K-pot's fucking fire. We're gonna grab Amanda and head down."

I can only hope that the food doesn't taste like glue. "Sounds good."

I feel better once I see Amanda in her deep navy sundress. She waits down in her building's lot, brushing nonexistent wrinkles from cap sleeves. I haven't seen her, physically, since it happened.

She gets in the back seat with me and gives me another long hug. I lean against her and breathe in her perfume. "Is it too much too soon?" she asks.

I think she means the dinner. "No...I really needed to get out of the house."

Too soon, she lets go and buckles her seatbelt. She painted the stubs of her nails, I notice, a soft silver. "You're still packing up the house?"

I shrug. "It's what he wanted. I can't... afford to keep it, long term. Not if Matt actually wants his half."

Amanda snorts. "He's trying to get money?"

"...Dad never actually took him off the mortgage. Hard to, when Matt paid for most of it."

She rolls her eyes. "Exactly what you need to be dealing with."

"...Yeah. Tell me about it."

"I'm–*tired* of talking about boring adult shit," I say, fidgeting with my sleeve. "*Please,* anybody say anything else."

Charlie hoots. "That's what I'm talking about."

Amanda takes my free hand and squeezes once, softly.

***

This restaurant, one of a bunch that sprung up while I was away, serves Korean hotpot and barbecue in a cool stone room lit with pink and yellow neon lights. The smoky, fatty scent of frying meat fills the space, and it is bustling with both the dead and living. As I know now, some spirits still have a sense of smell. Do they hunger, or just yearn for food? I would. I've never seen any of them attempt to eat anything, and drinks in hands always remain full. At our large booth towards the back of the restaurant, a spirit looks longingly over Amanda's shoulder at the menu.

It's the sort of meal that requires your full attention; everyone gets their own soups on hot plates to boil meat and vegetables in, with a grill plate in the center of the table for the more adventurous. Charlie immediately orders three steaks and sets them on to sear.

I'm glad for the busywork, honestly. Despite my desire for companionship, I have no idea what to say. Easier to cook thin cuts of meat than to engage with our shared reality. The soup *does* taste like more than paste, even if it's hotter than hell in here because of it.

If I weren't chronically and mentally ill I'd probably be unstoppable.

Amanda laughs at some joke Nellie made, scattering a handful of cilantro into her boiling pot. I look away before my eyes wander, and see who else but Dmitri leaning so casually against the edge of Charlie's side of the booth.

At least I'm in public, and I don't have to acknowledge him. His empty eye socket has that dumb flower in it again. I notice someone about Jenna's age look him over and shiver.

"Smells good," he says. "Is that miso?" He leans closer to Charlie. "The–*really* spicy stuff, that I can almost taste."

I fumble to reach for the sauce plate, almost knocking over Nellie's mojito. Amanda smirks at me and passes it over, her skin brushing mine. The goosebumps on my arm were not put there by her, but she blushes anyway.

"Is now really the time?" Dmitri asks. "All the shit you got going on, and you somehow manage to feel–"

"Where's the bathroom?" I ask Charlie.

He gestures in a wide arc to our left. "Past the party room, through the tapestry. You'll see it."

I get up, and Dmitri follows me closely. After checking the stalls for feet, finally I turn to him. "I'm here to fucking mourn, okay? Can we not do this for two hours?"

He raises his hands. "Strong surges of emotion summon me. What do you expect me to do?"

"Can you *not?*"

He scowls. "No. I can't."

I press my fingers to my temples. There appear to be no paper towels to blot at the sweat on my face, and I'm all blotchy.

Dmitri drifts over to me, almost touching me. "It really does suck about your dad. I'm s–"

"Don't you dare," I hiss.

"He didn't deserve it. Really. I thought you wanted me to be nicer to you."

I cross my arms. "Well, if I had listened to him, neither of us would be in this scenario, would we?"

Dmitri starts back, a hand over his dead heart. "Youch. Claws are out today." He smooths back a strand of hair into its funeral slick. "But hindsight's 20/20, isn't it? What would we do without all our lovely memories?"

A pulse hotter than a brand stabs me behind the eye, and I grip the edge of the trough sink to stay upright.

"Is there more you're forgetting?" he asks. "Might be worth considering."

Some guy comes in to pee. I force myself to stand back up and wash my hands, though that familiar shaky blood-pressure plummeting feeling is back. Not to mention my head fucking hurts. Back to dinner. Back to dinner, with my friends supporting me–

I'm in the car, in the back of the Subaru. All three of them are laughing, and Jon Lajoie's "Everyday Motherfucker" is playing on the stereo. I do not know how I got here. If I fainted, the mood would probably be a lot more somber.

Amanda catches my eyes and smiles, the sort of smile that makes you feel like it's just for you, but something about my expression must clue her in that things aren't quite right. "You alright?"

"It was just–hot in there. That's all."

She raised an eyebrow. Slowly, her hand on the seat fingerspells D-M-I-T-R-I? And she draws a question mark.

I nod.

She purses her lips. "You have to go straight home?" At some point in the night the bobby pins holding curls out of her face began to slip, causing the hair to pull free and cup her face.

"No. Not really."

"Want to come by for a little while? I can take you home."

My face flushes. I know she means only to speak of Dmitri. "Sure, sounds good."

Charlie makes eye contact in the rearview mirror and smirks. Waggles his brows. I roll my eyes in response.

He has to get out when he drops us off–another coolant juice box for the Subaru–and only then does he let the lightheartedness disperse. He holds me tight, tight. "You need anything, and I mean *anything*, you tell me," he says. "Don't be a stranger. Especially now."

"I won't. I promise."

The furrow in his brow indicates he doesn't fully believe me, but he gives my arm one last squeeze and climbs back into the belching car. Nellie blows us a kiss.

For a moment, we only hear peeper frogs chirping.

AFTERPARTY

Amanda clears her throat. "My aunt's not home. It's a city day for her." She gestures for me to follow up the stairs to the second landing. Her apartment is one of four in the building, and it has a balcony with a wicker chair and coffee table, a few plants spilling from window boxes. More herbs.

"Must feel like having the place to yourself."

She cracks open the door, her keys jingling too loudly. "Mostly. But when she's here her presence is very noticeable." She makes a swirling motion by her temple. "Her anxiety could give yours a run for its money."

"Then that really fucking sucks for her."

Amanda laughs a little. I follow her across the threshold. While the walls are an undeniable landlord beige, the place is full of color; from the burnt orange sofa by the kitchen pass-through, to the sunset-colored crochet throw draped over it, to the bold prints on the wall (O'Keefe, Kahlo, Klimst, Mucha). A small, octagonal kitchen table has a bouquet of peonies on it, somehow still alive despite it being late in the season, and I smell their perfume. A flatscreen TV sits on a white cube unit, each full of pale pink baskets; one on the bottom sits half-off the shelf, yarn spilling from it.

Near the door is a wooden shoe rack packed with more pairs of heels than any one person needs; bejeweled, animal print, patent leather, shiny, matte, thin-strapped and thick-heeled. Amanda notices me looking and grimaces. "Those are mostly all hers," she says. "Her boyfriend is a designer. Selling the ones she doesn't wear anymore helped pay my medical bills." She takes off her own modest pumps. "Shoes off. We keep a Japanese household."

I obey. One of the neighbors is watching TV with the volume on stun; *The Office,* I'm pretty sure. "A designer? Fancy."

"Hence why she can afford to live in two places," Amanda says. "She only pays her half on our place." She sets her purse down on a small buffet table. "I guess when they finally tie the knot, I'll have to get a roommate, or something."

"I thought you had like three jobs?"

She raises her eyebrow and crosses into the kitchen to wash her hands. "Cancer and student loans. Enough said. I've paid off... most of it." She grimaces. "My insurance decided that one of my oncologists was out of network. After I had most of my treatment."

"I really hate it here," I mutter.

"Anyway, dropping down to just one job will feel like a vacation, I'm guessing."

"You said two "and a half" jobs. What's the other job and a half?"

"Don't laugh," she says.

"Okay, I'm not laughing."

"I'm a personal assistant for a CEO of a pet talent agency."

A smile pulls at my lips, but I resolutely do not laugh.

Amanda's eyes glitter. "It's remote, and it has benefits. Makes up for the kinda crappy salary."

"And the half?"

She shrugs. "For me to know and you to find out. Maybe." She turns towards the stainless steel fridge. The barest edge of her bra, fine lace, is visible over the low back of her dress, and I blush fiercely. "You want anything to drink? I finished the last of the wine, I think, but I have tea, coffee..." She riffles through a drawer of cans. "Some kind of adaptogen drink?"

"Water, uh, water's fine."

She cocks her head. "You don't have to just stand there. Get comfortable."

I ease over to the couch. The neighbor's TV regales us about Jim's antics. "...That must get old real quick," I say, gesturing to the wall. The cushions, soft and squashy, almost swallow me.

Amanda sighs. She gets two glasses of water from the panel on the fridge. "I've almost stopped hearing it, to be honest. When it stops at night, that's usually when I notice." She joins me. This couch is smaller than the one at home, almost too intimate. She tucks her legs up under her skirt.

The water is cold, sweet, and buys time. I figured this would come up eventually.

"So... how are you really?" she asks in a low voice.

"Oh, I'm just peachy." I bite my lip once, hard. "Without him, or Jenna, the house feels... too big. Like a corpse. I hate everything I've been doing, but if I don't, like, do it, then..." I don't want to cry. Not again. "It's keeping me from thinking too much about what comes next, though."

"...That's right. I guess you'll go back to Scotland?"

"I really don't know."

"Well, there's nothing keeping you here, is there?"

She kind of has a point. "It's almost like you want me to leave." I put it teasingly, but find I mean it more than I want to.

"Yes, Aaron, I would invite you over to my house because I don't want to see you," she says. "I just figured–well, you must have built some kind of life. You never seemed to want to leave, anyway."

"And you know why that was," I retort. "If not... for him... I probably wouldn't have left here at all. Not like that."

Her shoulders droop a little. "Is he... here now?"

"No. I don't think so."

She looks around quickly, as if she'll see something. "That must be horrible..."

I rub my upper arms. "Yeah. You're telling me."

"And that was... what made you–"

"Yeah."

Smoothing down her hair, she drops eye contact. "Sorry. I know talking about it must be hard."

"It both is and isn't," I admit. "My uni friends were really, ah, fascinated by gun violence. They think all Americans have guns. So long as I haven't been, like, immediately triggered, it's usually okay." I have to think of it like a story, and not feel the whisper crush of memory.

She knots her hands. "When did he start coming to you?"

"Pretty much immediately. And things were so–fresh–I wasn't entirely sure I wasn't hallucinating from all the drugs. I really wanted it to be a delusion." I take a deep breath. "Nobody ever talks about what it's like to..."

"See ghosts?" she offers.

My knee jiggles. "Well, yes. And I..."

When I don't continue, she prompts, "...and you?"

I brace myself. "It's going to sound… really fucked up. But when I woke up, and I learned he was dead… I just wanted it to be over. No more him hurting me, no more games, but then it just… continued. Just like it did when we broke up."

Amanda takes my hands. "That's not fucked up, to not want to be abused again." She rubs circles into my palms. "Was it really… that bad? Him and you?"

I want to lie to her. To tell her that our breakup was mutual, that I only tolerated him in my life after that to keep the peace, that yeah, everyone could see it was toxic, but it was never that, he never did that. "I mean he shot me," I say. "I'm pretty sure he meant it, too."

But she's not surprised. "That's what I thought."

"I tried to save him and the fucker shot me." Back. I have to go back to the place-where-this-is-a-story. I pull in a breath through my teeth, tasting the peonies and her perfume and my own saliva. "And apparently my spirit promised him something."

Amanda sits up very straight. "Are you sure?"

"I mean, he told me, so I assumed it wasn't true, but everything–all these symptoms–I think he's right."

She pulls her hands through her hair, ruffling the perfectly sculpted curls. "This is–this is bad."

"Yeah, no shit."

Knotting her arms together, she gets up and starts pacing. "If you have that level of karmic bond, if he has that power over you… are you working on it?"

"Well, Dad kind of died, so, no."

Amanda pressed her face into her palm.

"Do you know anything about this?"

"I know we should probably get you to Leah as soon as possible. I could put you in before her first appointment..." She feels for her pocket and takes out her phone. "People with these sorts of bonds..."

My heart skips a beat. "...What?"

"Well, they tend to not *live* very long."

MEDIATOR

"*T old* you so," Dmitri says, right by my ear.

I scowl. At him, not her. "I can't exactly remember making a promise when I was *dead.* So... how does this work? How does it kill me, exactly?"

"I don't know for sure," she says. "I'm just–the receptionist."

"Reception manager."

"*Whatever.*" Her honey-brown eyes are practically burning. "Look, you get your skinny ass down there *first* thing tomorrow morning."

Dmitri steps away from me, splits the distance between us. He looks her up and down with his single eye, the other gaping socket gruesome in the apartment's soft lighting. "See, I kind of get it," he says. "She looks pretty good."

I don't know if it will make it better or worse, to mention he's here.

"Though if you plan on taking the route she's thinking of, this *will* be pretty interesting," he says.

"I'll go. I'm going to go," I assure her. "I don't exactly want to die."

She shoots me a look, then softens. "I wish I could just see…"

A bit of spectral gore, a flake of bone, drips theatrically from his empty eye socket. I flinch. "You really don't."

***

The next morning, bright and early–no sleep to be found–I do as I promised and go down to Leah's shop, stopping only to get us some coffee. Dmitri stayed with me throughout the night, but didn't speak much. He just watched me. Smug as a snake.

Amanda looks slightly less immaculate than she did yesterday, bags under her eyes, her skirt wrinkled in patches. She fumbles a set of keys with a purple pom-pom out of her bag and unlocks the shop door.

I offer my flimsy cardboard tray. "Coffee?" I startle her; the keys fall to the floor with a jangle. She stoops to snatch them quickly. "…Sorry, I thought you saw me."

She shakes her head. Her eyes are glassy. "I'm a million miles away. Not much sleep."

"Yeah, same. Hence…" I gesture to the coffees. "Toasted almond, skim milk, one sugar?"

Is she blushing? Is it just her makeup? "Yeah. You remembered right. Thank you." She takes the cup and sips, leaving behind a mauve-y print.

"How could I forget? If I had half the money we spent on Dunkin…" So many almost-dates, huddled close together in candy pink and orange booths. We were so bright, so happy, we felt endless.

"Maybe I wouldn't need two of my jobs," Amanda says. She gets the door open at last.

Only one small, dull lamp has been left on, and given the darkness of the walls, the shop feels like a lot less of a shop and more like the spirit center it is. Even the shadows on the floor seem to wiggle a bit. Amanda crosses over to a small panel on the wall, inputs a code, and presses a few buttons. Soft gold and white lighting flickers on, and the shadows vanish.

"She texted me before I left. She'll be here soon," Amanda says. She settles in at her desk, stuffing a tupperware container into a previously unseen minifridge and booting the POS system.

My own coffee is depressing: flat and weak. I lean against the counter. "Maybe some time we can go back to that cafe. I should know better than to go to the Hyde Park Dunkin."

She cuts her eyes up at me; the screen leaves a bluish imprint on her iris. "You should. But... that would be nice."

I didn't mean to imply it like that–butterflies swarm my stomach. I forgot some anxiety can be pleasant.

Before I can dwell too long on that, Leah arrives, her arms full with a lunch box and knock-off Stanley cup. She appraises me closely, blue eyes harsh in the otherwise gentle light. "I'm glad you're finally listening to sense," she says. "Come on back."

In the office, Leah flicks on some lights and boots a desktop computer, angular, crisp movements. "How are you feeling?"

"Well. Pretty shitty," I admit.

"Emotionally, physically–?"

I squirm. "Both. My... my dad died."

She nods sadly. "Amanda told me. I used to see him around town. I'm sorry." She gets up to retrieve the kettle. "You'll want some tea."

"Oh, I've got my coffee."

"Not that kind of tea." She sloshes it, to see if there's water left, then places it on the induction plate.

"It won't get me high, will it?"

"...No." From the basket under the kettle, she grabs a mug and a tea-tin. She takes out, of all things, what appears to be a dried flower, bud shrivelled tightly, and drops it into the mug. "Have you had any more medical episodes? Worse headaches, organ pain, anything you can think of?"

I clear my throat. The water in the kettle roils loudly. "I did have another seizure–but just the one."

Shooting me a scolding look, Leah crosses her arms. "And how often are these episodes occurring? How often do you see him? I don't see him with you, so I assume it's not constant." She hands me the tea, which smells somewhat lemony, and sits back down.

"He said something about strong surges of emotion. I've been banishing him like you said, but it's getting shorter and shorter each time..."

"Is there anything else that I should know?"

I don't want to meet those icy eyes.

More softness creeps into her voice. "There's nothing to be ashamed of."

Running my fingers back and forth against the textured walls of the mug, I admit, "he says... I'm his domain."

For just a second, her face contorts, but then she manages to smooth her mask back into place. "The thing about domains... rarely, if ever, are they other people. And the fact that you are essentially acting already dead is a hugely complicating factor."

"Is that what is allegedly going to kill me?"

"Well, it begins to weaken the tethers to the body," she says. "That debt, his own length of time lingering on this plane... he's going to start pulling you with him, if he hasn't already. Hence: headaches, seizures, organ pain, of vague medical veracity."

Now here's "a surge of strong emotion." A crackling sensation smarts in my belly, and I bite the inside of my cheek hard enough to draw blood. "So he gets to kill me *again,* and I somehow fucking owe *him?*"

"It doesn't really make sense, considering what I know and have seen..." She cups her chin. "I don't see or feel him. Perhaps instead of banishing him, you could try summoning him?"

"What, like, right now?"

"It will be worse if you put it off." She cocks her head. "I'm here to help you."

I draw in a deep breath. Two. I guess if I really want to see him calming myself won't help much. Maybe it's the tea, or the anxiety, my skin feels... weird. Not quite attached to me. "...Dmitri?"

And there he is, making this small room feel even more close. "I cannot believe," he spits, "you brought me to couples' counseling."

ASTRAL PROJECTION FOR DUMMIES

"You must be Dmitri," Leah says. She gestures to the only other seat in the room, a plain plastic chair. "Have a seat." If his mangled, gruesome appearance bothers her, she doesn't show it.

He scowls, but listens; it'll probably get him what he wants.

"So it sounds like we have a rather complicated karmic situation going on here," she begins. "Dmitri, can you, and will you, tell me anything about the bond between you and Aaron?"

"What did he tell you?" Dmitri asks in response.

Un. Believable. He's not seriously going to–

"He says he interrupted your suicide, and he was mortally wounded in the process."

He crosses his arms behind his head. "That's all true."

"...Are you able to tell me anything about the promise?"

He grins, revealing the edges of mortuary wire holding his jaw together. "Nope."

She sighs. "Worth a try."

"I already tried that," I say.

"Well, I'm not you."

That itch, that ache, kicks up behind my eye.

"How would you describe your relationship with Aaron?" she asks. "When was it, for how long? Were there any... obstacles, any sources of conflict?"

I expect more petulance, but he winces. "Going right for the sore spot, aren't you? What happened to the "I" statements?" He looks at me. "Isn't she supposed to be a therapist?"

"I am a medium first," she says.

He looks away from her. "I'm not–proud of what I did, okay? But I don't think–being trapped in between for three years is fair, do you?"

"Say more about that."

He points at me. "Yeah. I am bound to him. But I'm also not able to get too far from where I died. When he went abroad, I couldn't go with him. But I couldn't stick around, either."

Leah glances at me. I don't know what to read into that expression.

"Isn't it reasonable, maybe, to be a little frustrated? That maybe it makes us even? That maybe I didn't want to get crushed out of existence, so yeah, I might've bound myself a little harder than I should have."

She blinks a few times, but holds her face neutral. "And that promise must be fulfilled for you to move on? You don't have any other options?"

He scoffs. "I thought you were supposed to be an expert. *Yes.*"

I don't want to, but I'm shaking.

"Well, it sounds like you both want the same thing; for this bond to end. What can we do to facilitate that?"

"Remember," I whisper, barely conscious of it. "The promise, I mean. But I wasn't–in my body. It's not like I can..." I can't look at either of them. "It's not like I can leave it without dying, can I?"

"Well, you're going to die anyway if you don't, so–" He hisses.

"I'm not dying for you again. I don't care–"

"Excuse me," Leah says crisply.

He scowls and scuffs his shoe on the industrial carpeting.

"Dmitri," she begins. "That's not really what your spirit looks like, is it?"

"What do you care," he mutters.

"Show yourself to me. For a moment."

He exhales. Slowly, like putty reverting to its natural shape, his right eye fills in, his hair puffs out of its gel, and his funeral clothes fade to an ambiguously dark t-shirt and basketball shorts.

"That's a bit better, isn't it?" she asks. "A little less stress? Less pressure?"

"So you were just doing it to fuck with me," I spit.

"Screw me for wanting an authentic haunting, if I have to do it at all–"

"Excuse me," Leah says again.

I force my shoulders back down and glare at him.

She takes a gulp from her fake Stanley cup. "It *is* possible, to leave the body, though it's not what I'd call easy, pleasant, or even–recommended."

"What do I do?" I ask quickly. "I'll–I'll try anything."

"Anything?"

I nod so hard my neck hurts.

Leah pinches her nose. "Alright. So long as you understand the risk…"

"…What risk?"

"Well, there's a chance that leaving your body will immediately drag you to the other side."

"And if I hold him here?" Dmitri asks. "He can't go anywhere without me."

"He can once the bond is broken."

I am so tired. So tired. I lean forward against my elbows. "So how do I do it?"

"We give you a few types of drugs to facilitate the experience. Then we ward a space—a safe space, or a space that has meaning to you—to protect your body from harm."

"Witchcraft?" I ask softly.

"It is at least partially driven by belief. Some of these things only work because we think they do," she says. "The spirit… well, it's incredible, what it can or can't do."

Back when I lived with my grandparents at the very beginning of my time in Scotland, they dragged me with them to church a few times, long, miserable, Catholic masses. It had been a real sticking point, apparently, when Matt and Dad elected not to have me baptized. "There's no greater power than faith," the priest said, over and over again. Yet they insisted that the soul entered the afterlife immediately after death, despite the evidence to the contrary. There were even spirits there praying with us. Maybe prayer was even holding them there.

"And you're telling me the answer is… to get really fucking stoned?" I raise an eyebrow.

"To put you in a state where you can directly communicate with your spirit. You can't think about it so logically," she says. "Even if you don't realize it, what keeps us here... often has little basis in what's right for us."

Dmitri stares out the small, shallow window of this office.

She turns to him, a quick, jaunty move. "Will you let us speak privately?"

He shrugs, and vanishes.

Leah leans forward and tries to catch my eyes. "What was your relationship with him like? What are you comfortable telling me? I understand it's uncomfortable, touchy. You clearly speak as though you've done some work on it. You understand it was abusive."

I'm shivering, but I'm not cold. "I mean, it starts... how it always starts." I speak barely above a whisper; she has come closer to hear me. "He was the first boy I ever dated... ever *loved*... I was supposed to fall neatly into this box of what he expected me to be. And it was good. For a while it was really good." In my ears, my pulse thumps like a bass drum. "But his parents couldn't know about us, which caused all this paranoia, and it started to... get to him. He snapped at me, a lot, and then I didn't really know how to stand up for myself, so I just sort of took it. As he got... sicker, it started taking up more and more time."

"What did?"

"Making him feel better. Keeping him from killing himself. And I know, I get it, that it was a way to isolate me from everyone else, and there was always the love-bombing, the *I'm the only one who could ever love him,* and I..." Memories, concrete examples, won't quite come; I squint into the tatters of my mind. "He hit me, just the once, and that was when I walked away." Where had he hit me? How hard? When? The room seesaws a bit. "I can't... *remember.*"

"It's okay. It's alright. Breathe. You're safe with me."

It would've taken a lot of strength, willpower, from seventeen-year-old me, to cut him off. And evidently I didn't cut him off enough, to still try to save him two years later...

"Aaron? Breathe."

My lungs are crumpled and shrivelled in my chest. It was real, I know it was all real—

There's an abrupt jerking sensation behind my navel, and I fall out of my body.

THE VEIL

The world, the world as it really is, not how my person-eyes can see it, overwhelms me, colors existing nowhere near a perceptible spectrum. I feel the starlight and the rays from space and good god is the earth more alive than I even thought–

A hand seizes mine. His hand, I *feel* the touch, the contact, our skin doesn't look like skin, why does it look like that–

Dmitri snaps in front of my face. "You can't think about that. You'll go too far."

"Too... far?"

Is this "the shimmering"? I don't even know if I could quantify it as shimmery, if it even looks like light. Everything I could ever want to know, could ever hope to be, is right here. "You have to come back where they can see us," he tells me. "The living."

And still I recognize panic. Taste it. "Did I–"

"No." He sighs. "All that jabbering on about fucking rituals, and you just fall right out." He tugs my hand gently. "Come look. It's trippy."

I peer through layers and layers of dense reality, like lace encapsulating the world. I feel both weightless and rooted. Things as I know them start to take shape again. Walls of buildings seem thin and insubstantial, and everywhere, the bright flames of the living, each trailing a long, long way down into the earth. I see the burning-hot spirit still within Leah.

And then I see my own body. My hands–my real hands–cover my mouth.

Dmitri observes me. "Weird, right?"

"Why does it look like that?" Hollow, a puppet, it barely has more shape than old spirits do to my person-eyes. I think I'm laying down. I think Leah's watching over me.

"Because you're not in it."

I always expected it to be peaceful, here, but it's downright horrifying. I'm not supposed to see this, any of this–

"It's just because you're still alive," Dmitri assures me, smoothing hair out of my face; I jolt away from his touch. "The dissonance fades once you transition. It's actually really cool once you stop freaking out. Ahh! We're pieces of meat!" He shrugs. "Gets old quick. You can't–stay long. Already your vitals are dropping."

Vitals. My meat vitals, my sick body.

"Focus, Aaron. You have to go back soon."

I wheel around. Moving is weird, too easy, too floaty, I'm not thrown off balance the way I usually am by sudden movement.

I see him. At last, I see him. These strings, these chains, run between us, I don't know how he doesn't stumble under the weight. I pluck one, gently, feel the vibrations travel along it. He flinches. "What is all this?"

"What you forgot."

"I forgot all this?" I go to touch another strand, but he stops me.

"I said I would hold onto the pain, didn't I?" he asks me.

Right. The stupid promise.

The hollow puppet of my body twitches. Leah. Leah can probably see all this, right?

I taste rather than feel the sudden shift in conviction. No. It wasn't stupid. Isn't. So— "But I... remember... pain," I manage.

"You know what happened logically, yes," he says. "But the actual impact it had on you... *this* you, the real you... You can't take it all in. Not at once. It already almost got to you."

"When I overdosed a few years ago..." I murmur. "I could never figure it out... why I... tried to do it. They said I was psychotic..."

"And you were. That's not all of it."

"How do I... do we...? What else did I promise—" The answer comes to me right as he says,

"I asked you not to forgive me," he says. "That, you've done pretty well."

I think I'm crying. I think this is what it feels like. Tears fall upwards like petals. "...And?"

"This is where... I fucked up," he admits. "I thought I could do this forever—indefinitely, until you die naturally—but I realized there are limits."

Truth might as well be gravity.

"You were supposed to die that day," he says, as if I don't know, as if it isn't brutally clear to me in this weird and perfect form, "I would take your pain; I would give you an anchor to this life. I didn't realize—that would make you owe me."

"So... in order to even things while also living..."

"You'll have to remember," he says. "That way you break the bond with me and become your own anchor."

There are so many chains. So many.

He shudders. "Here I am hurting you again. I can't even repent properly."

Something like calm settles over me. "I guess we can start... piece by piece," I murmur. "I can try to keep coming back..."

"It's risky," he points out.

"Well, it doesn't seem like there's any other choice." I look back at my meat-puppet. At Leah. "How do I go out and tell her?"

He unwraps a few of the chains, plucking them wincingly from himself. They are dull with rust. "Take this with you."

My hands tremble when I hold them out. The rust burns into my not-quite-flesh, worming into me, and I fall away from the terrifying splendor back down into my body.

PIECES 1, 2, AND 3

1.

The first time I had to stop you from killing yourself was a Thursday, a frigid winter afternoon the bright color of a bruise. I missed your calls while I was ironically at therapy, sobbing to Fitzl about the flavor of misery of the day.

The drop in my stomach when I saw all of the messages missed was new but becoming familiar. You didn't like it when I didn't respond quickly. Being left on read gave you anxiety; worse still was when I didn't read them at all. You started slow and escalated quickly in your own deathspiral, each damnation a few minutes apart–

Having a bad day. Please call me.

I need to hear your voice. I don't know how much longer I can keep doing it. I've had all this weight on me so long, I can't keep doing it.

This is serious. Please don't ignore me.

I guess nobody loves me. All the more reason to go with it.

Although so recently sated by Fitzl's careful ministrations, I started to panic, an animal terror taking root. There were more messages–paragraphs of them, some outlining your own faults, others chastising people around you for not *being there*, still more detailing what you will miss from your life–but there was no time. I called, praying that it wasn't too late, that I could still–

"Where were you?" you asked muzzily, and I could tell by the way the words were drawn out that you were drunk. Possibly high. Maybe even overdosing.

"I was in therapy–Fitzl doesn't like when I have my phone–are you okay?"

"Oh, he doesn't *like* it, does he?" Liquid swishing against glass. "Of course I'm *not okay*."

"You don't mean it, do you? Dmitri, please–"

"I just don't know what the damn point is." You sniffled. "Nothing good is *ever* going to come from this. The news, my grades, the fucking climate, I can't even... be with you. Nobody loves me. Nobody needs me."

My breath tasted like a scream. "I need you. *I* need you."

"Then why didn't you answer the damn phone?"

2.

On an unseasonably balmy spring morning, a bout of the flu took out my painting teacher and left us with an unexpected study hall, without even a sub to keep order. The class, already rowdy, immediately descended into complete madness; Monica and Shannon made a paper football, and it became a game to see who can get it farthest across the classroom. A whiff of competition was enough to set everyone off the edge. For me, it was convenient; I could work on the trig homework

I hadn't gotten through last night, fuzzy with insomnia. I was only good at math when I could see the practical applications; I'd helped Dad balance the accounts since I was thirteen, so things like money and statistics come easily enough. Trig was another ball game.

You had lunch right now. You would want me to text you. You *always* wanted me to text you. You would crawl into my skin if you could.

There was a whole worksheet here that literally had my name on it. I took out my graphing calculator, resigned, and found its battery died. I could probably find an app or a website or something to do the job.

Or I could slack off.

From her spot at the desk next to mine, Phoebe nudged me. She deftly slid her weed pen up her sleeve. "Unisex bathroom?" she whispered.

I shook my head. "I have a quiz next period."

She shrugged. "Suit yourself." She snatched the bathroom pass—a battered Vermont license plate—off its hook by the door.

Another one of my classmates, Saima, perfectly nailed the plastic anatomy skeleton we used for still lives, Alejandro, in its nonexistent crotch. The best shot. Everyone cheered. I took out my sketch pad, thumbed to a clean page, and picked up a piece of charcoal. Bones always made sense to me, and I'd drawn Alejandro approximately one billion times. I knew his bones better than my own. With a small *swoop*, I added the paper football flying from his pelvis and wrote *"One day I will have my revenge"* in a speech bubble. Snapping a quick picture for Insta, I send it to our shared friend Discord.

You texted me. Instantly. A flicker of irritation crept up my back. I turned back to my sketch and habitually filled in details around the skeleton; the blackboard behind it, the trash can, full of old pieces of crumpled paper towel, the shelf where we place paintings to dry.

Another message. *I'm not bothering you am I.*

It was bait. The realization was quiet amongst the rowdy classroom. This was my cue to assure you, *not at all.* I reached over to lock my phone, but my fingers moved across the keyboard of their own accord.

3.

The end of year art contest had already come and gone three times, but it still managed to shred my nerves even though I'd placed every year. There were rumors that whoever gets in the show in our painting class would automatically land a spot in AP Art. I should be, am, a shoo in. And yet I did what I do best and fret about it.

The problem with anxiety was there was a nonzero chance that fear was warranted.

My undoing came in the form of a softly cleared throat from the art teacher, Mr. Sanders. He was young—only in his mid-twenties—but very competent. His black beard and swarthy skin would make him look like a pirate, if not for the pastel polo t-shirts and khakis. "...Aa ron?"

He usually only called us by our last names, so I was immediately on edge. A few of my classmates trickled around me, our portfolio cases bumping awkwardly. "Um, what's up?"

He tapped his fingers together. Didn't quite meet my eyes. "I wanted to talk to you about your submission. Are you—okay?"

Vibrating with terror. But I knew that wasn't what he meant. "I'm fine."

"Your... piece. I like to think I've worked with you long enough to divine some personal meaning from your work. There was a lot of pain in it." He leaned forward a little more. "Whenever you submit pictures of... that boy, there's an element of pain. Is..." His eyes crinkled, and I could tell he felt terribly awkward. "Is someone... hurting you?"

I blinked. Truth be told, I had no idea how he divined *pain* from my submission. I'd hedged my bets very safely, sending in a pointillist-inspired landscape of Vanderbilt park's view of the Hudson river, you and I reddish-brown blurs on a blanket. "...Hurting me?"

"Like... doing something you don't want them to. You look... exhausted."

I touched the skin under my eye. It was a bit swollen to the touch, but I wasn't the only junior with puffy eyes. "I have trouble sleeping sometimes," I said. It wasn't exactly a secret; I painted about it often. The warning bell rang briskly. "I'm fine. ...I should go."

"I'll give you a pass," he said quickly.

"No, it's really fine." Why did I feel... weird? "What do you mean about pain?"

Mr. Sanders sighed and gestured me over to his Mac. He sifted through a desktop cluttered with files and opened a file with the years' submissions, photographed or scanned. He plucked open mine.

The painting was not nearly as rosy as I remembered.

"I know you know all about color theory. Do you see how... cold, the colors you used, are? The sun looks almost sickly, the light almost... greenish. Look at the subjects' hands." He wheeled his mouse over. "Even with the blurring effect, I see one grips the other tightly. See how he looks away? The fact that you *chose* to do it dot-by-dot makes it almost impossible that this is just a mistake."

Weird. That was the only word I had for it. Like the ground was about to open up under my feet.

"I wouldn't think anything of it, but this isn't the first time I've seen something like this from you."

"...Pain?" I echoed again.

"I wanted to make sure you were okay. Are you? Are you okay?"

A panicky sweat crept down my back, making my shirt stick to my skin.

The final bell rang. I saw a student's face at the window of the door, looking to come in. "I'm fine. I'm really fine."

Those pirate eyes were skeptical. "Okay. I understand that. But you can talk to me, Aaron."

My skin tingled. Would you look at it and *also* see pain? "Can you... take it out?"

He looked puzzled. "You mean withdraw your submission?"

I nodded, once, then again, my skull on puppet strings.

"I'm—I definitely can, but you wouldn't be able to submit anything else. It wouldn't be fair to the other students."

"That's fine." I was at the edges of my body.

"Um—okay, sure. Consider it done. You'll be able to showcase next year with the other seniors, anyway."

"Does this mean I won't get in?"

He glanced at the door. "That dumb rumor goes around every year. The contest—*is for fun*. You don't need to worry about getting into the class. At all." He grabbed a pad of late passes and jotted one off. "Think about what I said. My door is always open. Okay?"

I brushed past him, ghostlike, the paper a sickly pink in my hands. The next period's class filed in, grumbling about me holding them up, but I barely noticed.

Pain.

This isn't—this isn't how I remember it going. This isn't right. This isn't *true*—

GRAVITY

I slam back into consciousness, my body so heavy and painful and my breath gasping loud in my throat. I can feel my blood moving and every twitch of my muscles and organs as they work together. It's too much. I need out. I want out–

Leah abruptly stuffs something in my mouth. Sticky, overly saccharine, and flavored with artificial strawberries, it takes me a few seconds of chewing before I realize it's a piece of taffy, and it's meant to distract me.

It works. I knead the candy free from my teeth.

"Sorry," she says.

I swallow. The taffy pulls down my throat. "It's fine." Did my voice always sound like that? I hadn't thought my accent had changed, but it's there, slightly at the edges. You would have to look for it.

She grasps my wrist and takes my pulse. The same thing is happening in her body, in all the bodies in all the people in–

"Don't make me give you another," she says. "All I have left are licorice. You don't want that."

"How'd you—"

"I could... see you. At the edges."

Meaning my spirit. It feels worse than being caught naked.

"Breathe. Stay with me. What did you see?"

"Everything," I murmur, but much like a dream, true reality is fading fast from my mind. "I saw... I saw him, I saw... memories, but they were... not... right..." Or too right? "I-I'm so..."

"Your heart rate's really high. I want you to lay back and rest."

Like an unbalanced washer on high, my heart *thu-thunks* in my chest. Without even thinking about it, I prop my legs against the chair to will the blood back into my abdomen.

"Before I—forget—" Has talking always required this much effort? "He said—when I was there—" A dizzy wave of pain crashes over me and takes up residence in my head. "He... he took away my pain and made himself an anchor for me, so that I could—live."

"Take away your pain? What does that mean?"

"The worst of the memories." My ribs feel like they might buckle under the strain. "I mean how things really were. It's why I can't—remember concrete details."

She straightens her glasses, which have fallen askew.

"And he told me not to forgive him." The taffy hits my stomach like a brick. I'm soaked through with sweat; curls stick to my face.

"And to go—*through*—" Words. What are words? The walls are shivering. "I have to—keep leaving my body—to get the pieces—all at once—too much." I try to sit up. I might as well be trying to make a nuclear bomb; each is equally impossible. "I... I think I'm going to—"

***

I half expect to wake up dead. I'm still in my body, but it's a bit less overwhelming. The back of my throat tastes like taffy and bitter spit.

I'm not on the floor of Leah's office. Below my cheek, I feel scratchy canvas and padding, the stale smell of an old futon. One of them draped a crocheted blanket over me. It smells like Amanda, and I relax a little.

The air is cold, dank, and musty; boxes upon boxes in are in neat rows, each labeled, surrounding a black-topped work table with a mortar, pestle, and some kind of juicing machine. A few incandescent bulbs break the gloom. My skin is crackly with dried sweat.

I sit up, and I manage to not pass out, but my stomach churns. There's a garbage bin next to me presumably for this reason, but I am determined to make it to a bathroom. At least I'm in luck. At least there's one tucked in the corner, a shop sink barely visible in the semidarkness.

I can't help but catch sight of that flower from the tea, somehow undigested. What had it done to me? I wish, I *wish* I had just been tripping balls, but I'm not that lucky. I rinse out my mouth with some rusty-tasting water and see myself in the cracked mirror. Not the hollow meat-puppet or the resplendent spirit.

I both do and don't recognize myself. The unruly celtic curls/yes/washed out gray eyes/yes, but something seems off about my features, like someone tweaked them slightly.

I realize part of me was seeking my teen self–rail thin, petulant, exhausted–and not the current "adult" me. My features look different because I am older. Is it because I "died" at eighteen? Is that how I instinctively am interacting with myself?

I have to think about *anything* else.

Those memories...

Suicide. Bait. Pain.

Suddenly I'm furious. How deep does it go? How much did he warp my memories, my mind, my *self*? I want to break something. I raise my fist and see the thin silver line of the scar on my palm.

From up above, I hear *thumping* on the steps, and I tense, but it's just Amanda, her expression sad and cautious.

"I heard the pipes," she admits. "How... are you?"

There's so much I could say. I come away from the bathroom, back towards the couch. "How much of it was real?" I ask her. "How much did you... see? Of him with..."

She closes the distance and takes my clammy hands in hers. "It's okay. You're safe."

Safe. I am the farthest thing from safe.

She brushes her finger against my cheek. "You're safe with me. I won't hurt you."

It is so *cold* down here. "You won't hurt me."

Picking up the blanket from the futon, she drapes it over my shoulders. "Come on. Let me take you home."

***

I wish I could have taken Amanda back under better, more normal circumstances. Apparently I've been asleep most of the day. I'm too shaky to drive, so I'll have to go with her tomorrow to pick up the Honda. We drive most of the way in silence, though I feel the questions practically bursting from her.

"My paintings," I whisper.

"What?"

"My paintings. Mr. Sanders—he said—he saw *pain*, in my pieces with Dmitri in them. Do you—know? Did you... notice?"

She looks back at the road. "Your work carries a lot of grief," she says. "The comics alone... I could barely read them."

Grief. Is this all I am? When was the last time I made something beautiful?

"I thought it would help," I murmur. "Why are you doing all this for me?"

"Everyone needs someone," she says softly. "I still... I still care about you."

"Even though I abandoned everyone?"

"I seem to remember I did too." She huffs. "How about this: you won't abandon me, and I won't abandon you. Can you do that?"

I nod. I feel my raw edges.

When she drops me at the house, she asks if I want her to stay with me for a little while. I do. Desperately. But Matt's car is in the driveway, and that's a whole can of worms. "I think I'm just going to smoke and go lay down," I tell her. "I'll see you tomorrow." Carefully, I fold the blanket and hold it out. It shouldn't feel heavy to me.

She shakes her head, the ghost of a smile playing along her lips. "Keep it. I have tons. Besides, peach suits you."

I haven't even noticed the color until now, to be honest; I was more focused on using it to not fly apart. But yes, the weave is a sunset peach, and very soft to the touch. Another diamond-flash of memory: I used to wear colors like this often. Pale orange. Pink. Baby blue. I'm a "spring."

And then he said that the colors were too soft, *too feminine, it might arouse suspicion in his parents...*

I vow to buy something pink the next time I need clothes.

"Thanks," I say, almost belatedly. "I guess I'll see you tomorrow."

Inside the house, Matt is cutting himself a piece of Stouffer's vegetarian lasagna—the box sits guiltily on the counter. He starts a little when he sees me. "Well, help yourself, it's hot. Hey... you don't look so good."

"Water's wet," I retort. "I had a... bad day. That's all." I do need to eat, even if my stomach is still in ever-tightening knots. There's only so long someone can subsist on protein shakes, coffee, and cigarettes. I carve a slab and, feeling too weak to get up the stairs just yet, join him at the table. After a few bites, the nausea loosens its hold on me, just a bit.

"Do you want to talk about it?"

"About what?"

"...What made your day so bad?"

My fork seems extra loud against the Corelle porcelain. "Sick, bad. Not... bad, bad." Though it was that, too, I really am not about to get into that with *him*. Unless... "Matt?"

He brightens when I address him, reminding me too much of Jenna. Jenna, who's taking our father's death about as well as a punch to the face. I should text her; practice would be over by now.

"When you were with... Dad. Did he ever do anything that made you... doubt what was true?"

He frowns, skirting a spare shred of carrot around the plate. "In what sense?"

Crap. "It's just that since I've been home... there have been a lot of reminders about... you-know-who. I've had reason to doubt how true my memory is."

Matt traces a finger around the edge of his glass, which seemed to be mostly full of brown soda. "You know he didn't tell me much about it. You and the boy, I mean. Just kind of mentioned it offhand when I asked how you and your sister were. All I *know*... is that he hurt you that day."

His spirit unspooling from his body his spirit unspooling from his body

"It was a lot more than that," I mutter. "I guess I..."

"You want to know if your father gaslit me," he asks.

I take a tiny bite. My lips are dry and cracked from all my sweating.

He leans back in the chair; it creaks slightly on the old linoleum. "Alan was never deliberately unkind to me," he says. "That was part of the issue... I felt like I was on the periphery of his life. All that man ever did was work, and look where it got him."

"He's at peace," I say.

"At what cost? He doesn't get to see you or your sister make something of yourselves. He doesn't get a retirement. Hell, we never even fully talked about what happened between *us*. Did he–" Matt sucks in a breath. "You... saw it. Didn't you?"

I look down, but I feel my blood stinging in my cheeks. "Yes."

"*Jesus.* That must've been–"

"But you know what I mean, right? About being so *sure* something is one way, but it was really... another?"

He shoots me a look. "Try being a trans man growing up in Reagan's America."

I wince. "No... that would do it. So you... you knew, then?"

"I think it was more that I didn't have the words for it," he says. "Something always felt *off*. When I looked in the mirror. Or did makeup, or when men hit on me. I thought I was a tomboy, low maintenance..." He seems to turn inward. "I never really wanted to be a mom. I found pregnancy disgusting. Still do. But all of a sudden... there you were, two little blue lines."

"Why didn't you get rid of me?"

He turns pink. "We said we wanted a family... I felt like it would be... *wrong* of me, in my thirties. Marriage and kids is something you do. And then I held you, and I swear I was never so terrified. This was a world I brought you into that wasn't safe for either of us. I think I knew you were queer before you did, and by then it was—more common, and I researched, and I realized, I didn't fit me right. And only when... Jenna came, did the pieces start to come together. When I was setting up her nursery. All the *pink...*" He shudders. "To get back to my point: I realized it, consciously. I thought, "I wouldn't want to be a girl, either." And then I immediately thought, "no, can't be.""

I cast my mind briefly to my own coming out process. Bisexual was just something I was, same as Scottish or gray-eyed or batshit crazy. It never caused *dissonance.*

Not until Dmitri made it.

"I guess what I mean is... if you have enough motivation, all it takes is a little *push* for someone to lock in the lie." He jabs the salt shaker, making it skid across the smooth table. "And the lie *has* to be true, or else..."

We'd fall apart. We'd lose it. We'd be shattered. "...We'd realize how much we'd been wasted."

"Exactly." Matt scrapes up the last few bites. "I can't... pretend to understand what that was all like. Frankly, I'm shocked you even shared that much with me. So... thanks."

I laugh dryly. "Yeah, well. Another perspective on an unhealthy relationship is useful."

I was. I was wasted.

Shamblingly, I go up to my bedroom, open the window, and lean out of it, smoking. I thought I'd *done the work.* Of course I was *angry* and of course I dwelled on *who I would have been* if not for him. My existence swivelled around his. Literally. I swear I can almost feel the places where our spirits are linked, right under my scar. My broken heart, broken blood, do nothing but emphasize all the fractals.

Careful not to drop any ash, I reach into my mostly-empty suitcase and pull out my sketchpad and pencils. The smooth, creamy paper is a little warped from the trip and from any amount of times I toted it around in the murky Scottish cityscape. I see the last drawing I started but never finished, two days before Dad's heart attack, featuring my old neighbor's Russian blue cat as it peered from behind a wrinkled linen curtain.

My hands shake, making the pencil tremble. A hand, then two, one reaching for the other, soft charcoal. Around them, like a wreath, words:

They said at some point it would stop hurting
–a necessary lie to keep the peace
How to make truth?

FIRSTJOB

I can't sleep.

It's a feeling I know well, but if I take too much Ambien, it stops being effective. I toss. I turn. I doomscroll. Around one AM I accept that this will be a sleepless night and lay, feeling the pebbly weight of exhaustion scrabble under my eyelids. Apparently my body ruled that passing out yesterday morning counts as sleep.

I might as well get up and do something.

I go to turn on the lamp, but the moon is nearly bright enough on its own. Outside, reflected in the silver rays, Teddy plays by himself near the yard.

I breeze downstairs and out the back door, barely aware of the motion. At least I feel much better, no longer like sludge, though I swear the taste of strawberries has resisted being scrubbed out of my mouth. "Hey, bud."

Teddy grins. He's conjured some sort of string-game, the kind kids used to play before screens melted our brains. "Wanna play?"

"Sure. What are the rules?" It doesn't occur to me that I don't have any of my own string, at least, not until he ties some knots and drapes the cool yarn over my fingers.

And I feel it.

Don't freak out. Don't freak out. Definitely do *not* freak the fuck out. This is a dream, a very realistic dream, and I am in my body and *this is normal this is fine–*

"Are you the real you?" he asks me. "'Cause the other one ignores me."

The sensation is not the reality-is-too-much that I saw earlier yesterday. I don't see the burning hot threads of everyone's ghosts. I see the little boy in front of me, his cheeks no longer that weird transparent pinkish. He looks real. My hands look real. "I'm not—sure," I admit.

He shrugs.

We play the knot game. Somehow my hands know the rules. I know what to do and what not to do, the fine line of letting a little kid think they're beating you at something you can do easily. "...I guess I must be."

"I can tell."

I look at my hands, really look. I don't have the scar on my palm and my metacarpals are almost visible in the back. "How long have I been doing this?"

He shrugs again. "A while."

I let him win the game. He pulls out jacks, smooth and shiny, and even though the dirt would ordinarily not be conducive to a bouncing ball, it somehow works. "You're... really strong, you know that?"

"I know," he says, unbothered.

"Most spirits can't do what you do."

"Well, I can't have my iPad." The ball seems to linger in the air when it's his turn; he grasps quickly at jacks. When it's my turn, the ball falls comically fast.

"No fair, Teddy."

"What toys did you have?" he asks me. "When you were small."

It shouldn't be hard to remember. I was his age once, and I'm not exactly old. "I liked Legos. Building things."

The jacks disappear, and a pile of Legos spawns. We spend a few minutes stacking the bricks; he's making some kind of vehicle. I don't know what I'm making. Maybe a house.

"I'm sorry about your dad," he says softly.

I pause. I can't lose it even more. "Thanks, bud. I appreciate it."

We play for a little while longer. His car gets more complex and crazy, more like a *Mad Max* vehicle than anything, including pieces that make no physical sense.

"I'm bored," Teddy says.

"I can only imagine." Time used to feel so long back then. It still does now, but in a different way.

He grits his teeth, then admits, "I want to–go."

My hands, working on a fake roof, still. "You mean move on?"

"But Mommy... I'm worried about my mommy."

"I can talk to her tomorrow. Would you like that?"

He nods, fidgets with a block. "What do you think it's like? On the other side?"

I hesitate. Even disembodied as I am now, I can't quite remember my time *over there,* just that it was too much and objectively larger than this. "Things... now. Can you see more than you used to when you were alive? Is everything... big, and burning?"

His eyes widen. "Burning? Like... like *hell?*"

"No–ah–poor word choice. Like bright and... shimmery?"

Teddy shakes his head. The moonlight reflects his cowlick. "I can see where it starts, but... everything is just... flat."

"You'll be happy there," I tell him.

He looks down, his expression oddly blank. "Why do I get to be happy when she doesn't?"

Oh boy. "Life—life isn't always fair. Death is."

"Why?"

"I wish I knew, Teddy. I really do."

***

At least returning to my body the second time isn't quite the same dick punch as it was before. I still feel crappy, but at least I don't pass out and puke.

I spend a few hours digging through more of the crap in the attic and setting up Facebook marketplace posts. By then, it's late enough to have breakfast, and Mrs. Graham's car is in the driveway.

Right. I steel my nerve. She already thinks I'm a nut, so worst comes to worst, she just thinks I'm even worse than before.

Or else she'll think I'm a total asshole for bringing up her dead kid.

Teddy tails me as I walk up their driveway. "You remembered this time?"

"You bet."

The Grahams' house is a squat beige ranch house, and their property is as scraggly as ours was until I hired the guys to come clean it up. The trash and recycling cans are overflowing and stink badly. I brace myself, figuring the inside of the house will not be much better, and press the doorbell. It tries its best to ring, but I resort to knocking.

From the inside, I hear someone scrambling, objects falling over, and then finally the door opens.

Now that I know him better, the resemblance between Teddy and Mrs. Graham is undeniable. They are both painfully blonde, with the same round eyes and pointy chin. She looks exactly like someone deep in grief, with glassy, pinched eyes. Her hair is pulled into a messy topknot. "Oh... hello." She sounds sleepy. "I thought you were the Amazon driver."

"Sorry to disappoint." Even after poring over it all night, I still don't know how to approach this. "I know this is strange... but would I be able to talk to you?"

She rubs her eyes. Just behind her, I can see how dark and dank the living room is, blankets spread over a sectional sofa, dirty coffee cups. "Oh... right, you're moving, aren't you? I saw the sign."

"Yes, but..." I shut my eyes for a moment. "It's about... Teddy."

Mrs. Graham seems to snap out of her reverie. "You wouldn't have heard, would you?"

"I am so sorry." It feels strange to say when Teddy is right next to me.

"And I'm sorry about your father," she says. "We saw the obituary in the paper. He was a good man."

"Yes."

She looks over her shoulder, appraising the mess. "Won't you come in? I can make some coffee."

"Sounds lovely."

The depressive mess is more obvious now. It's not so much clutter as neglect, surfaces visibly dusty, windows foggy with dirt, and the general stale smell of too much habitation. The kitchen is adjacent to the living room. She fusses with an old Mr. Coffee. At least the coffee pot seems reasonably clean; I would feel like an asshole not to drink anything she offers me. Teddy goes over to the sofa and lays down.

While it brews, Mrs. Graham hastily clears me a spot at the small dining room table. "I'm sorry for the mess. I don't... it's just us, usually, and–"

"I understand. I've also been depressed. You've gone through a lot."

Two reddish circles form on her pallid cheeks. "I didn't realize how... hard things would be. Without him here, I..." She trails off. The coffee machine gurgles.

"I am here, though," Teddy murmurs. I wonder how many times he's said this to her.

She fakes a laugh. "I'm sure you don't want to hear about all that."

I sit up a little straighter. "It's kind of why I came to visit." I've never *willingly* admitted this before to someone not in the know. "I see... I see spirits." Almost immediately the guard slams down in her eyes. "Just–hear me out. Okay? I had a... near death experience, and I see them. What everyone says, about *us*, it's not true."

Mrs. Graham composes herself. "So you see ghosts. Then what?"

She's going to lose it. "Since I've been home, I see Teddy."

Abruptly, she stands. Teddy shoots up, too, crossing the distance in two big leaps.

"You were always unwell," she says. "Please, *please* don't start with this–"

"Tell her about the orange I flushed down the toilet," he blurts. "I'm sorry. I didn't realize how bad it would be."

"He says he flushed an orange down the toilet, and he's sorry about it," I say quickly.

Mrs. Graham freezes. "How did you..."

"He's also sorry about the peroxide in the laundry soap," I repeat as soon as the little boy gets it out. "He was playing scientist. He... he figured if maybe he wasn't so bad, he would still be here. With you."

God.

Her face falls slack, and she shudders so deeply I see her bones through her clothes. "Where... where is he?"

"Right in front of you."

Mrs. Graham kneels. Her eyes drip, almost as an afterthought. "Baby?"

"Mommy," he's sobbing. "Mommy."

This isn't like interpreting for Jenna; it feels much more intimate. I repeat what he says verbatim.

"I'm so sorry, sweetie," she says. "We didn't–I should have been paying better *attention*–"

"No, no, you told me not to play over there–I miss you."

She keeps feeling at the space that, to her, is empty. "Oh, we miss you so much."

"Will you be okay?"

"Me? Sweetheart... if you're here with me I will be just fine."

I flinch.

Teddy turns away. "But I... I want to go."

"Go?" she looks at me.

I knot my hands. "He means on."

"I just... I just got you again."

"He says, "I've been here the whole time."" As calm as I've tried to be, their sadness is a palpable entity.

"All by yourself?" she murmurs.

"I've made some friends," he says, and tells her about some of the other child-spirits I've seen wandering around. "But... yeah."

"My brave boy..."

"So can I?" he asks her. "Can I... if I go, will you be okay?"

She presses her face in her hands. "If that's what you want, Teddy... I'll try."

He sighs with relief. "I love you."

She says it, over and over.

He looks over at me. "I'm going to go now."

"We'll see you one day," I tell him.

He says he loves her once more, and like my father, disappears into the light.

***

Mrs. Graham stands, shamblingly. "He'll be–he'll be okay?" she asks, her eyes wild.

"It's very peaceful."

She abruptly scoops me into a hug. She smells like not-quite-clean laundry and dirty hair and grief. "I'm... I'm so..."

"It's okay, Mrs. Graham. I was happy to do it." I pat her back awkwardly. Vertigo is making my vision seesaw. "I'm glad you believed me."

"Please. Heather."

"...Sure, Heather."

She lets me go and looks around again. "Where do I even begin? It still... he was here so long, and now... I only know now that he's *not*."

I consider. "We could start by cleaning the house."

"We?"

I sigh. "He was my friend too."

BACK TO OUR REGULARLY SCHEDULED PROGRAMMING

That evening, sore, stinging, my hands still smelling like bleach, I sit on the porch and chew on grief. Even though it's a little too warm, I hold Amanda's blanket on my lap.

Dad. Teddy. And of course Dmitri.

I text Jenna. The school suggested she enroll in counseling, but was loath to actually find a counselor that could sign. She's trying to pretend she's in good spirits (ha ha), but even through text I can see through her. No friends, no family, in a new environment, under a lot of pressure by her team, already, and the semester hasn't even officially started. Suggesting that she might come home and go to the community college for a few semesters as she grieves led to her icing me out for most of a week, something she never does.

I can't *do* all this.

Before I can give into the madness, though, Amanda texts me. *Hey. Just wanted to see how you were feeling after all that.*

I should just lie and say I'm fine. But I promised.

Before I can stop myself, I call her.

When she answers, she sounds a bit startled. "Hey."

"Hey. Is this a bad time?"

The phone scuffs against her cheek. "No, not at all. So?"

"Well—not great," I admit. "Head trip aside, I can't say I would *recommend* it."

Immediately her interest is piqued. I remind myself this is the same girl who watched endless disaster videos to try and gain the sight. "What did you see?"

I squint. The more time passes, the more it seems like a very intense dream I've just woken up from—fading at the edges like an old photograph. "...Have you ever had nitrous?" I ask instead.

"What, laughing gas? No, they put me out for my wisdom teeth. But..." She pauses here for a moment. "For one of my surgeries, I was only sedated."

Lighting another cigarette, I take a deep drag, the familiar burn in the lungs. "That feeling of... oneness with the universe. Reality is so much *bigger* than what we see." When she doesn't say anything, I add, "I know that sounds like every "I'm 14 and this is deep" post, but that's... mostly true. There were all these... colors... I couldn't even begin to describe. It was... kind of terrifying. I *saw* my body from the outside. Yeesh."

"Did you see God?" Her voice is low, scratchy.

"...No. You might have to actually be dead for that one." If God even existed, which was a whole other can of worms.

"Do you think *I* could do it?"

I glance out at the street. This time of day, town has quieted, and most people are home. A few kids are out and about on bikes, and the sweet smoky smell of someone's barbecue drifts over across houses. "It's risky, she said. Chances are you might not be able to return."

"But could I?"

"I'm sure you *could*." She could do just about anything. My lip quirks. "I'd rather keep you around, though."

"You *do* owe me a coffee," she says, and a chill shoots down my back.

"When can I see you?"

I hear a thump and some footsteps. "I should have time... oh, Tuesday night, my first job's office is closed for some event. They asked if I wanted to go, but..." She sighs heavily. "It's all the way in the city, and I'm *tired*."

"Not too tired for me?"

"*You* won't make me commute over two hours for an hour-long fundraiser," she points out.

"Well, when you put it like that."

"So–Tuesday, meet me at the shop when I get off?"

"I'll be there."

"So it's a date."

It is, isn't it? No exploring weird spiritual bullshit–unless she brings it up. An actual, honest-to-god date.

The euphoria lasts about five seconds before it's replaced with utter *terror*. "Yeah–a date." I clear my throat and cough after my next drag. "You wanna hear something else cool?"

"Always."

"Did I tell you about Teddy–that little boy spirit? My neighbor's kid?"

"The one that drowned last year? It was all over Facebook."

"He's been around. I'd been... talking to him, on and off, he was pretty lonely." Not to mention, apparently leaving my body for indeterminate swaths of time to play with him. In the setting sunlight, the scar on my palm is almost invisible. Were there other times that happened, and I wasn't aware of it? What did I say? What did I do? I've only blacked out drunk a handful of times, and always dreaded not knowing what happened. This couldn't exactly be *good* for me, anyway. A headache starts to gnaw and pound near my temples, and I try to rub it away.

"...You there?" she prompts.

"Yeah... I... sorry." I wonder if this is how it feels to have a brain-eating amoeba. They *say* the brain has no nerve endings. I think that's a crock of shit. "Sudden... headache." What I probably need is a dose of the oil; the ramifications of what I did today can't be insignificant. "I'm fine, I'll... call you back. Just ghost stuff. I think."

"Uh–sure–"

The ground seesaws underneath me as I move, and I feel that ashen *whoosh* as my blood pressure plummets. Why does this ghost shit have to worsen my already-tenuous relationship with my own vascular system? I wish someone could just rip it out. Replace my veins with copper tubing. Something.

I manage to not pass out until I get to my room, by which point my stupid and very ballsy decision to *walk up some stairs* leaves me splayed half in the threshold. It's a miracle I haven't had a concussion in my life, I swear.

My GP in Edinburgh used to admonish me for not exercising enough.

When I come to, Dmitri is standing over me, and the resultant surge of *you're not safe* makes my chest hurt. "What did you *do*?" he hisses.

My vision is all doubled, and it takes me a second to realize it's not just from the orthostatic *fun*. I'm both in and not in my body.

"No, *no*, stay where you are and don't move." He admonishes me like you would a pet that chewed something it shouldn't. "Just stay still."

I look down. Try to, anyway, I can't tilt my head properly. There's a heavy, leaden weight around my waist, pinning me–my ghost, my spirit, fuck all this–in place.

"...Good boy."

Chains. I am covered in chains. I can only see them when I squint. They quiver, twitch like snakes. He used to call me that, sometimes, when we slept together, thought it was hot–

"Ah shit," he says.

PIECES 4, 5, AND 6

4.

W e were in my room. You held your phone like a knife, Instagram open.

"What were you thinking?" Your voice was level. All being told you did not *yell* often.

"It's a... group picture. I didn't think–"

"Yeah. Exactly."

Within the last six months or so, I'd gotten taller than you, growing pains sharp and severe enough I asked for painkillers. Nothing wrong with me, the doctor said. Take some ibuprofen and get over it.

I slouched in my chair, pressing back against the corner of my drawing desk. I liked the feel of the corner against the small of my back.

"You coulda just cropped it," you said. "Or even... run it by me."

"So your parents are going to fault me for *standing next to you?*" I cross my arms.

"Your arm was around me."

"...And the other was around Phoebe. That's what people do in pictures." I saw flickers of it on the screen of your phone, of the group of us at the county fair, smiling, happy, the velour arms of a stuffed prize wrapped around Charlie's neck. "I'm sorry, okay?"

You huffed. "Look, just–just delete it, okay? I don't think she's seen it yet, or I'd have gotten an earful."

"Are you not supposed to spend time with your friends?" I asked, gently.

"Just—delete it, please?"

"I will, but–"

"Now?" You furrowed your brows.

I hesitated, but pulled out my phone. "There are just so few pictures of us together. I really think it looks inconspicuous–"

In a flash, you yanked the phone from my grip, unlocked it, and swiped onto my account. I blinked, for a second not entirely sure that had actually happened. You placed it, gently, back in my palm.

"I didn't delete the original," you said, looking relieved. "You've got, like, a million DMs from Charlie, though."

I looked from it, to you, to it again. I was feeling something. I took a deep breath, like Fitzl always told me, and tried to classify what I was physically feeling and what emotion it might actually be.

Other than, you know, blind fury. Shame, maybe. Tasted like parsnips.

You folded your arms behind your back. "What?"

It was–should be–silly. It was just a phone. I had nothing to hide, you could search to your heart's content and not find anything that needed to be hidden. The way you did it, so quick and matter of fact–

I didn't tell you the passcode.

I had nothing to hide, I had nothing to *hide*, but you've *gone through my phone*, I could just tell from the look in your eye, crinkled slightly at the corner. Maybe when I was in the bathroom. Or went to get us snacks, when we hung out. "...How did you know how to open it?"

Color floods your face, but your expression remains a little too impassive. "What do you mean?"

"Just now. You wouldn't know my code."

"Of course I would, silly, I see you put it in all the time–I think you're–you're overreacting." You rock on your feet. "This is about my safety, and of course, I trust you..."

My chest spasmed.

You tutted and moved towards me, cupping my face. "I wouldn't do that if I didn't think I needed to. It's not a big deal."

You had so much fire brimming right below the surface; sometimes I swore I even felt it on your skin, which was always overwarm to my touch. All that made being burned inevitable. But I could drop a hot poker, or let go of a hot pan. I flinched away. "Have you done it before?"

"What do you mean?" You were going to make me say it.

"Gone through my stuff," I said shakily.

"Don't be crazy."

I stood abruptly, making you step back.

"No, you didn't," you said, meeting my eyes. "This isn't how it happened."

"You're lying," I said. "I know, I know you did–"

"You didn't say that."

I feel dizzy, I feel sick, I–

"You're right," the memory-me said. "It's not a big deal."

5.

Sunday mornings were a mixed bag in my house. Dad didn't work Sundays, so he was always there, hovering. Sometimes he even tried to make us breakfast, and burned the bacon every time. I'd caught him this time before he could ruin another pound, and instead made pancakes. My sister, away at a sleepover, usually provided a buffer between us.

He waited until I had my back turned over one of the pans.

"Sweetie..." His voice was husky from one too many late-night Marlboros.

Nothing good ever came after "sweetie." He only dug out "Sweetie" when he meant business, when shit hit the fan, a broken leg or a panic attack or a relative dead. Or a mom gone. I braced myself and poured out another pancake.

"Are you gay?"

My hand slipped, spilling some batter directly into the frying bacon grease; it spattered and hissed and I had to fight the urge to swear.

You told me to dread this moment. To keep it to myself as long as possible, a white-hot secret behind my breastbone. There would be screaming or yelling or worse *disappointment.* You painted a good picture; you even brought up Matt's trans-ness, making out Dad's broken heart into something evil it wasn't. "What makes you say that?"

"That... boy. That friend of yours. I really didn't mean to–" He exhaled. "I saw the two of you in the pool. I saw you kiss him."

I froze, a familiar panic gathering in my belly and palms. "No," I said quickly. One of the pancakes was burning; I couldn't get my hand around the spatula. And it was an honest answer. I was not gay.

"I hope you don't see this as a phase–"

I whirled around, wanting to be strong enough to tear into him, to fight *back*– and I see his face. He didn't look angry or disappointed. What he did seem was anxious.

"--sexuality is a spectrum. A beautiful thing. I'm glad you're learning about yourself."

I couldn't fight the panic attack anymore. It was one of the embarrassing kinds, where I cried and cried. He got up and hugged me, assuming a different reason behind the tears.

"You're not–mad?" I gasped.

He pulled away, confused. "Why on earth would I be mad?"

"I–I thought—*he* told me—you would be mad."

Dad frowned. "I see..."

I wiped my face, clumsily, and went to shut the burners until I could compose myself.

He rubbed his arms. "I'm sorry, I... I should have let you come to me, first. Why would you think I'd be mad? I just want you to be happy with–whoever. Unless... they're an axe murderer. That would be a different story," he tried to joke.

"But... but *Matt*," I said.

He jerked a little, and his eyes took on that shuttered look they do whenever Matt is mentioned. "There are things... I don't understand," he admitted. "But it was–never because he was–if *you* told me you were a woman, right now, I wouldn't care about that either. Well. I *would,* but only because this world is dangerous for trans women–" Babbling now, he cleared his throat. "Whoever and whatever you need to be yourself, I want you to know I accept it."

Sometimes relief is painful, like pulling out a splinter.

"His parents are homophobes," I said, to explain my erratic behavior. "He was worried for me."

"And it's awful, he has to go through that." Dad touched my shoulder. "Why don't we go to the diner? You can get whatever you want."

"...Okay."

6.

When I started to come out of the anesthesia, I first saw my hands—wrinkled, shriveled, a disconcerting shade of yellow from the blood loss and studded through with IV catheters, deep red stranger's blood creeping through one—and I wondered, briefly, if this was another sleep paralysis nightmare. I didn't get those often, but with the sleeping pills, it could be a crapshoot, and if I didn't take them at least three times a week, who knows if I would ever sleep again.

I blinked my way back into myself. Directly across from the nearest bed was a TV, playing some kind of news footage of a bunch of guys crawling all over the capitol building. I tried to let my eyes fall shut, to fall back out of the nightmare.

"Aaron? Are you awake?" Dad's voice. It lent less credibility to my dream. I tried to turn my head towards the sound, but it felt so horrifically heavy.

There was a weird... niggling, sensation, in my leg, not quite pain but the precursor to it, almost more itchy than anything. I was *so* itchy.

His hand, when he took mine, was clammy and hot. My eyes weren't working right; everything was blurry. He had a mask on, his own eyes bloodshot, and he smelled like smoke. Something stunk of dirt and that acid copper of dried blood.

"Can you hear me?"

A flash of adrenaline, which shook the worst of the grogginess. I shot up, my head spinning, but my leg wouldn't work–

Dad grasped my shoulders, eyes crinkled and wet at the edges, and gently forced me back down. "You need to rest, sweetie."

The deep-shit word. "What happened?" My words were slurred. "Where–"

"You got hurt. You had to have surgery." Level and calm, I wondered if he used this voice on anxious clients. "You're safe now."

Safe from–

I couldn't see the totality of the situation. As much as I tried to remember, to think back, all I knew was my brain felt like concrete. "Where is he?" I hissed. My throat was hoarse; I'd learn later they'd briefly intubated me. "*Where* is he?"

Dad flinched. "What do you remember?"

A bright-hot crack, and the blood, and the *snow*–

"That isn't how it happened," Dad said, and adjusted the blanket on my chest.

Near the door, you linger, your spirit a torch in the cold sterile room.

CARRION

A steady *rowr, rowr, rowr* brings me back into consciousness, obligingly re-woven into flesh. I feel like I've been beaten with mallets.

Somewhere near my face, Rascal screams, her tuna-scented breath complimenting my tableau of misery. "I'm alright, girl," I try to tell her. "You need to shut up."

She licks my face, catching some of the sweat. It's all wreathed in my hair, down my back. I prop myself up on one shaking arm.

Dmitri's nowhere to be found. Typical.

Seconds later, Matt clatters upstairs, a barrage of steel-toe booted steps. I hate when people wear their shoes in the house. He sees me, and that I obviously have just passed out. "Good girl, Rascal," he tells her, tersely. Without asking permission, he tries to help me to my feet.

Gamer tip: you should not force anyone with dysautonomia to make any sudden, fast movements.

I crumple like a carnation, and when I come to–again–he's managed to get me on the bed and get a pillow under my feet. I recognize the expression on his face, all worried; the wrinkles on his forehead, wary round eyes, I saw him make it hundreds of times as mom.

"We should get you to urgent care," he says. "Your pulse alone is–" He flops over my hand to get a better look at my manacle, which is of course brightly alerting. I swear I feel the individual parts of my heart working.

"Nothing they can do," I say, all grumbly and full of dust. It would be almost hot if I didn't feel like death warmed over. "Salt. Get me salt?"

"...Salt."

"Helps. *Please.*"

He disappears without further convincing. Rascal struggles to get onto my bed, finally drawing herself up the covers with her claws, fibers tearing loudly. She lays at my right thigh and purrs fiercely.

My arm weighs a million pounds. I check the numbers for myself. Almost 200. Must be a new record. "I made the leaderboard," I mutter, half delirious.

The bottle of tonic sits on my nightstand, three feet and a world away.

That day lingers in my dreams, my memories, but the moment of crystallization–the moment I woke and knew he was dead *and* I saw him–has eluded me until now.

Matt returns with a glass of water and the big container of Morton's salt. My hands tremble badly when I reach for it. With no time for niceties, I dump a few teaspoons in my mouth, my tongue puckering at the onslaught, and force it down with a few mouthfuls of water. Rinse, repeat. He watches me with something akin to horror. "And that does... what, exactly?"

I cough. "Helps stabilize the blood pressure."

He tuts. "And here *I* have to avoid excess sodium, and you can eat it straight."

It would take a little while for the salt to do its job. Gingerly, I sit up. He moves towards me with his arms outstretched, the way you might for a toddler that has just learned to walk. "I'm alright. I'll be alright."

It took me weeks to figure out that I was really and genuinely seeing spirits. I figured it was hallucinations. Blood loss, brain damage, hypoxia, the like. Fitzl put me on Seroquel and upped the dose and scrambled my exsanguinated neurons. But still, I saw and I saw and I saw—

And I see.

"Matt," I begin, slowly. The excess salt has left a bloodlike flavor in my mouth. "Who was it you... when did you..."

He starts a little. "Must have been about three years after I left home," he admits, not quite meeting my eyes. "There was a trucker, Jackson, that I was pretty friendly with. We happened to be at the same truck stop one evening, so we got dinner at the little diner it had. He went to the bathroom, came back, and... dropped dead." Matt shuddered. "I saw later in his obituary that it was an aneurysm. The way they—curl, get up, I thought I had a break with reality."

I nod. I should say something to acknowledge how horrible it must've been, but instead swat sweaty hair out of my eyes.

He hesitates, rubbing his upper arm, then asks, "He's still... he's still with you, isn't he? After all this time?"

I shudder. "He convinced me of so much," I say instead. "I'm just... finally remembering how it really was..."

He puts an arm around me, unsolicited, but instead of flinching away, I lean exhaustedly into his flesh. He smells like Old Spice, cat, and dust. "Don't let him win," he says, fervent.

***

That night, itchy with exhaustion, I sit with my stupid sketchbook on the front porch with Amanda's blanket spread across my lap. All the talk of seeing spirits has just made me miss Dad, the sudden raw barb of his death joining the rest. I don't fight the tears, have no reason to, other than the fact they'll smudge my pastels. I forgot that grief feels like being stabbed regardless if you're a little kid or a grown ass man. I tilt the smooth white paper against my knees so it won't get wet, and let my hand move however it wants across the paper.

What results is... paper. Stacks of sheets, lying on top of one another like leaves. Charcoal doesn't allow for such fine details to see what is *on* the papers, but I know. A crow comes to roost on top of the pile, snatches the topmost piece in its beak. I write "CARRION" at the top, and then, on impulse, grab a picture and upload it to Instagram, something I haven't done in months. I know I should write a post with it, something to explain *what* this meant, to wax poetic about the nature of grief and how Dad *was a good man.*

But everyone who matters knows that, so what I write instead is, *Dad always did say somewhere under the paperwork were people.* I post it without letting myself hesitate, and then I do something I've been dreading.

I know I picked him up myself. The funeral home, Sweets, does it nicely, discreetly, cremains into a padded box with the label *human remains* into a black bag you might get while shopping. I left him–on his chair–in his office–unable to decide *where* to put him, especially while I was packing everything up.

I pick him up. He's light, even with all the padding, even in my weaksauce noodle arms. I bring him out onto the porch. He was happiest here, I think. After a few minutes of rummaging in his desk,

I find a few last stale Marlboros in a squished box. I bring them here too, and then finally, finally open the urn's box.

I thought he would've gotten something dead simple, in a flat black or maybe a burnt red like the walls of the office. The vessel was a smooth, almost burnished blue stone, agate or something like it, the size of a small jewelry box. The lid opens, I know, but I don't bother. I set the package on top of him and light up myself.

This isn't him. Not really. Yet this I will carry wherever I go, wherever I move. Nobody will leave him ever again.

PERSEIDS

Tuesday dawns hot and unbearable. I forced myself to crash and sleep and wake with the usual Ambien hangover. As I lay there, the house is heavy and quiet, central AC churning softly in the rising light.

I fear today will make or break me.

For at least an hour I lay still in bed, trying to calm the rampant terror. There should not be any uncertainty. She likes me. She was practically the one to suggest this whole thing, and she helped me with Dad, and I can't pretend I haven't noticed the *staring*. There's a nonzero chance I will wake up with her tomorrow, and that scares me so badly I have to go throw up.

One thing at a time: it will be a small miracle if I get through the date without fainting or crying on her. Again.

I go through the ordeal of washing and diffusing my hair, iron three shirts, decide I don't like any of them, actually, before choosing a deep blue one that's smashed in the corner of my still-very-much-on-the-floor suitcase. So long as I manage not to sweat too much, I am very nearly attractive.

Embarrassing to admit, but I used to love the way I looked, especially after I no longer looked like a starved crow. I'll give anyone $5 if they can guess what happened.

In a dissociative fugue, I make the drive to the shop, somehow find a parking spot without much trouble, and stand there staring at the closed shop door and steeling my nerve. A minute passes. Then two. Someone brusquely bumps into me, throwing a glare over their shoulder, and finally I get out of the way and enter the store, breathing in the now familiar herby-sweet smell.

There she is. Her hair, soft and glossy, is in looser curls than normal, pinned back with a simple enamel clip that matches her mauve lipgloss. When she sees me, she smiles easily, the light catching her scar and making a dimple appear on the right side of her face. Her white, short-sleeved blouse is ruched in the front, drawing focus to her bare collarbones and the single, tiny droplet pearl on a delicate silver chain.

"Um, hey," I say. "You look pretty." All of the words I could've chosen and I go with *pretty.*

"Thank you." She clears her throat. She stands too quickly, tottering off balance, and blushes furiously as she rights herself. She's nervous too.

I look around quickly, but Dmitri isn't here. Thank God.

Picking up a small black purse, she hurriedly locks the POS. "I'm... I'm ready, whenever." She slides the long, thin strap over her shoulder. Her nails, still bitten to the quick, have been painted to match the clip and the willowy, swishy skirt. And she wears the ring I gave her.

"Right... so... let's go," I say. "Before they... run out, or something." *Idiot.*

I follow her to the door, and neither of us says anything as she locks up shop. Finally, she manages, "It's been a long day. I'm glad I had something to look forward to."

"Oh? Like what?"

She shoots me a look.

"Right—um—me, too." Gee, I have so much rizz. "What... happened?"

She groans. "First I spent all morning taking inventory, *three times,* because I was sure I made a mistake, but the buyer had their entries all wrong, and then our system was down all afternoon, and then I kept emailing this one client back and forth because they couldn't understand that August has a 31st day." She rolls her eyes. "*And* to top it off we need to go get another delivery before long." Almost absently, she slips her hand into mine somewhere throughout this story. Her skin is warm, dry to the touch, almost tingly against mine. I've held her hand dozens of times. But we look like... any couple on the street.

He never let me do this.

I clamp down hard on the thought. I would not let him ruin this for me. Instead I wonder at the feeling of her skin on mine and try to not let my hand get too sweaty.

We get to the cafe without disaster. This late into the afternoon on a workday, there aren't many customers. A pair of spirits—a couple, perhaps—pretend to browse menus at a spot not far from ours. We get coffees and split a sandwich.

"How's packing going?" she asks.

"It... it goes. My sister's room is almost empty, and Matt's taken care of most of his shit."

Amanda furrows her brows. "So he's still here?"

Sipping my coffee, I look towards my half of the sandwich; a Reuben. "It actually... isn't as bad as all that," I say. Red splotches are forming on my elbows from the heat and the coffee; I turn down my sleeves a little. "We... we've been working through it. I don't know. I think I see it a little differently now."

"How so?"

"Well, I ran, too."

She cups her hands around her mug. "You didn't leave behind two small children."

"...I guess not. Anyway, he'll be gone before long, I'm sure. Once the estate is squared away." *Estate.* I hate rendering it down to that word, and shudder.

"Have you thought about where you might go?" she asks.

I pause. "...I have no idea. But it... sounds like I have time on my side. Something about this not being a seller's market." I trip over the words. "I guess I could—crash on Charlie's couch, or something, until I find something more permanent."

Her eyebrows shoot up. "So you're not going back overseas?"

I straighten. "Well, I..." Then it hits me... I am no longer thinking of Edinburgh as home, if I ever did. Jenna might be at school, but she still needs me. And if I'm being honest with myself, it doesn't have *nothing* to do with the girl sitting across from me. "No. I don't think so."

Amanda cocks her head. "But weren't you happy there?"

"To the—degree I could be, I suppose." I swish the brown liquid around the small cup. "Are *you* happy?"

Amanda drops her eyes, wincing a little in apparent sheepishness. "I guess it is a stupid question, isn't it?" She picks up her spoon and stirs the remains of her drink around and around, though I saw her put no sugar in. "Maybe... if I could have one less job... or if I didn't feel like such a time bomb..."

I cock my head. "Time bomb?"

She shrugs, her shoulders curled inward. "You must understand, considering you have POTS."

After a moment's hesitation, I reach across and take both her hands. She leans into my touch as if exhausted. "Did... did it come back?"

She shook her head. "No... no, with the interventions I took, it's unlikely... but a small chance isn't *nothing,* and..."

"...You feel like... you can't really start your life. Because *if* it happens again..."

"Bingo," she says softly.

I run my thumbs across her fingers. "Well, like you said. I'm not going to let you disappear again."

She smiles, wrung out and tired like a threadbare towel. "I guess I never really realized how alone I felt until we started talking again."

"...No. Me either."

She sits up a little straighter. "There really was no one? No one else?"

"Nothing... *lasting,* anyway." Bracing myself, I meet her gaze. "What about you?"

"Well, I was pretty immunocompromised for a while," she says. "Most Tinder dates aren't exactly enthusiastic about wearing a mask. And I told you about my ex."

In the low, warm light, she couldn't look farther from sick; her eyes are bright and clear and her skin has a healthy glow to it. "I know what you mean."

She takes a moment to tuck her hair behind her ear, her gaze darting nervously from side to side. "Can I ask you... what are you... looking for?"

My heart stutters. "What do you mean? This is a... date."

She pulls one hand from mine and traces the edge of her almost-empty cup. "I mean... are you *ready* for something? Especially given... everything that's happened lately?"

This I didn't account for. "You mean..."

"You just lost your dad. You're dealing with a massive headache with the house, and everything. And... you're still affected by what he did to you."

Blood rushes to my face. "But it's been years–"

"And trauma isn't dealt with neatly."

I pull my hands away, crossing my arms tightly. My underarms are damp with sweat. I have to hope she can't see it. "I'm... I'm *stable,* Amanda, it isn't *like* back then–"

She cocks her head. "That's not what I said." She clears her throat. "I can–*keep* being your friend, I can *keep* waiting–"

"And if it ends like it did before? And we just... drift apart? Would you really be okay with that?"

She bites her lip. "...No."

"I... can't pretend I'll be perfect at this. But I... want to try." I swallow, feeling the tightness of the lump in my throat.

She softens. "I do too. I don't really know how. We can... figure it out."

I slide my palm along the table, and she places hers against it. "Good deal."

She blushes furiously and smooths already perfect hair behind both ears.

A few beats pass. A cafe worker comes to take away the empty plates and cups. Somewhere over the course of our conversation, the cafe has started to clear out. "I guess they're, um, closing soon."

"Yes."

We haven't discussed plans further than this. I've been so focused on surviving that I didn't think I'd get this far. "Maybe we could... catch a movie, or..."

"There's going to be a meteor shower tonight," she says instead. "We could... find somewhere to watch it."

I wonder at what point the anxiety will pass. "Well, I have a yard. I could make you some dinner later–"

"I would *love* some of your cooking," she says. "It's been ages." Her eyes light up. "Do you think–do you think you could make that skirt steak thing? With the–"

"Mushroom risotto?" She never seemed to get enough of it. "Sure. Just have to pick up a few things."

Amanda follows me to the store, even though she really doesn't have to. Her hand in mine feels so conspicuous in the bright cheap fluorescents. Eyes of people and spirits alike gloss over us without disaster. Only when I feel my shoulders finally start to relax did I realize how freaked I was about it. Being seen. Being *exposed*. As cis-passing, straight-passing people, there's no threat to *holding hands* in public.

Nobody should feel threatened, but that's a whole other thing.

It shouldn't feel novel, thrilling, even, to go shopping with someone like this. She shows me an almost perfectly round, red apple, so shiny with wax you can see our faces in it. She spends a few minutes meticulously searching through the rows of table bread, examining each for perfection. After way longer than the task really needs, we go back to the house. Back home. Matt's made himself scarce, not that he knew where I was going or what I was doing. Last I heard he's really been enjoying watching the game at the local bar, Darby's.

Only a few steps through the door, she appraises the fruit of all my labor, her heels louder than usual on the old hardwood. "It's a lot... emptier than I thought," she murmurs, her voice still carrying.

"I've been busy," I say.

She ghosts inside, her fingers brushing against a section of the dining room wall, darkened in spots where frames used to be. "Are you going to miss it?" she asks softly. "This house?"

I haven't been able to give much thought to it, really. I've only lived here–here and that shit flat on Chambers Street, anyway. The cold blue solace of my room, the porch. "It's too much for me to maintain on my own, especially the yard," I tell her.

She turns slightly. "That wasn't what I asked," she says, almost teasingly.

My face colors, and I clench my fists reflexively; I find I have to consciously force myself to let go. "I... I will," I say, tasting the thoughts as they form. "I... I don't know. I didn't move around a lot like you or Charlie, and I didn't... have a bad relationship, with this place." I stand at the precipice of Dad's office, the boxes of papers still awaiting the paralegal's pickup. "I think I... felt bad, that I didn't."

"Because *he* did?" she offers, leaning against the other half of the doorframe.

I shake my head, a few curls swaying in front of my eyes. "I shouldn't be talking about him. Not now."

"You can, you know," she tells me. "I don't–it's fine." She cants her face towards mine, trying to catch my gaze, but I don't relent.

"You would think–at some point–I would finish inventorying the damage." All the damn *chains*. "All the therapy, the meds, and now all this ghost work. You would think–"

She touches my arm, and I flinch, again reflexively. For a moment she stands there, her lips slightly parted. "I won't hurt you," she reiterates. "Is he... here?"

I shake my head. "He tried to... mold me, into something I wasn't. It was... it was damn *oppressive*. When he died, I thought... I would be free."

"What did he make you do?" she asks me.

The concrete examples must be among the chains; I can't quite grasp specifics. "I wanted to wear pink," I tell her, the words lamely falling between us. "The... softness, the femininity–it drove him crazy."

Her brows pull up. "It's one of the things I like about you. You're not afraid of... who you really are."

I exhale harshly, feeling the jagged edges of tears. "You must be, um, hungry, right? The risotto will take a while–"

"Aaron," she says, firmly.

I promised myself I wouldn't cry. And yet I'm hanging on by threads.

She takes both of my hands in hers. "You don't have to give in anymore."

"I know." I clear my throat. "And I, um, meant it, about the risotto. The, uh, onions. Have to caramelize."

And when I cut them, I pretend it's the acid making my eyes water.

***

After dinner, both of us digging the remains of the risotto out of the pot with pieces of bread, I spread an old wool blanket on a piece of grass not far from the pool. Overhead, the sky has already darkened, stars peeking out timidly. We lay side by side, not quite touching, and don't say anything for a time.

"When did you get so into astrology?" I ask her. "You never really seemed to care whenever Phoebe would get into it."

"A*stronomy* and ast*rology* are two different things." Amanda folds her hands across her waistband. "Let's just say I started to care a whole lot more about... my own significance."

I wonder, again, if her condition then was more serious than she's let on.

"Every time I would feel scared, or overwhelmed, I would just think about how much more of the universe there is aside from me. We *know* that, and there are ghosts. *If* I end up not being here..." Amanda trails off.

I lean partially onto my side. "Were you... suicidal?"

In and around us, crickets and the peeper frogs punctuated the oncoming night, and now and again, fireflies. Amanda lifts up a hand and one brushes past her fingertip. "Did you used to catch these, as a kid?" she asks. "In jars?"

"Matt always made me let them go," I say. "There... used to be more, back then."

"Do you think we're bugs?"

I tut softly. "Just because something seems small doesn't mean it has no meaning." I stumble over the double negative. "We... we found ways to linger after we die, just to keep being in and around the places and people we love. Maybe bugs *do* do that. But... I dunno. Bugs are pretty cool."

I think her lip is quivering; it's hard to see in the semidarkness. "Will you stay?" she asks softly. "After you die... will you stay? If you could choose?"

I bite my lip. Should've used more chapstick. "I... can't say for sure. That could be tomorrow or sixty years from now. If I live that long, I'll be a whole different person."

"What would you choose now?"

I trace the silhouette of her face with my eyes and lean onto my side. "I'd stay for a little while," I tell her. "Make sure Jenna is okay... watch over... well, you. Even if you couldn't see me."

"You really would?"

"Of course I would. What would you do?"

"I..." She exhales. "Maybe I'd stay, for a little while. You *can* see me."

"Now that's a long distance relationship if there ever was one," I say.

"You think we couldn't make it work?" There it is, again, the smell of her perfume, soft like a sweater.

"I'm sure we *could*," I murmur. "Let's... maybe focus on the "both of us alive" thing, okay?"

Across the sky, the first flashburn of fire blooms across the horizon, then another, then another. I am not watching the meteors burn; but the rise and fall of her breath. Tremblingly, I reach to cup her face and find my fingertips come back wet. "Amanda?"

"Stay with me," she whispers.

I wrap my arms around her and pull her towards me. She grips me tightly, all smoothly corded muscle, yet is trembling like a leaf. I hate that part of me is hesitating, part of me still does not want to crack open fully. Cannot fully let go.

I want to. I want to so, so badly.

She holds me, and I hold her, and above us, bits of stardust blink out of existence.

At some point she stops shaking. My skin feels thirsty and I breathe her, feeling the places where we overlap. She presses her forehead against mine. Our lips almost, but not quite, touch.

"I-I want... something real," I whisper. "I want something that isn't..."

"It won't be," she says, and kisses me.

I know this. I remember this, how it felt, those few hushed times. This doesn't boil or burn under the weight of unbearable tension. It's more of a promise than a kiss, though when I begin to pull away, she loops her arm around my neck and draws me in again. It is the opposite of pain. My heart beats fast and crackly and I burrow my lips against the soft inside of her throat. I think I can almost do it. I can give in, welcome the blush of love and desire. Her skin is so smooth and the way she's kissing me–

–is threatening to make me pass out. I lay on my back, trying to stabilize what is surely very fucked up blood pressure, because God forbid I feel something good for once, and she instead gets on top of me. Her hair tickles my face and I'm sure she can feel *exactly* what this does to me. I cast my gaze, briefly, towards the sky again, and as my head cants back, I see him.

There. At the edge of the property, near the trees. Sunken eye wide, hands over his mouth, as if fighting back tears.

"I can't," I tell her. "I'm sorry. I can't. Not now."

Amanda leans heavily onto her her elbows. Feeling the warmth and weight of her hips is *not* helping. "Too fast?" she asks.

This is such a shitty time to lie. To bury myself in half-truths. I can't admit he was watching us on the verge of– "Maybe... maybe a little..."

"...Oh." She smooths mussed hair. "You're more of a... second date, type person, then?"

His eye seems to glow in the darkness.

"Maybe..." I can't get air in fast enough. "Next... next time?"

"Whenever you feel ready," she says. "It's not... not like last time."

"I'm sorry–"

She kisses me once more, softly. "Aaron. It's okay."

"It's not because I don't–I-I mean–"

Amanda nuzzles against me. "It's really fine." She means it. "Just... watch the stars, okay?"

ACCOMPLICE

S ome time later, I walk Amanda out to her car. We hesitate there
for a moment.

"When can I see you again?" I ask her.

"Maybe we can have dinner some time this week?" she asks. "That
delivery is almost ready for us."

"I'll be there." I clear my throat.

She smooths my collar. "Don't... worry about it, okay?" she tells
me.

It would be easier to let go if she stopped telling me it was okay to let
go of it. She's probably just reassuring me because of my prior traumas,
but still, it stings. "I won't if you won't."

We kiss once more, softly. With less urgency, less *hunger*, more of
the intimacy bleeds through.

Matt chooses exactly then to pull back into the driveway. Amanda
pulls away, blushing. Matt's car door creaks nastily when he opens it,
and he looks haggard and puffy. I wonder briefly if he drove drunk.
"Oh... ah..."

"Amanda was just leaving," I say. "We had dinner."

She beams with the appropriate level of wattage for a customer service interaction. "It's nice to meet you."

"You're the girl from the pictures," Matt says. His voice is level, unslurred, but there's still a looseness to the way he speaks.

"We're old friends," I say.

She looks him over once. "Well. Have a good night." She gets in her car, offers an awkward wave, and drives off.

"I didn't know you had a girlfriend," Matt says. He rubs the scruff of his neck.

"...This was our first date."

"Oho! Sorry to... spoil the mood."

I shake my head. "It wasn't like that."

"I thought you were, you know, gay?"

I shoot him a look. "...No. Are you *drunk*?"

"Me? Never. N-ever."

I exhale heavily. "Look, there's enough going on without you also getting a DUI. We live like five minutes from Darby's. Just fucking call me next time." I really just wanted *ten minutes* to sit on the porch and have a smoke and digest *everything* that happened before inevitably fighting with Dmitri. My luck for the evening has officially run out. I go to push past him back upstairs.

"I spoke to your grandparents," he says to my back. "They called the landline."

I freeze. "Gran and Grandad?" I've been trying to be better about emailing with them, considering the whole "Dad's dead" thing. As far as I knew, Matt hasn't had anything to do with them hardly ever. They didn't even come to his and Dad's wedding. "What happened? Why did they call?"

"Well, first we had a just *lovely* conversation about me and the divorce." He leans heavily on the still-open door of the Subaru. *Creeeak.* "They're worried about you. Your sister. Something about "you always have a place there", et cetera."

That didn't warrant the level of urgency to call and incur international fees. "What actually happened?"

"She wanted to see your face. Nancy," he says slowly, and I hear now the slosh of more booze. "Hear your voice. You look *just* like him. You know he used to wear his hair long, before he took the bar? Curled up just like yours."

He might as well have punched me in the stomach. "...Oh."

"I got to... I got to thinkin', it must be so *hard* to lose your baby."

"Not so hard you couldn't walk away," I say.

"'Nd that's why I got drunk," he mutters.

I put a hand up. "Look, it's great you're *doing the work* and reflecting and all that. Really. It only took–how many weeks of being here? First of all, don't drive drunk. Second..." I feel all the emotions scratching like thorns in my throat: humiliation, frustration and now *grief.* "I don't know. I'll call Gran back tomorrow when it's not three AM for them." What I need is a damn cigarette before I deal with Dmitri. "Give me your keys and go lay down."

He obeys and wobbles up the porch to sit on the wicker couch. "You think you could forgive me?"

It occurs to me that not everyone thinks deeply or critically about their own actions, and therefore shallow revelations can feel like bombshells. "Do you want my forgiveness, or do you want to stop feeling guilty?"

Matt's face goes slack, like he didn't even think of this.

"We can talk about this when you're not drunk. I'm just– I'm *tired.*"

He nods.

My feet feel like lead as I climb up the stairs; the cat waits for me at the top, howling. Today has wrought havoc on my vascular system, and I can feel the blood pooling downwards. Sleeping pill for me tonight. Maybe two.

I give Rascal a gentle pat. "He's downstairs," I tell her. She tries to roll on her belly, but given how old she is, she kind of flops over and stays there. I have to help her get back on her feet.

Dmitri at least has the decency to wait until I've smoked most of my cigarette, hanging out the window. A few sparrows have come to pick at the shingles.

"I remember when you used to feed them," he says, his tone surprisingly levelheaded and calm. "Scatter the seed right out of the window. You can almost still see the bird shit."

Shit was right. The birds did come–in droves. I did it because I liked to draw them, and if they were fed they tended to be a captive audience. Sixteen-year-old me hadn't necessarily thought of the impact of bird shit on roofing. It was one of the only times Dad really yelled at me.

"Do you still bird?" he asks me.

"...I used to go sometimes with my roommate."

"What's that one?" Dmitri leans against my dresser, his spectral elbow pressing against the old wood. He's still chosen to have his eye blown out, but the wound looks smoothened somehow, almost blurred. The tone of his voice arouses goosebumps; too gentle, too inviting. He gestures towards the bird determinedly pecking for seed that doesn't exist.

"...A sparrow."

He stands up straight. "Look, I... I just want to talk. No fighting."

"Dmitri, after the day I've had, I'm really not in the mood."

"It seems like it was pretty good until about ten minutes ago."

I stub out the cigarette into a glass that needs to be washed anyway and turn towards him. "*Really* appreciate you turning up to watch, by the way."

He holds his hands up. "How many times do I have to tell you? *Strong surges of emotion.* You want to get laid? I will theatrically pan away. Girls never did it for me anyway. God, I wish they had."

I look at him. His stupid dyed hair, the ugly suit, the *guise* he's chosen to show me.

"Incredibly based of Matt to do that, by the way," he continues, conversationally. "I wonder what it feels like."

"Drunk driving? I wouldn't know. Yeah, he's... Look, what do you want?"

He rocks back and forth a little, knotting his hands behind his back. How many times have I seen him do that before? He somehow manages to surprise me with what he says next. "I don't know you anymore," he says, words pitching over themselves. "I listened to you talk to her, and I... It was so bizarre."

"I grew up," I say.

"What do you want, Aaron?"

"What do *I* want?" I scoff. "Since when have you cared?"

"I've always cared."

"So much so that you tried to *kill* me."

He drops his eyes. "Ah. That."

"*Don't* tell me that wasn't how it happened." My heart thrums, and I don't have to look at my wrist to tell what's happening. Dizziness encroaches the edges of my vision.

"Oh, no, I very much did shoot you," he says. "Sit. Your face is white."

I don't want to, but I have to. Too much blood in my legs.

"But I don't want to go there. Not yet." He winces. "There's... so much to *do*."

I can almost see the complex waves of chains; perhaps lessened from what they were, but still numerous enough to stir up the sense of dread.

"I want you to... be able to love her," he mumbles. "*What* do you want?"

Wrapping my arms around myself, I realize he's loath to meet my eyes. "What do *I* want?"

"Yeah."

I haven't even really been able to *think* about it. There was the house, and Matt, and Jenna at school, and of course Dad dropping dead.

"You let go of Scotland. Why?"

"Without my student loans, I wouldn't have enough income–"

"Why did you *really?*"

"What, are you trying to be my therapist? That's kind of ironic."

He gives me half-a-glare. I have to fight not to be cowed.

"It didn't feel like home," I say to my knees. "Maybe... maybe if I'd found a job, or done a post-grad... things would be different."

"But you chose not to."

"Well, Dad was *dying.*"

"You still made a choice."

"What would you have done?" I spit back at him. I'm so sick of this shit. Is this all we did? Talk ourselves in circles for hours?

"My dear, you spent a not-insignificant amount of time today talking about *bugs.*" He comes closer to me, and I hold my ground, though my hands tremble, some half-dead memory catching in my nerves. "I would've left the old man dead. But I didn't love my father, did I?"

"You loved me, and look where that got me."

Dmitri goes towards the window, the spectral funeral pants catching in the carpeting. "You don't know how much I wish it didn't happen," he says. "How much I–*wish* I hadn't hurt you. And then I made you scared of being loved. I *made* you so many things, but somehow, you found another way out."

"I *had* to." My jaw pulses with pain; I force myself to relax the muscle. "And now we're here and it's made no difference."

"It's made all the difference. You're strong enough now to face it, at least. You weren't always."

The tremors have found their way to the rest of my body. My room has become as cold as an icebox, despite the fact that I still feel the summer sweat under my arms. "I really don't want–"

"Breathe. Try to stay in your body."

Is that why I'm freezing?

"Tell me: what do you want?"

"I just want to be free," I whisper through chattering teeth. "Free of it. Free of you."

He's so close now that if he were corporeal, we would be touching. A piece of his hair intersects with a piece of mine. "I want that too." He holds out fragile filaments of memory, coiled together like spun sugar. "Was there... was there any good?"

There must have been, for me to take so much. Right?

"If I give you–*these*–" He gestures with the fine pinkish strands. "I want to give you... this, as well."

He imparts the memory in my open palms, less effectual than steam; it sinks into my skin and leaves a vaguely tingly sensation in its place. "Before... the heavy one. I saw what you did to help that little kid. Tenacious little fucker."

I smile despite myself. "He found what he needed to let go."

"Couldn't be that easy for us, of course," he mutters. "But who do I have to blame for that?" He reaches out, almost as if to touch me again. "I'll see you on the other side."

PIECES 7, 8, AND 9

7.

The rain disrupts our picnic plans, an unexpected summer thunderstorm. At that point, we fumbled along the trail, getting gradually wetter and more agitated, until a too-close-for-comfort peal of thunder made you uncharacteristically shriek. Somehow, I saw something vaguely shelter-like in the distance through the curtain of rain, and we ran towards it.

It was a barn, or what was left of one, with chipped old red paint and missing doors. There must have been a property nearby, but all we could see, at that moment, was a viable place to not get struck by lightning. We hurried inside. The sound of the rain intensified.

"Remind me to never go hiking with you again," you muttered, pulling the blanket from over your head down around your shoulders. We were both soaked through.

"It was supposed to be clear today."

"*Sure* it was." You glanced upwards at the rafters. "It's a tin roof. Must be why it hasn't rotted away."

I looked up, too. There was a storage loft, an old ladder leading straight up. I set down my backpack and headed towards it. "Must be someone's hideaway."

"More like old storage."

I mounted the first step. It held, seemed less worn than everything else.

You tutted. "You'll break your pretty neck."

"There are worse places to die," I remarked. "It can't be more than fifteen feet. That's more like a broken leg."

"...Suit yourself."

I kept climbing. The ladder was steady, and I realized that what I'd construed as rot was actually age; the deep brown of the wood belied how long this place had been here, half-protected by the trees around it.

Up on the loft were some signs of habitation; an abandoned camping lamp, a few empty and crumpled cans of soda or beer, a moldering sweater, a wicker chair missing most of its seat. Something was stuck to the back of the chair. Tentatively, feeling for rotted beams, I worked towards it, but the wood was solid. It was a photo, rolled and nestled between pieces of cane. As gently as I could, I unrolled it. Bits of emulsion flaked off against my fingers. There was a date on the back, 1991. I flipped the image over.

Two white boys, maybe our age, maybe a little older, in this very loft with sleeping bags. One had the arm slung around the other, pressing a kiss against a bearded cheek. I gasped.

"Did you find something?" you asked..

"Yeah. Get up here. It's cool."

You grumbled but obeyed, dragging the blanket with you. I showed you the photo and your breath caught..

"...Who are they, do you think?" you asked.

"...I'm not sure. There's only a date on the back."

"Guess this was their hang out spot."

"Looks like." I handed you the photo and grasped one of the empty cans—it had an expiration date of 1993, almost perfectly preserved.

"...I hope they're okay," you whispered.

The evidence pointed to the couple not coming here in over twenty years. Whether that was because they'd broken up, or moved, or passed away, was anyone's guess. Still, their presence lingered, ghostlike.

"Well. It seems like we're going to be a while," I said. "I'll get the bags. We can still have our picnic."

You nodded, still looking at the photo, transfixed. But by the time I'd climbed down and back up, you'd spread out the wet blanket, taken off your shirt and shoes. My pulse spiked; not what I had been expecting to see. Noticing my gaze, you blushed. "...I was hoping some of it could dry."

I set down the bag and tried to quell the shaking of my hands. Trying to feel unembarrassed, I peeled off my own clothes, down to the underwear, laid them out flat, and joined you on the blanket.

Water snaked from my hair down my neck, and I shuddered. Tentatively, you reached across and brushed the droplet away. I should've said something. Cracked a joke. Maybe it was the residual energy from the lovers, or from a good storm. Your finger trailed down along my shoulder, to my chest. Before I could let myself hesitate, I kissed you, and very quickly things were going farther than they had before.

"I-I want to do this," you said against my collarbone. "Please."

Before I could let myself get bogged down with the reality, with the logistics of what *this* implied, I heard myself speak. "Yes. Yes."

***

After it all, the storm started to subside, losing some of its frantic violence. You traced patterns along my stomach and broke the silence.

"Are you okay?"

"Yes," I said. Woozy. Flushed and alive and already, somehow, sore.

"I tried to be gentle—"

"I know." Truthfully, it had been the longest time we'd spent without talking. Later I'd think about why you'd brought condoms and lube with you on a picnic. You'd tell me it was "better to have and not need."

"...Did it hurt?"

Truthfully? It had, a fair bit, considering nothing'd exactly been *up there* except for the odd finger, but the pain very quickly hadn't mattered. "Not really."

"...You're shaking."

"I am?"

You brushed some loose hair out of my eyes. "Oh, right, you haven't eaten." You fumbled for the bag, liberally doused your hands with hand sanitizer, and started digging for the snacks.

I sat up. I did feel shaky, but not from low blood sugar. Truthfully, I hadn't expected this moment to come so soon. Hadn't expected to feel so vulnerable. We'd done almost everything else, it wasn't like intimacy was a new mystery. My heart felt... raw. I almost wanted to cry. Was this normal? Was this how it happened?

You found the sandwiches I made and turned to offer me one with a dopey smile, but something in my expression must be giving it away because you set the food down and quickly crossed over to me. "Hey. Talk to me."

"I'm fine, I'm really—"

"You're crying."

I felt so *young*. "I'm not upset," I tried to convince you. "It's just, like, I'm feeling so much."

You pulled me close, shushed me. "Did I force you? Were you not ready?"

Yes. This was how it happened.

You're not understanding. That wasn't it, at all. Had you not ever felt so much love you thought you might burst? Felt so loved it practically hurt? "I just love you so much," I said. "So much. Happy tears." *Gravity,* I realized, was almost the right term. Gravity of connection.

This is how it happened; it was consensual, I took the plunge willingly. I tied myself to you so completely before I understood what that meant. What that would do. Sixteen–horny, too young, too much in love–even my body seemed to be trying to reject the gravity of the moment.

Maybe I was trying to give myself a warning.

8.

"Run away with me," you said, whisper-close next to me before we get into school for homeroom. "Let's go on an adventure."

My pulse skipped. With you, "let's go on an adventure" could mean driving forty miles east to go to an obscure independent bookstore or walking to Taco Bell in the middle of the night. It could mean building cairns near old property lines in the woods, or slipping into clubs we were too young to listen to edgy punk bands so underground they might as well not exist. Then, it was mostly wonderment. "What kind of adventure?"

"I want to go hiking," you said. "I read about this trail–up in Washington County. Tell me you want to be here *today*." You gestured up at the sky. It was one of those fall days gifted on us by the Hudson Valley, sunny, slightly cool, the sharp crunch of leaves in the air.

"You'll get caught," I cautioned you. I was no saint; I played my fair share of hooky, but only infrequently enough that Dad really *would* buy I'd gotten sick. When the school called him, he trusted me enough to have taken myself home and gotten into bed like a big boy. If I really needed to sell it, I left half-empty bottles of ginger ale and cough syrup on the kitchen counter. Most of the time, he himself was too tired to see through my bullshit.

Only Jenna, with her sharp, knowing gaze, unusually smelled bull-shit; luckily she was at an age where Starbucks Frappucinos could buy her silence.

"Au contraire, mon ami," you said. You had by then done badly enough in French to not get pushed through to French IV and V. Despite the fact that you have "at least an eighth" French somehow mixed into your very Russian pedigree. "I already got that taken care of."

I waited for you to elaborate, but you didn't. "Uh–yeah, I mean, I don't really have anything going on today." It was still early enough in the year that I hadn't yet been mobbed with schoolwork. The beginning of our senior year was as fresh and crisp as an apple, with as much potential.

You slung your arm around my shoulder, almost making me jump at the contact. "Let's go!"

"Yeah–let's go," I said, feeling the edges of a smile.

Driving upstate in the middle of the day, we felt very grown up, and we grabbed some water and overpriced deli sandwiches along the way. You smoked two of the cigarettes you'd stolen from your mother and managed not to cough this time, before trying to offer me one.

I grimaced and shook my head. "It smells awful."

You blew a smoke ring in my face. "Don't you want to be one of the *cool* kids?"

"I'd much rather have functioning lungs."

You navigated us, with *printed* directions nonetheless, to the place you had in mind, only getting lost once. Only one other car is in the small lot at the trailhead, not entirely unlike our barn.

Out here, on this small, ill-known trail some two hours north, the world felt both much too large and very far away. The air was fresh and open and I liked the strain on my lungs. I felt more than a little smug when you wheezed your way up this section of the winding path.

"It's just 'cause–you were on the soccer team," you huffed, leaning heavily against a young sapling. "Okay–okay. Uncle, I need a minute."

This time of day, the afternoon light had a silky sort of quality to it, dappling through the treecover and freckling your face. I saw the brutal softness of your bone structure–your brown-gold eyes mellowing and relaxing now that we were away. If only I could catch this moment in a jar and leave it to flicker.

Once you caught your breath, we continued up the winding path, which was gilded with pine needles and fresh moss. Birds flitted in and out of the trees; black-capped chickadees feeding in their transience.

"Just nine more months," you said.

"Until?"

"Until I'm free. I'm going to try to get–early admission to wherever I can." Your eyes sparkled with a rare earnestness, and it brought the boyishness back to your tense, guarded face. "Take whatever summer classes they'll let me. Maybe–New School, or Pratt, or... even a SUNY, at this point."

I hated to be practical at this rare moment of optimism. "...Have you... started to prepare your portfolio?" My grades were stronger than yours, and even I was worried about my prospects. "Would you go for film, then?"

"Film or photography."

Trying not to tense, I smoothed my tone as best I could. "...You should have already decided. Early admit needs to submit by November. Even earlier."

"I–I *know* that, and I'm working on it." You offered me a glowing smile. "Point is–I'm going to get *out* and it–it will be different." You seized both of my hands; yours were fever warm. "You do know that, right? I–I'll be different. I promise. I'll be a better–partner. As soon as I'm not in that fucking house..." You let out a long breath. "Do you believe me?"

I wanted to hesitate. To confess, *things don't feel right anyway*. To say my dreams were supposed to lead me in an opposite direction: to RISD, maybe, or Champlain in Vermont, one of those art schools out west– "Dmitri..."

"I promise, Aaron, I *promise*..." Your gaze was beseeching. "It'll be–this time will be different."

And you've said that *so many times*. I went to pull away–

Your grip was firm. "We both know that isn't how that happened."

My child-self melted. "I believe you."

9.

By the time I got to you, the March wind had turned bitter and rank and cold. After so many days in a row at home, the trip down Route

9 felt alien, dead and empty. The Taconic–an incredibly windy and active commuter route–was even worse; for a moment I felt like I was the only person left alive.

The lot of the little trail was devoid of any well-meaning hikers. Made me wonder how the hell you got here, if you didn't borrow your parents' derelict truck. You *would* hitchhike when we'd all been told to stay the hell home. Maybe you'd even walked.

Here I paused and considered just walking away. Just driving off. Just *letting go* as Fitzl so often tried to impart in me.

But then I smelled smoke.

Wary, I got out of the car. A particularly nasty gust of wind only brought the smoke nearer to me. Bracing myself, I walked the short way up the path towards the clearing.

There you were, at the makeshift fire pit among all the tall grass; perched wraithlike on a chair dragged out of the barn. In front of you, the fire had that hot, hectic glow of burning paper or textiles. Your puffer jacket hung heavily on your shoulders, your face was puffy, and your hair–which had needed a dye job prior to the lockdown–sprouted white-blonde half to your ears. You reached for a bottle at your feet and took a long swig. "Hey."

I looked towards you, and the fire. "How the hell did you get here?"

You waved your hand at me sort of dismissively. "Details, schmetails… I just needed… a few hours…*away.*"

Wading through the heavy, dead grass, my scarf pulled free from my jacket and slapped me in the face; I tucked it away. As I made my way towards you, you shuffled handfuls of stuff from a box into a fire. Papers with glossy writing on them. "What are you–"

The next handful kicked up a wave of embers; you spread your arms wide. "It is a *funeral* of *dreamssss,*" you announced. "I figured I needed a witness."

"Dmitri, we are both supposed to be *home*."

"What, is it dangerous, outside, or something? I'm not sick, you're not sick." You used the bottle to point to us respectively. "Come on. Kiss me."

I shook my head. You knew I didn't like to kiss you when you drank; you stunk. "I'm not taking my chances."

"*Kiss* me," you intoned. "I haven't seen you 'n... how long? And this is how you act?"

A furrow of frustration crept up my spine. "I don't owe you anything."

This isn't how it happened.

I crept around the fire and gave you as close-mouthed a peck as I could; Stoli's has made the air practically flammable. Is that what this is? Another attempt?

Closer now to the fire, I could see the detritus within; glossy college pamphlets, offer letters, paper mockups of applications, old schoolwork. "What is..."

"I ain't going," you said, with a theatrical sniffle.

"A lot can change between now and June–"

"And I could be dead by then. You could be dead by then. And if it–goes on?" You laughed once, a bubble of pure hysteria.

"There's always Zoom–" I started, this being an immediate mistake.

"*Fuck* Zoom!" you yelled. "An' *fuck* FDR, and *fuck*.... *Fuck!*"

I reminded myself to take a deep breath. "It's going to be okay. Maybe you might have to wait a little longer–"

"*I am sick of waiting.*"

This... this rawness, this was new, hard and desperate from the alcohol. "What do you expect me to do? I can't fix this."

"Even if it weren't because of COVID, my... my aid packages came in and *they're not enough.*"

I closed my eyes. "Dmitri. We've been through this. There's SUNY. I said I'd help you apply for the grants, Dad would too–"

"'Cause everything just comes up roses when Daddy gets involved," you muttered.

"...Excuse me?"

"Everything is just so *easy* for you. All the time."

Within the sleeves of my jacket, I clenched my fists. "Yeah. Some things *are* easier for me. But at some point you have to stop dwelling on how *shit* everything is and take steps to, you know, *do* something. *Let* people help you instead of biting their heads off. *Everything* sucks right now for *everyone.*"

You hiccupped. "At this rate I might not even pass the year anyway, so. Guidance counselor called me about it. Skipped too much gym."

"Then maybe you shouldn't have skipped so much gym," I told you.

"It's all so *fuckin* stupid," you hissed.

I closed my eyes and counted to ten. "Look. Let's just... put some dirt on this fire and I'll take you home." I reached to take the bottle from him, and you grasped my wrist. Hard. I jerked my arm once, twice.

"I'll finish it. I'll finish it, okay?" In one fell swoop, you downed the remainder–what probably amounted to three shots. "We can... we can go." You stood, stumbling. "Okay?"

"Dmitri..." My eyes drifted over your red, swollen face. "Dmitri, you can't keep doing this. You said you didn't want to be like your parents."

"Oh, shut *up* about parents," you slurred.

I was starting to lose patience, hot flickers of irritation starting somewhere near my tailbone. "If you get in the car I'll take you back to my house. Will you go?"

The neck of the now-empty glass bottle falls slack in his hand.

"Dmitri. Things will look better after you have some water and sleep it off. It's going to be *fine*. Remember? Remember what you promised me? You can start doing that now."

You looked down and were very still, breathing through your mouth. More vodka fumes.

My chest was tight, shallow. "Dmitri... I need you to start committing to that. Or..."

Your eyes flashed hot as that fire. "Or?"

"Or...I'm not sure how much longer I can keep doing this."

And this is how it happens:

Your hand flew out quickly, catching the fine skin of my cheek. A sudden *whoomf* of betrayal had barely started to catch up to me; I stumbled, had to take a moment on my knees. The skin of my face felt weary and hot and I touched the spot where–

You'd hit me.

I forced myself to a stand.

You looked at your palm, horrified. "Wait... Aaron, I–"

The thing I told myself would never happen.

My cheek was bleeding; not badly, but enough to be felt. The zipper on the edge of your puffer must've broke the skin. Everything in me was like ice; it had gone numb, and I shivered. I cast one last glance at you.

"Aaron–"

"I'm done," I said softly. "That's... I'm done. No more."

I forced myself to start walking away. To ignore your frantic apologies; because all of the things I'd suppressed, let go, forgotten, were welling back up.

I got in the car, and I left you there, and when I wept, the tears burned the mark on my cheek.

WALKAWAY

When I come back into myself, Dmitri has that cowed, curled-in look of a pet that's been bad. And he's equally as anxious for my reaction.

I was out–away, whatever–for quite some time; it's nearly dawn, the sky that tired drawn gray that precedes sunrise. My eyelids burn, and I taste the familiar nausea.

He waits for me to speak first; when I don't, instead gently dragging my body upright so I don't faint, he says– "I want you to remember what you promised. That you wouldn't forg–"

"Do you even *remember* that?"

He flinches back. His chest rises and falls rapidly. "...No."

I nod. I figured as much. I take my phone and pack of cigarettes from the bedside table. My skin has that greasy, slightly sandy feeling because I slept in my day clothes and haven't showered. "There's so much you say I haven't remembered. What about all the things *you* don't remember? When you were drunk, high, worse? Do you get that back?"

"...No."

"So why do *I* have to take a bunch of your bullshit back, and you don't even have to deal with it at all?" I'm struggling to keep my voice soft; Matt must be trying to sleep.

"It has nothing to do with physical memory, it's the bond–"

"Yes, I *know* that." I huff. "I swear, I can't get rid of you *soon enough.*"

His face pinches. "I'm sorry."

Sorry doesn't take it back. Doesn't fix the broken plate, any number of tired metaphors. Sorry doesn't erase my PTSD or make me the person I was. I shouldn't say what's burning on my tongue. I should just *walk away.* "Go to hell."

For just a second, I think I see pride in his eyes; and then he's gone. My chest seizes, not in anger or panic but a sensation that evoked the word *hospital.* It passes quickly, but not quickly enough to reassure me.

I wonder how it will happen. Aneurysm. Kidney failure, liver failure. Poetically, a heart attack like Dad. Everyone will say, *well that's a damn shame, but he was* so *sickly.*

The last thing I need is more nicotine, but I'm sure fresh air can only help. I move as delicately as I can downstairs, out to the porch, and sit with my head in my hands for a long time.

***

When I feel something resembling calm, I check my phone and discover a barrage of missed messages.

From Amanda–*I had a good time tonight [heart emoji]. Talk tomorrow?*

From Charlie–*Thinking about you. I know it's Amanda's birthday soon, maybe we can all get together again?*

At least a dozen messages from Facebook marketplace, wanting to buy stuff from the house I've listed.

And from my sister–*Do you think it ever gets better?*

I sit up straighter. Her communication has been mostly unpredictable, which I know is unlike her. There's only so much I can do if she isn't willing to come home. I send her the usual worried-parent texts often: how has she been eating/how is class going/is she getting along with her roommate/classmates/team? And receive single word responses if any.

She's probably asleep. I hope. *It's not that it gets... better. But it gets easier.*

Immediately the message is read. *So everyone has been telling me. But I don't KNOW.*

I don't want to risk driving her off. *Can we talk?*

Let me go to common room. Eleni is asleep

Contrary to popular belief, conversations in ASL are not *silent*. They usually come with audible exhalations and the snap and slip of skin. And, you know, stuff like laughter and tears.

A minute or so later, Jenna calls me. She sets the phone down awkwardly on some surface in front of her, and behind her I see the fake-leather stiff couch I remember from move-in day.

Hunched over in her school branded sweatshirt, this version of Jenna is not one I've seen before. Her slick, greasy hair is pulled into a loose knot, and the skin under her eyes has that purplish-gray of exhaustion.

"Hey," I sign.

"Hi." She sniffles.

"Why are you up so late?"

"I can't sleep. Eleni gave me some melatonin, but it didn't work."

"Oof. Been there." There's an awkward pause; I thought she would say more, given she wanted this conversation. "So... what's on your mind? I've barely gotten a hold of you–"

"I can't do this," she says, and starts to cry.

It never gets any easier seeing her cry. "I know how you feel."

"I kept–*pushing*–" She signs messily. "Maybe if I studied more, or worked out more, it would... I can't stop *seeing* him. I just walked away. I just–"

I wish I could just be there to give her a big hug. "There was no way we could've predicted that he'd drop dead *the day you moved away.*"

She starts sobbing harder.

I get up and start towards the door, to the buffet table that holds the mail and my keys. "I can be there in two hours. We can get breakfast–"

"No. No," she repeats. "No, don't drive all the way out, I'm just... I don't know how to *do* this. How are you doing this?"

I cross into the living room and sit on the couch, which is currently earmarked by someone named Donna online. "...By keeping busy. The counseling center... did they ever get back to you, about a grief counselor–" She's already shaking her head before I finish my sentence. "...Great. *What* exactly are we paying for?"

Jenna sits on her hands for a minute. "Eleni's mom died two years ago and she seems *normal.* I just don't know how to be *normal.*"

"When was the last time you slept?" I ask her.

Jenna squints.

"It's not good if you have to think about it."

"I just–haven't been able to shut off my *mind,*" she laments. "I don't know how to stop thinking about it. I feel so *alone.*"

I think for a moment, absently rubbing my hand against the stubble that had formed on my cheek. I remember that I also promised that I would call Gran and Grandad... Before I can slip under into panic, I force myself to re-center. One thing at a time. My heart is already starting to do that two-step. "Don't try to stop thinking about it," I tell her. "Just... sometimes it's just healthy to *sit* with it. Feel it."

"Because I'm sure *you* have."

"Hey, I'm *allowed* to be a hypocrite at this moment."

She swipes at her streaming eyes with the cuff of her sweatshirt.

I take a deep breath. "I'm going to tell you a secret."

"...A secret?"

"Yep. That's right." I clear my throat. "I can... Ever since Dmitri died, I can see spirits. I saw Dad."

Her eyebrows momentarily pull up. Then, "Why didn't you *tell* me?"

"...I wasn't sure how you felt about it."

She crosses her legs. She's wearing cotton shorts, and her knee is skinned. "I always would have believed you."

My throat is tight. "I'm sorry, Jenna."

She sniffles. "You really saw Dad?"

"Yeah. We spoke. He... he was at peace. He said how much he loves you."

The tension in her shoulders eases slightly. "I really wish you would have *told* me."

"Well, I'm telling you now. And I've been dealing with my own shit too."

She wipes her nose. "He's really okay?"

"He was ready. It was... weirdly beautiful."

"I wish I could have been there," she signs.

"Yeah. Me too." The sun is rising in earnest now, brilliant persimmon and gold above the trees. "Listen, I... I know how to make you sleep. But I also didn't tell you."

She perks up.

"Get some Z-quil–I think you can buy it at eighteen–and also some magnesium. And some tart cherry juice. Crush in a melatonin or two."

"...Are you sure I can take that all at once?"

"It'll work," I promise her. "Better, ah, clear your schedule, though. And... Jenna?"

"Yeah?"

"I want you to come home. At least for a weekend. I think... I think you need it."

She nods. "Okay. I'll see if they'll let me out of weekend practice."

"And Jenna?"

"Yeah?"

"I love you."

She flashes an "I love you" at me, and hangs up.

***

I don't exactly sleep, but I sort of doze for a few hours, my body heavy and unwieldy. I wake on the couch disoriented and badly needing a pee. Grateful that the downstairs bathroom works now, I wash my hands and catch sight of myself in the mirror. I'm pale and puffy–grayish–and my hair is lank. A trio of zits blooms against my chin. Even though I've been careful as usual, my heart surges–I brace myself against the onslaught. My watch alerts me. Vision swimming, I try to stand and lose my balance.

I'm running out of time. With shaking fingers I text Amanda: *me too. Date 2 soon? Also: what do you want to do for your birthday?*

Again I'm feeling weak, not in myself. I breathe in deeply. My blood thumps in my veins and under my skin.

She writes back: *I don't care as long as you're there [cat with heart eyes]*

This should woo me. Does. At least until my body decides I've had enough.

PIECES, UNDEFINED

? ??

We stood there together on the prickly ramshackle of Phoebe's back porch, sharing one cigarette between the two of us. You behaved yourself tonight, meaning: you were only drunk and not blackout.

You rested your hand on my head, stroking the curls softly in a way that made me feel like a marionette. You could be so gentle sometimes. I think that was the gist of it; there was so much *potentially* good.

"What do you want?" you asked me. You had recently dyed your hair, and a splotch of skin behind your ear is still red.

"What, in general?" I asked, muzzily. I leaned against you, relishing in the kiss of contact. This was about the only place I could do so. "I guess... what I want is..." Stability, sure. Freedom, but from what? "I want to *be* with you. Just... *be*."

You smirked and chucked me under the chin. "Pretty sure Ann and Phoebe are already at it in the back room, but I'm sure we could figure something out..."

"Not... not like that." Things had yet to escalate beyond furtive over-the-clothes rubbing. The sheer *weight* of that feeling was draining. "When you think of us in the future, what do you see?"

You took too long of a drag. I still didn't like the way they tasted, not really, leaving a bitter taste in my mouth for hours afterwards. "Well, alive, for starters."

"And?" I breathed you in, the sting of your deodorant, the hops of cheap beer, Irish Spring soap. "Where would you want to live? What would you want to do? Would you want... marriage?"

"Easy, tiger. I'm sure the good ol' fascists down in Washington will get rid of that before we're even old enough."

I blinked around the fizzy feeling in my stomach. "But would you?"

With your free hand, you cupped my cheek. "You're mine," you said. "What else do you need?"

???

My insides still ached the next day and for several after. Sources seem split as to whether or not this was *normal*. Some soreness was to be expected. Even the next time? I wasn't sold on this. It took *practice*. Why did everything require *work*?

I tried not to let the discomfort show, but that night at the party—so many parties, so many indeterminate hot smears of inebriation—I couldn't fully relax until I had at least two beers in me. Alcohol, I knew, was pretty inflammatory.

Amanda sidled up to me with a Solo cup filled with white wine. "Long day?"

"...Sort of. I, ah, worked out. It hurts to walk."

She took a slug. "*You?* Worked out?" She was really feeling braids lately. French, fishtail. She had a strand of some shiny silvery stuff woven in. I brushed my fingers against it, briefly. "Ann said it looked a little too "DC Fair." What do you think?"

"It looks nice. The contrast, I mean. Maybe more *Renaissance* faire."

Amanda snorted. "Okay, no more embroidery thread in my hair."

"No. Keep it." I cleared my throat and lowered my voice, but between the chatter and the movie Charlie had put on in the other room. "I, uh. We..." She raised her eyebrows. "I had *sex*, okay?"

If she was surprised, she hid it well. "Oh... and... how was that?"

"Kinda... not great."

"Usually isn't the first time. So they tell me." She rubbed my upper arm. "Tylenol? Maybe some ice? I think I have some in my purse–"

"I think that's *enough* about my ass, thanks."

She smiled a little. She hesitated, then, "Aaron, are you *happy?*"

"...Happy?"

"Like... with him."

I glanced inside. You were on the couch next to Charlie, talking about *something*, gesturing widely with your little cup and slopping a little of it onto your jeans. You seemed not to notice. "Well... of course."

Amanda tilted her head. "Why?"

"What do you mean?"

"What *about* him makes you happy? What do you find attractive?"

I pulled away from her. "That's a mean way to talk about your friend."

"That's not what I–just *humor* me, Bateson."

I looked towards you again. "Well... he's brilliant."

"So are you. And?"

This was categorically not true. "Well... the way he sees the world, and..." Death, gloom, nihilism? Not quite. "He's a talented photographer–" When was the last time I saw him hold a camera?

She leaned in, slightly. "This is not *quite* how this happened. But maybe it should've." She took a delicate sip of her wine. "What about him makes you happy?"

And I looked at you, in the dull glow of Phoebe's living room. "Well... I love him."

???

We were raised in a culture that valued *love* as a force that could overcome it all. *Love* as the harbinger of tragedies, the sword of Damocles. Love, a wasting thing, that tuberculic intensity. Cling to love because you'll never know when it's gone.

"How do you know when you're in love?" I asked Phoebe one of those endless evenings. By then she and Ann had already been together at least five years; an eternity, in high school. If anyone could tell me how I felt, it would be her.

She reclined back in one of the battered porch chairs. Her hair was in its usual short blunt bob. "Well... you just sort of know."

"I mean... what does it *feel* like?"

"It feels like love," she said, amused.

In my seat, I fidgeted; a piece of broken wicker pricked at my back. "When did you know you loved Ann?"

I expected Phoebe to have to think about it. She adjusted the sleeve of her tank top and answered relatively quickly given her state of inebriation. "I had just dragged them to go see *Divergent,*" she began. "We went to get ice cream after, and they had this long-suffering look on their face, so I thanked them for coming with me. They said, "for you, I'd watch a thousand more shitty YA adaptations," and I was like, damn, okay, they must really love me. And then I was like, *shit,* I love *them.*"

"So it kind of crept up on you, then?"

"More like it was made clear." She grinned. "What you feel... what you feel *is* love."

"It is?"

Sagely, she nodded. "I see the way you look at him, Aaron. That's love."

I bobbed my head, and looked towards the yard, where fireflies had come to roost.

UNEVEN

I come to on my bedroom floor, my cheek inches from my suit-case. I'm honestly not sure if I fell; I can't remember if I had the wherewithal to lower myself to the ground. My head sure hurts badly enough.

Dmitri stands at the window, hands tucked in his pockets as though pensive. "You didn't fall," he informs me.

I glance towards my wristwatch. My pulse has slowed; meaning it's only like I've recently sprinted. I lay in repose for a few moments, watching the early morning sunlight dappled on the ceiling. The carpet smells like dust. Easing myself gently to a sitting position, I look at him guiltily there in his basketball shorts.

My suitcase is only a few feet from me. I scoot towards it and give it a push; it's so empty that it moves easily. Brownish specks are sprinkled across the bone-white piece of carpet, which is the same color as the scar on my palm. "I can't imagine a life without you in it," I say. "You're just... you're just everywhere. All this talk about *freedom*..." I trail off. "I don't know. I really don't have anything else to say."

It shouldn't look strange for him to have both eyes, and yet he does. "If it hadn't shook out the way it did, do you think... we would have ended any differently?"

"I don't," I tell him.

"Maybe–maybe there's a version of me that deserves you," he murmurs. "In the multiverse... somewhere..."

"I don't want you to deserve me," I say. "I just want to... be who I am without you. Don't you... don't you get it?"

"I do," he says.

I pull my knee up under me. "So what's after this? The big one?"

Dmitri folds his arms behind his back. "Yes."

"...And I'm sure I'm *wrong* about that too."He says nothing.

"After... Jenna's gone. After Amanda's birthday. We'll put it to bed. Okay?"

"Aaron–"

"It's not open for debate," I say woodenly. "Enough. That's it. Now–go away, or something, my head really hurts."

I heave myself up into my bed, dizziness washing over me, and watch the pallid light dance for a while longer.

***

Throughout the next few days, I curl into the familiar lushness of depression. The world seems slow and still even though it's practically on fire. I pull a Bella from *New Moon* and sit for several hours staring outside my bedroom window listening to sad music. I think about the meaning of *mourning* and make a few bad sketches which will never again see the light of day.

More people buy our things. More people take our things for free. Matt rents a small dumpster for the useless, shitty stuff and tows it himself with a rented U-haul. In it go boxes of moldering clothes and blankets too chewed by mice to be used even by the needy, unneeded old schoolwork, women's clothes. I am surrounded by hollow rooms and feel even hollower.

I've so far avoided cleaning out Dad's room. I've gone in to dust, but little else; even the trash can still has trash in it. With almost everything else mostly squared away, I can't put it off much longer. He was the one who wanted this, after all.

I flirted briefly with the idea of staying here, getting two or three roommates, but that would cause a whole host of other issues. I can't, don't want to, deal with other people in this corpse of a house. Easier to cut and run, and then... what? Everything beyond that–beyond *dealing with Dmitri*–seems to be behind a wall I can't comprehend. The *after.*

I thought I knew who I was without him–I spent nearly a year before the [accident] and three since. All this *memory* has done is further confuse things. Which may very well be what he wants.

I stand at the doorway of the master bedroom, looking over what's in front of me. Dad was always ludicrously neat; I think he found a sense of control that way. The bed's sheets and comforter are tucked tightly enough to bounce a quarter off of. The stack of books–one fiction, one nonfiction, always–are straight and neat. Propped near them is a moleskin journal with a reddish-brown cover, pages creased with use. I pick it up and hold it in my chapped, dry hands. Before I can convince myself to open the front cover–he isn't here to have his privacy violated–I instead set it aside and start cleaning out the dresser. Socks and underwear immediately in the trash, except some wool socks

I know were pricey. I am not here, I remind myself, I am just doing a job.

Pajamas. I remember when he wore these on Christmas/on birthdays/on New Year's/on first days of school. Most of it still smells like him—Tobacco and Ivory soap and that sweet sticky smell of printer ink. These were *just something worn,* no memory sticks to them, just mere objects. His beloved, battered Ramones shirt finds its way to the top of the pile and I hold it close against my chest and will myself not to cry. At least I know how I feel about Dad's death. At least those wounds won't leave such a dreadful scar. Three things, I decide. I will let myself keep three things. The shirt, for one, and the cardigan from the office. I breathe in the smell of dust, carpet fresh powder, and lingering Marlboro smoke that wreathes the room.

I manage to fold and put away most of his things for donation. If I'm being honest with myself, most of it will probably fit me. I scavenge a few pairs of the least dad-looking pants and one of his black suits, because as I've been made brutally aware, you can never be too prepared.

Mixed in with the clothes and pairs of shoes in the closet are a few other boxes. One seems to be keepsakes; seashells and crumpled concert tickets and museum pamphlets and even a handful of old Euro bills, pre-plastic, slipped into a clear plastic sheet as though for display. His expired UK passport is within the detritus, worn at the edges. I flip through, seeing stamps from London Heathrow, Paris, Amsterdam, Berlin, and of course Edinburgh; there were plenty of those, as that's the closest airport to Gran and Grandad. There's the facepage, with his name and photo, and he wasn't much older or younger than me. He had light in his eyes, still.

Plane tickets. Train tickets. Polaroid and disposable camera photos from adventures from years past: often there was a young man I recognize as one of his former best friends, a white guy with striking dark hair named Jonathan, and a few other faces with scribbled names on the backs. Old churches. Leaning against a sign outside the Beatles museum in Liverpool, one arm slung around a woman with auburn hair. I blink, squint. Well, not a woman anymore, anyway.

I flip over the photo, seeking more of his meticulous dates. *Alan and _____, Liverpool, 1999.* Matt, in an overlarge sweater, beams up at him. Were they really that happy, once?

A small white cloth album holds their wedding photos. Matt has on this white silk thing and heeled pumps, his then-long hair in a messy updo, yours truly making a slight pucker in the front of the garment, outside of the Poughkeepsie courthouse. His knuckles, around a small nosegay of asters and goldenrod, are white, and his face is pinched and uncertain. Perhaps he was even sick that day.

Fewer of those friends are present in the small album, candid in the poorly-lit community center where they must've had their reception. John, passing Dad the cake slicer for an unimpressive sheet cake; Matt's sister, adjusting the sleeves on the white silk thing, her square face serious and also impassive; my maternal grandparents, who I barely remember, looking on almost disdainfully from a pair of plastic chairs, potato salad and ham on their plates.

"...He still held onto that?"

Matt scares me badly; my heart lurches in my chest and I scramble to shut the album. He makes a dismissive gesture. "It's alright. You can look." He has on another one of those tacky wolf shirts, stubble poking out from his chin.

"...I didn't know you had a reception," I mumble.

"We didn't want to, but Mom and Dad kind of twisted my arm," he admits. Hesitantly, he sits on the bed, and when I don't react to this, he pats the mattress for me to come sit next to him. He mimics a deep, rumbling voice. ""If you have to have a shotgun wedding, at least do it right.""

"They don't exactly look happy to be there," I observe. "Neither do you." I hand him the album.

He observes himself as the bride. The resemblance stops at the auburn hair. Matt just holds himself differently, his shoulders turned out instead of in. "Well, I was dealing with horrific morning sickness," he says. "That's why we tried to get away with just the ceremony. Mom said I had to have my cake and eat it too—only to throw it up an hour later." He continues to flip slowly through the album. My parents almost looked happy during their first dance. A toast, Matt with orange juice; more people I don't recognize in various states of intoxication.

"You have a cousin, you know," he says. "Not too much younger than you."

Kate's twenty; we're friends on Facebook, but she hardly ever posts there. The most recent photo of her I saw, she was doing one of her ballet recitals, the cords of her long neck evident above a pale pink shrug. Kate has Matt's gray eyes.

"I kind of wish things hadn't shaken out the way they had," Matt admits, his face downcast. He shuts the album and passes it back to me. "When I was a kid, we used to—all get together, at least a few times a year—twenty, thirty of us. Don't you—wish you had family?"

I shrug. "It kind of all washed away," I tell him. "First—I don't need any more fascists in my life. And I never felt... really *part* of the family when I was overseas. And before that, you left. So..."

"...You never really missed what you didn't have?"

I trace the soft edge of the album with my finger. "Not really."

Matt puts the photos down and takes both my hands in his. Unsure of where he's going with this, I let him. "I hope you can find it," he says. "Friends–that girl–I hope you can find people who make you feel at home. I'm not sure we ever gave you that."

I look away from him, towards Dad's keepsake box. "Well–you tried. I think that amounts for something."

Matt lets go of my hands. "Oh, you think?" he asks. "At least it wasn't for nothing."

DISTANCE

As I wait for my sister's much-delayed Amtrak train to arrive at the Poughkeepsie station, Amanda joins me for a long lunch (I may have bribed her with a roast beef sandwich). On the lookout deck facing the Hudson river, she rests her head against my shoulder, and we watch the pleasure-boats go by.

And it shouldn't be a relief for this to be easy. Sandwiches and casual touch in public with no meltdowns. I shouldn't be waiting for the other shoe to drop.

"The shipment comes in on Tuesday," Amanda says softly. "It's about time; the shelves are looking barren again."

The day is overcast and tepid, but her skin glimmers anyway with some kind of highlighter. It occurs to me I haven't seen her bare face since the last delivery, a thought so all-encompassing I have to restrain myself from kissing her right there and then. We are still nebulous and undefined. "Tuesday's your birthday," I point out.

She smirks. "I'm an adult who has no problem working on my birthday."

"Well–I was just–"

She raises an eyebrow.

"I was hoping–to do something–with you."

A hint of real blush emphasizes her makeup. "Then it sounds like we're spending the day together." Amanda bumps her hip against mine. "I'm sure we can find some place to have lunch or dinner, and then... hang out at yours? My aunt will be home, *ostensibly* to spend time with me, but..."

Goosebumps form along my forearms. "If... that's what you want."

She yawns theatrically. "Besides, I'm too *tired* to do anything crazy. What I wouldn't *give* for a vacation."

"Where would you want to go?"

"Somewhere with a beach. And those drinks with the little umbrellas."

Given the choking heat and humidity, the *last* thing my POTS ass needs is to sit somewhere on a hot beach. "Something fruity would be pretty refreshing. You don't... you don't get any time off? Ever?"

She guffaws. "You're funny."

My face colors. "Even a day? Two?"

Amanda reaches up to tug at a loose strand of hair. "I guess I... *could*," she says at last. "It hasn't all... gone towards debt and medical bills."

I cock my head. "What are you saving for?"

She averts her eyes. "It's going to sound... silly."

"Knowing you, I'm sure it's dead sensible."

"Well, I'm full of surprises," she begins. She goes to elaborate, but the wail of the incoming train drowns her out. "That's your cue. I'll keep you in suspense until Tuesday." She kisses me once, quickly. "Give your sister my love." Amanda waves, and quickly makes her way towards the stairs that lead down into the parking garage.

For a moment, I listen to the familiar *clack, kuh-clack* of the Amtrak train as it comes into the station, looking like a round and somewhat dented tin can compared to Metro North. I make my way down the stairs, dodging city commuters who have also been dislodged from their respective train, and see Jenna searching for me with wide open eyes.

In the few days since I've seen her on video, she's shaved half her head in an artful and unambiguously queer undercut, the exact type of hairstyle a college freshman out of their depths would get. Against the pinkness of her scalp, the auburn tufts look prickly and itchy and, I have to admit, not unlike Matt's beard. She lets me squeeze her in a tight hug for ten seconds before she breaks away brusquely and says, "I really have to pee. The bathrooms were out of order."

Five minutes and a trip to the women's room later, I brush my fingers against the bare side of her head. "That's new."

Jenna looks down and shrugs. "Eleni did it for me the other day," she signs. "She figured I could use a change. Something about... cheering up."

"I like it. It's edgy."

"My head feels *cold*," she admits, "But it makes me feel butchy and strong, so."

Interesting word choice. "Yeah?"

While her face stays relatively pale, her ears burn brilliantly. "I'm, um, starved. Can we go get something to eat?"

"Sure—whatever you want—"

Jenna shoulders her bag and starts towards the parking lot, going the complete wrong way.

When I finally corral her into the car, I weigh the information that I've been not-quite trusted with. I have two options: push her on it, or let the situation unfold as it would. Jenna never expressed interest in anyone, but honestly I kind of figured that was because of the lack of people who are fluent in ASL at her school. It might also be a gender thing, or maybe I misinterpreted her sign incorrectly altogether. It just *seemed* very distinct to me.

We end up at a local Mexican place. Jenna inhales most of our chips and salsa and half of her burrito as soon as it's set in front of us.

"...Do they not feed you there, or something?" I ask. "I saw the dining bill."

Jenna gestures with a fork. "No time. Early train. Delays. I didn't feel like paying fifteen dollars for a dry sandwich."

While I'm happy her spirits have improved so recently, I have to wonder if there was a catalyst. "...So... how are you doing?"

A mouthful of rice and beans. "Oh, you know. Good."

I blink. "Excuse me if I'm a little skeptical, considering the reason you're visiting."

"I'm just kind of glad to be home, to be honest." With her fork, she draws the small plate of guac that came with the chips over and starts shoveling spoonfuls onto chips. "This is like, so good."

I appraise my sister a little more closely under the warm-toned lights of this restaurant. What hadn't been immediately evident before: her glassy, red-spoked eyes. "Jenna..."

She looks up amid a hasty slurp of her coke.

"...You're stoned, aren't you?"

She huffs and crosses her arms for a moment. "Eleni... gave me something to help me sleep," she admits. "Because frankly your concoction sounded illegal."

Weed is illegal at her age, but I figure now is not the time to mention that.

"And I didn't realize that if I took it, I would... *still*... feel it the next day. Sue me."

Butch haircuts, pink dye, and weed: I have to admit Eleni is the poster child for a "cool" roommate. On the other hand, Jenna is my baby sister. "Just... don't make a habit of it. Don't they drug test you?"

"Weed is legal in Massachusetts. And I looked it up. I should be *fine* if it's a one-off thing."

"...So is it?"

"...Huh?"

"Is it a one-off thing?"

Jenna scowls. "Like you're one to talk. How many legal benzos are you on, again?"

"None." Clonazepam is a benzo, but I don't take it regularly enough for it to count the way she means.

She scoffs. "Tell that to the bottle of Xanax I found in the bathroom cabinet."

My heart skips. "...Xanax?"

Jenna gave me an exaggerated look of surprise. "I found it behind the toilet paper. Nice hiding spot."

I shake my head. "Then it must be dumb old, because I haven't been able to get that stuff since–"

"May*be*, but it also had an expiry date of 2024. As long as you don't... take too many again." She cringes. "I like, get it, or whatever."

"Jenna, I genuinely don't remember getting that."

"O-kay," she drawls in English. "Are you going to eat that?" She points to the neglected half of my quesadilla.

Appetite soured, I push it towards her. It *has* to be old; that's all. But I never hid any of my stash in the bathroom; those were amateur spots. No, for me, it was under the floorboard in the closet, and I haven't had to do that in years. Maybe it was Dad's prescription? But then why hide it? Perhaps even Matt's?

It has to be one of theirs, otherwise... I really don't want to know the alternative. It's *possible* I hid it there in one of my fits of psychosis, but in that case, the meds *should* be long expired. "...Do you remember if there was a name on the bottle?"

Jenna shrugs. "Not really. I didn't want to touch it more than I had to. I assumed it was... from that guy you used to buy from."

"I *swear* I wasn't stashing it."

She stifles a laugh. "Do you think it's Matt's?"

"Maybe... I don't know." Fluttery tremors of panic are making my skin prickle. "Uh... dessert?"

"*Oh!* Yes, please." She seizes the menu and peruses with gusto.

I manage to remain some semblance of calm until we get It helps that Jenna is currently very distractible. Unfortunately, I can't investigate right away, because she insists on taking a real shower in a clean bathroom (which I can't totally fault), and she's in there for almost a solid hour. When she emerges smelling strongly of her Pantene shampoo, all she says is, "Can we watch *Blown Away?*" as if our conversation was entirely forgotten. Which it may have been.

A glass blowing reality TV show. "Uh–sure–go pull it up."

As soon as she's safely ensconced downstairs, I wade through the fog her shower left behind, thrusting my hand far back against the wall of the little closet that holds our linens and toilet paper. Fumbling, my hand closes around the familiar knobbly surface of a pill bottle. Trying not to shake, I fish it out and bring it into misty light.

Alprazolam 0.5mg

I drop it as though bitten. The bitter taste of those pills–they work faster if you chew them. The bottle falls with a clatter to the tile floor. I stoop to pick it up, my vision seesawing with vertigo, the steam from her shower collecting on the fine hairs of my arms.

The label is half-peeled off–exactly what psychotic me would do–leaving the name of the prescriber and prescribee conveniently absent. The expiration date is indeed somewhere in mid-2024.

Mystery solved. An old stash. That's all.

I sit heavily on the lip of the tub, breathing in her overly sweet shampoo and trying not to choke on the humidity. Jenna surely hasn't been away from home long enough to forget to turn on the bathroom ventilation. My head is spinning and I–

Wrap my arms around myself, as if to coax my spirit into staying within my body. No. Not now. Jenna's gone through too much, and I don't *want* to. I just simply won't. That's all. I'll just avoid the gravity pull of memory, the little handful of pills still here after all this time. I open the bottle and pull out one of the tabs, holding it in my palm, small and white and inconspicuous and *when I was with you sometimes we would pop them like candies* and no. No. I breathe out through my nose.

It's not mist. There's a horrible *wispyness* over my arms and–

I press my nails into my free palm, hard. Breathe into the pain, lean into the pain.

Maybe none of this is real–

On the verge of–someting–I press the pill between my lips and bite down hard. The bitter taste is *so* familiar and I'm brutally reminded of why I'm not allowed to have them anymore. My tongue is half numb before I can even swallow.

I force myself semi-upright, my body protesting at the sudden movement. I push through the fog downstairs, try to immerse myself in artful glassblowing, and ignore Dmitri's single eye burning into the back of my neck.

REAL OR NOT REAL?

2 *022*

Amanda left after spending the day with me; I watched her drive her shiny Mazda off into the distance.

"...Mind if I join you?"

I jumped a little, but it was just Dad. "...Alright."

The chair creaked nastily as he sits down, and it took a few stutters from the lighter before he got it. "You seem lost in thought."

Unusually perceptive for him. "I guess I was."

"...Amanda's been here a lot. Is that... something?"

Chagrin socked me in the stomach, sizzled the tips of my ears. So much he didn't notice, and he caught the things I didn't want him to. I took a long drag in response. If he said something about being careful I thought I really would kill myself.

"She's a nice girl," he said instead.

"She is," I agreed.

"Much better for you. *Normal.* Then again, I think anything is better than..." He trailed off.

"Than... Dmitri?"

Tapping off ash, "I always worried about you. With him. With her I don't feel like I need to worry."

The chagrin solidified, turned sharp and thorny. I felt it scratch the inside of my stomach.

He inhaled, a wheezy sound. "I know you don't like talking about it."

My fingers were trembling so badly I almost dropped the cigarette.

"It's not because–she's a girl. He was just so..." A pause. Then, diplomatically, "Abrasive. I didn't like the way he talked to you. Sometimes you used to flinch--"

Smoke scraped and clawed at the inside of my lungs.

"I'm sorry," Dad said quickly. "I shouldn't have brought it up."

For a second, a flash–

Blood / snow / pain

And a cramp seared in my right leg just below the scar.

"Aaron?"

I blinked. Tried to shake it off. Snowflakes flecked against my cheek. "I was with him," I whispered.

Dad's face crumpled with a sort of pain. "I know," he said. "I know, Aaron."

I was slipping, I knew I was, I was scrambling for a sort of mental purchase. Smoke drowned out the oxygen. *He did this. He did this. He did this.* Memory rippled and cracked and almost broke through. The dead boy's name seeped out of my mouth on a cloud of tobacco. "Dmitri."

***

I was in the upstairs bathroom. I didn't remember getting here, but I still tasted tobacco, so it couldn't have been long. The air itself hurt to breathe, everything hurt, it ached.

"Oh, no you don't," you said. "I'm not hiding away again."

I coughed, tasted earth, and tasted petals. "What do you want?"

"How long do you want to keep playing this game? You can't do it forever."

"Just tell me." Petals and blood dripped into the sink and ran down my chin. They scratched me from the inside. "Tell me what you want."

"Remember, dumbass. Can you do that?"

"I don't think I..."

"Can't, or won't?"

I wanted to slip back into nothing. I tried to lean back into it, but consciousness was hot and raw.

"You know you're just hurting both of us," you said. "When you do it like this. I wonder what Amanda would think. If she knew you were seeing me. If she knew you were the reason I'm dead."

"That's not true," I hissed. Still bleeding freely, I limped out of the bathroom. "That's not true."

"Isn't it?"

I slammed the door in your face, but it made no difference; when I turned, you're there, brains oozing out of your right eye. Ozone and gunpowder and snow drowned out the ambient smells of my room, the candles and detergent, and cigarette smoke. I shivered. "I didn't kill you."

You didn't speak. Your face was still, placid, purplish and blueing. In front of my eyes you seemed to rot, the flesh glistening and sloughing off. I fell to my knees, covering my eyes and ears.

"It's not real. It's not real." Even the words don't seem to be words, loose and formless. I heard, felt his breath against my covered ears. "It's not real."

"You might as well get comfortable," you said. "I'm not going anywhere."

***

The weight of blood and gunpowder and the chill kept me locked up for a good long time. I whispered that it wasn't real until my mouth went dry, but I couldn't bring myself to get up, to get out of my little ball. I didn't know how long I'd been here. Time had to be passing, I had to be moving, my clothes had changed and my face had gone from smooth to stubbly. I didn't know or remember these interstitial moments. True dissociation came over me in longer waves, rendering the familiar into terrifying blurs.

At some point I went so long without sleeping I lost the ability to read. I was gone, I knew I was gone, I needed help, but in these small moments of consciousness, I felt the press of the corpse and felt the brunt of its weight, the scratch of thorns and stabbing pain. My whole room was flowers and the smell of death. I tried taking an Ambien and hoping that would make this all stop or quiet, but all it did was tie me down on the bed so you could scratch open my abdomen and tell me I have to remember.

I thought losing it would be a relief, but it was a whole new terror. Even the world outside my window was nebulous and nonexistent, endless plans of barren grass. I tried to scream. Tried to speak. I needed to call Fitzl, or Amanda, or Jenna or Dad, I needed help.

"Why should anyone help you?" you asked, peering over my shoulder at our reflection in the mirror. A piece of bone dripped, meditatively, onto my shoulder. "Help you like you helped me?"

I couldn't take it anymore. "Shut up."

"You might as well embrace it. You're not going to be anything. All these advantages, all this love, and still, you can't even keep your shit together."

"You're not real."

"Not real, or you wish I weren't real?"

"Leave me alone."

You laughed, a dry scraping sound. "That's rich, you know. Real rich. I wish I *could* leave you alone, Aaron. I don't like this either."

I took my phone out of my pocket.

"You haven't slept in days. Can you even make sense of it?"

I could because I had to. But the numbers and letters swam.

You took something silver out of his pocket. A revolver, heavy and blunt, an old Soviet piece. "I'll give you a hint."

Everything stopped. Unravelled. The ache in my leg was back and worse than ever. I looked at my thigh. And your face.

"Go on. The way it really was."

I couldn't breathe. My mouth tasted like a burn. "You... I..."

You smiled wickedly. "Yes?"

"You..." I swallowed more blood. "You... did this. I was with you."

I stumbled back. You twirled the gun idly. "I promised you..."

"What did you promise me?"

The room was starting to crumpleshatter, fade into a sickly black darkness. The mirror, I thought wildly. You were in the mirror. I squeezed my phone a little harder.

"What did you *promise* me?"

"*Shut up!*" I screamed it, harsh, hoarse. I pitched my phone at the mirror and it cracked, but it wasn't good enough. A book went into the mirror, then another, until glass finally started to fleck and fall to the floor. I had to make it stop, needed to, I picked up a piece of the glass and slid it along the lifeline of my right palm. The pain started to solidify some things and you made a low guttural noise

"No–"

And I went to make a second incision. It didn't even hurt badly, stung like a papercut, thorns and rot seeping through the wound and I took the shard of glass down along my wrist's artery and

"No!"

A real voice, a living voice, but I needed to do this, and all of a sudden I was being shoved bodily to the floor, my weak wrists pinned uselessly. I couldn't see, my vision was full of all sorts of colors but I could almost hear myself saying "make it stop make it stop" over and over and over.

"Aaron? Aaron, it's me. Can you hear me?"

The world trickled in a little more. The pain was grounding, so I tried to focus on it, the dull sting becoming a throb becoming hot agony. My assailant shook me a little. It was "...Dad?" My vision wouldn't focus, and I dimly felt the blood puddling.

"Did you take anything?" he barked. "Are you on something?"

I didn't *think* so, but I couldn't tell for sure. "Help me..."

"I'm trying. For the love of God, I am. Did you take any pills?"

This I suddenly knew was true. No. No pills, not even the ones I was supposed to take. "...No."

Periphery was focusing, slowly. He picked up a dirty T-shirt and bound my wounded hand. It throbbed in time with my heart. He grasped my jaw and made me look at him. Tears snaked from my eyes, errant, unintentional. "What is happening?"

"I can't stop seeing things..." I felt so dizzy.

"Things? Like a hallucination?" He spoke quickly, and when I didn't answer fast enough, he gave me another little shake.

"I don't know."

"Tell me what you saw."

"Flowers..." My vision started to reel again. "...A gun... He thinks I... he thinks I killed him..."

"*Who*?"

"Dmitri... he keeps..." I swallowed, tasting spit and snot. "Help me." Bright red seeped through the pale shirt, and I almost screamed again.

"We have to go," Dad said slowly. "Get your hand stitched. Get you some help. Okay?"

GOODBYE FOR NOW

I'm woken by a few brutal shoves, that hot, jabbing pain behind my eye back and more insistent than ever. Hot, sticky liquid runs down my face.

"You're bleeding like everywhere," Jenna says, her face illuminated by the glow of the *are you still watching?* Screen. She unceremoniously stuffs a dishtowel under my head in an attempt to stop further staining on the couch.

Nosebleeds. I used to get them a lot, as a kid. Really freaked me out, too. I grab the cloth and jam it against my face. Blood always looks more than it is, and the damage seems localized to the pillow I (passed out on) fell asleep on. Peroxide and some Oxy-Clean will fix it, and then Donna from Facebook can come get it, and then–

It takes me a minute to remember why I feel so spun, dizzy. I'm fucking stoned. "Oh... shit... Sorry." I forgot the way Xanax made the world feel like a smokescreen. I used to love that; now I just feel hazy and disconnected and dangerously not real.

"It's not *your* fault," Jenna says. "You want some... juice, or something?"

Unsurprisingly, blood loss is not something my deteriorated vascular system can handle very well. "Probably, ah, should," I say around the towels under my nose. Once at uni I was making dinner and sliced into the tip of my thumb. It only took about ten seconds until I passed out; Kiki had freaked and wanted to call 999. The wound didn't even need stitches. "Dry air, you know."

She shoots me a look that indicates I'm full of bull, but it's not like she can disprove it. Jenna scurries off to retrieve some orange juice, and I sit with my head between my knees, waiting for the flow to stop. Maybe even the Xanax triggered it.

Or I'm just an idiot.

Once the pillowcase is soaking in a peroxide mixture, Jenna exhaustedly puts herself to bed. It's very late. I should try to sleep. Need to sleep, still. Instead, I sit on my bedroom floor, leaning against the frame and staring down the stain on the carpet. While I know no further intervention will help, instead I sit and meticulously scrub at the carpet fibers with a nail brush.

"You're going to burn your fingers," Dmitri informs me. "At least put on some gloves."

I don't feel the pain, the burn of bleach or the sting of peroxide. The numbness has nothing to do with the drugs I took. Some of the residue from my nosebleed has caught in my hair; I can feel it on the side of my cheek, sticky and dry. "You know, in the hospital, they really only clean the area that needs the surgery," I tell him. "They'll wipe you off, but not much more than that."

He sits across from me. He's wearing his "true" spirit form, and I notice his knee is split. Why would anyone want a split knee for an eternity? Then again, I don't exactly like how my "true" form looks either. He remains silent, his face pinched.

The brush *hushes* against the plasticine carpet. "It took me three days to feel strong enough to shower. When I got home, I mean. It all washed out of my hair. Like a horror movie. I hadn't been expecting it."

He picks at spectral fingernails. Is that shame on his face?

"You bet I screamed murder. It was really... theatrical. Dad thought I had fallen, split the stitches, something. He found me naked and surrounded by a bunch of bloody water."

He says, "You remember that much?"

My brush halts. "Of course." He was right, about the chemicals; the tips of my fingers are pinkish and singed. After the effort of heaving myself to a stand, I go to rinse off the products in the bathroom sink.

He admits, "I saw it happen. Do you remember seeing me?"

"...No." That was the brutal moment I became aware of the concept of *flashbacks*. Though trying to see it now, there's just that ominous gap in my memory.

"It's getting worse," Dmitri tells me, unnecessarily. "Aaron, how long–"

"Wednesday," I say. "Let me get through until Wednesday, and then I'll–I'll fucking do it."

"...Wednesday."

"I promised Amanda I would help with the delivery."

He shakes his head. "Do you love her?"

I'm shaking. At some point it got deathly cold in here; the AC must be compensating for the ever-present heatwave.

He leans against the doorframe. "It's because you're starting to have trouble regulating your body temperature. I mean even more so. Your autonomic nervous system is starting to fail."

I want to punch something. "I'm not sure I know what love *is*," I tell him. "And who do I have to fault for that?"

Somehow, he manages to hold eye contact. "I know."

"But I... I want to," I whisper. "I want to know. I think–I think maybe I *could*." Shivering, I grasp my bathrobe and pull it around me.

"You remember AP bio?" Dmitri asks. "The autonomic nervous system. Think. What does that do?"

"You never paid attention anyway," I hiss.

"But *you* did. And the longer this goes on, the more of that I have access to." He holds his hand above my chest. "Those lizard brain functions... breathing. Temperature. Heartbeat." He emphasizes the last word.

"Maybe I don't care if I die."

"I *know* you do."

I want to live. I want to live so, so badly. Even once he's gone, though, I'm terrified that in a sense he will still remain. Scarring me always.

Dmitri kneels near me; I wasn't aware that I sank down. "You have to live," he says. "You promised me you would make this worth it." He wraps his hands around mine, and I swear I *feel* the contact. "Come *on*. Don't give up just yet."

I squeeze my eyes shut, and when I open them, he's gone.

***

Hot sunlight sprawls across my eyes. While I'm technically in bed, I'm more across it than in it, my neck at an awkward angle and wrenching badly. A second *thunk-a-thunk* startles me fully into consciousness. It would not be the first time Jenna woke me because she isn't aware of how much noise she's making. The thumps are followed by something dragging across the upper hall carpet.

Blearily, I check my phone; it's well past noon. Up. I have to get up. There's a text from the realtor requesting a showing next week for a couple "all the way from the city." Yet more messages from Facebook Marketplace. And from some guy to come get the junk that can't be sold, given away, or otherwise donated.

Thunk-a-thunk. Drag. And a distinct yowling.

Gingerly, I stand and cross over to the door. Matt's pushing boxes towards the stairs.

"Uh... hey," I say. "So... what's all this?"

He grunts. His face is red, sweaty, and the boxes skid along the carpet. "Going to bring these down to the car. I've got a friend who could use 'em."

"Use what–bricks?"

He gives the stack another incautious shove, his thin arms visibly straining. "I'm sure she could use bricks also. But no." He rounds the corner facing the stairs and unceremoniously pushes the stack down them. Boxes rain down, and I flinch. "Just clothes."

"Sounds awfully heavy for clothes."

"They're vacuum-sealed. In those packs." He huffs, then swipes at his brow with a red paisley bandanna. "There. Just have to get them in the boot with everything else."

Now that he's no longer standing in the way, I can see the doorway to the guest room. Gone are the piles of stuff; the bed is stripped bare. Rascal, still howling discontentedly, sits within a plastic crate on top of the mattress.

Matt notices me staring and blushes. "About... that."

"...Were you going to tell me you were leaving?" It's not that the sight stirs up something in me; it's that it *should* stir something up in me, but doesn't.

He bites his lip. "I meant to tell you yesterday–but you were dead to the world when I got home. I've got a... new contract. They want me to come out for some training, and then I'll get started right away. It was all very fast." He says this in a rush; I'm not sure how true it is. "That's just how these things go when you're a contractor."

My mind seems to be moving very slowly. "Oh... I just thought..."

Matt waits, his hands knotted behind his back. Rascal keeps complaining.

"...You would stick around until the house was sold. That's all." Like he told me he would. But since when has he kept his word?

He opens his mouth, closes it. "I... I know that. And I still–mean it. You'll still be able to reach me. I have to stay active enough in the company for the insurance."

This could very well be true. I can't jeopardize that.

"I'll be in the northeast corridor anyway, so, not as far as before," he continues, still speaking quickly. "I'm sure I can come by, when... when time allows. If you need a signature."

Everything in me has gone horribly quiet. My fingertips are still numb. "...Sure."

"You're not mad, are you?"

Nobody has ever particularly cared if I'm mad. "...No. Have you... spoken to Jenna?"

He shakes his head. "I will when I leave. If she allows it. We're not quite ready yet. I have to finish packing up Rascal." *Yowl.*

"I'll say goodbye to her." On my puppet strings, I cross over to the small bed in the guest room. The window is cracked open despite August heat, bringing with it a waft of humid air against dusty curtains.

When she sees me, Rascal meows a little louder, pressing her paws against the side of the carrier in a weak bid for freedom. I undo the latch, reaching my hand in to pet her scraggly head. Odds are I will not see Rascal again alive. "Stay cool, grandma girl."

She licks me with a particularly drippy tongue, her cloudy eyes meeting mine with perhaps an understanding. I know Matt will take good care of her. It's pretty much the only thing I can guarantee from him. I kiss my fingertips and scratch the underside of Rascal's chin.

Downstairs, Matt's moved the pile of boxes from the base of the stairs, the door wide open. I think this is how I will always see him, always glancing over his shoulder; one eye, one foot out the door.

Over the course of my breakfast, I watch him remove his remaining things. The smartwatch on the kitchen counter. The odd mug. The cat's litterbox. Jenna emerges from the pool long enough to cram a hasty sandwich down her gullet and see if I want to go out to the bookstore later.

I follow Matt and the cat out to the car. "Where are you going?"

He pats the roof of the red Subaru. "I'm going to stay with the friend who needs these first. Then, go pick my truck up. I'm used to living in the cabin."

I know I should say something else. But there's not quite anything left to say.

Matt clears his throat. "The ghost. The... boy. You deal with it, okay? Don't... don't do it alone."

How else am I supposed to do it?

"There's more people than us that are haunted. There has to be power in that."

Power. Sure.

He hesitates, then says, "it's okay to let go."

"Was it so hard for you?"

His sky-eyes glimmer. He watches the horizon for a moment. "I wish it had been harder." He squeezes my shoulder, once. "Take care of yourself." As he goes to get in the car, I'm surprised to see Jenna emerge.

She's a bit sunburnt, her hair slicked back from her face, the under-cut jutting out brilliantly. "Can I talk to him? Alone?"

"Do you need me to–" I begin, but she cuts me off.

"No."

And while it's probably a bad idea, I back off, instead observing them warily through the small window in Dad's old office. Jenna talks at him for what feels like ages; through the gauzy curtain, it's hard to see Matt's face. He says something. She shakes her head once, again; he says something else, then rests his hand on her shoulder. Jenna doesn't cringe away; her shoulders are folded in. She gives him a hasty hug, then lets go, stares at him, and darts up the front steps and pounds loudly up to her room.

Matt stares up at the house and I think he says something else, but he just shakes his head, secures Rascal in the car, and drives off a final time.

A cigarette later, I find Jenna huddled on the sole remaining beach chair in the yard. She's texting someone relentlessly, and when she sees me, she quickly puts her phone away.

"...So, what was that about?" I ask her.

Jenna pulls her knees up onto the chair, and for a moment, her hands are still. "I guess I just figure... you never know," she signs. "I'm–I haven't forgiven him. I feel like..." Here she falters. "Even if he never gets it, at least I got to say goodbye on my own terms. Eleni... Eleni told me what happened when her mom died, and then Dad... I just know I'd always wonder."

"That was very mature of you."

She shrugs. "I'm just oozing maturity. Is he really... gone?"

"For now. Yes."

She swallows and blinks wetness out of her eyes. "As long as *you* don't go anywhere."

"I'm not planning on it." And God, I wish that will be true.

***

Sunday evening, I take Jenna back to her train, the Facebook person picks up the couch (and doesn't notice the hasty stain job), and I sit in a lawn chair in the barren living room, TV perched on a plastic tote. Even after vacuuming, the lines where the furniture lived are stark as scars. I smoke, slowly, the screen door open to vent the smoke. Dad's urn watches me warily from the kitchen counter.

Earlier in the day, Leah texted me regarding tomorrow's delivery, normal-seeming stuff about addresses and costs, and I responded in kind. Only now, some hours later, does she add, *do you have this all in hand?*

I'm not sure what she means. *We've been before. It'll be fine, so long as there's no rain this time.*

I see the flickering dots, then, *have you seen him since? Have you made any progress?*

Progress. All I have are my half-shattered memories. *Some. Yes.*

I want to get you on the books. I don't like this lingering over you. Call it a gut feeling. Can you come in Wednesday?

To not agree would be senseless.

She adds, *let me help you.*

I feel I've already admitted too much. But this is what Leah does—this is her *job. I'll try.*

If I survive until Wednesday, then I will grieve and panic over what to do next. For now, though, with my shiny new sketchbook on my lap, I etch strikes into the smooth paper with a soft, cheap pastel.

Hush hush; green stalks gradually emerge on the pale cream. A petal, then another, and another. Baby pink and hints of yellow, the deception of creating white in a piece of art. On a tablet I can select these colors with a HEX value. Pastels must be blended, leaving my fingertips covered in splotches. These flowers, at least, won't die.

If I die, it will gut Jenna. She's already having enough trouble dealing with Dad's death, and he had a complex and thought-out death plan. If I die right here, right now, chances are nobody will know for weeks. Unless I walk out to Leah's and tell her what to do with my body.

I set the drawing of peonies aside, careful not to smudge the topmost layer. I found an old frame of Gran's that will be perfect, a soft rose gold. Amanda probably won't find what I've written on the back for a while, if at all.

On a clean sheet of the sketchbook, with one of the very heavy and official pens I found in Dad's desk when I emptied it out, I outline a plan. Just in case. I sign the paper and fold it up very small, cramming it into my wallet behind an old Oyster card and an alcohol prep pad.

BEST LAID PLANS

At first, Tuesday threatens to mirror our last delivery; violent rain beat the windows for most of the previous night, loud and unavoidable given that my bedroom is now sans curtains. I watch the sun rise as a hot red ruby, tie back my hair behind an old bandanna, retrieve Amanda's gift, and lock up my mostly-empty house. After the junk guys come, the little that still belongs to Jenna and me will end up in a storage unit outside of Red Hook.

Despite a thermometer already threatening to crack ninety before it's fully light out, I remain bone-cold, the tips of my fingers and half my palms numb. Because I don't trust my stomach, I sip on a chocolate protein shake that tastes like chalk.

Today I will work and be happy for her. Tomorrow... I can't know for sure.

Amanda is already waiting for me outside the front of the shop, wearing a French braid and a careworn Paramore shirt. Without lipstick or gloss, the scar above her upper lip is even more silvery and stark; it curls upwards when she sees me, her smile accompanied by something like concern. She has a canvas bag slung over one shoulder.

Despite exhaustion already sucking at my toes, I try to be cheerful. "Happy birthday!"

"Gee—you remembered?"

I pull her into an embrace, smelling her usual perfume and a rose-mary tinge. "'Course. How could I forget? Your present is in the car." When I kiss her, her lips are cold to the touch. I'm not sure if it's her or me.

Amanda leans heavily against my shoulder; I almost stumble under the weight of it. She breathes me in.

"Is everything okay?" I ask her.

When she pulls away, her eyes are dark and downcast, shoulders pulling forward. "It... it will be," she says. "I'll tell you later. Right now I really just want to go."

I wonder what could have possibly happened. Something with her aunt? Something gone wrong with Leah, or her other job? Or something worse altogether? I brush my fingers across her cheek, feel her lean into the touch. "You sure you're alright?"

Amanda blinks quickly, her eyes flitting around. "I'm okay. Enough."

There's so much about her I don't know. Before I can stomach that, she tugs gently on my hand towards the Honda, which I've street-parked given the early hour.

She slumps into the passenger seat. "I need *coffee*."

"Not much sleep?"

She shrugs and starts playing with the end of her braid.

Steering us towards the highway, I dig within my ever-depleting well and try to be sanguine. "Come on, lighten up. We're going to spend the whole *day* together. Kind of like a date, if you think about it."

"Sure… a date." She fiddles with the FM knob on the radio. "I don't know how you survive without Bluetooth."

"I've literally never driven a vehicle *with* it."

Eventually, she finds a radio station playing at least listenable music. After fueling up and getting some coffee and snacks, she leans back in the passenger seat and closes her eyes. At first, the rise and fall of her chest is a bit too regular for me to buy that she's just taking a nap, but eventually she starts snoring softly.

This ominous *news* shouldn't put a pit of dread in my stomach. I have to trust that she's mature enough to say what she means; and while I know intellectually she *will*, because she's Amanda and she's *normal*, still the fear hesitates.

It occurs to me that, should we keep going, should we do the whole boyfriend-girlfriend thing like for real, I'm going to have to unlearn a whole bunch of coping strategies I picked up with him. Unlearn and heal trauma responses. That will be lengthy and exhausting and frankly I don't know that I'm worth it. For her, she has nothing to gain; I'm sickly, unemployed, and reliant on an inheritance which will be pretty sparse once the IRS takes their cut. She doesn't need another thing to take care of.

Amanda bites her lip, causing that silvery scar to pucker a little. "You remember how I told you I was saving?"

"Yeah. 'Course."

"I wanted to… buy a van. One of those Sprinter ones, or like it. I want to mod the crap out of it and then…" Her expression becomes sheepish. "I don't mean to be like, one of those obnoxious vanlife vloggers. I just wanted to travel around, see what's worth seeing, and meet other people… like you."

She's been so staid and solid for so long that it does surprise me, at first. But I can understand her wanderlust; Amanda never got to go away from our small hometown for very long. "I think that's a great idea!"

She shakes her head. "Except it's not going to happen now."

"...Why not?"

"I was kind of relying on having a remote job to support myself." Her hands squeeze and release the steering wheel a few times. "They laid me off yesterday. Along with a bunch of other people. Financial problems."

"Holy shit, I'm so sorry." She also alluded to that being her source of health insurance. God bless the fucking USA.

"I can... probably scrape by with what I make with Leah. No idea how I'm going to cover my meds once my savings run dry." Amanda blinks quickly. "They couldn't even wait until September to give me the extra month's coverage. I was torturing myself last night pricing marketplace plans. I'm so–*tired* of working hard and nothing coming of it."

"I'm sure you can find a better job. You're–I mean, you're awesome. Look at all the shit you can do."

She smiles wryly, then sobers. "Aaron, I say this with all the love in my heart, but have you even looked at a job application recently? And I don't mean for like, bullshit part time work. Do you even have a LinkedIn?"

"I logged in once," I protest weakly.

"It's–it sucks. I'll still try. I have no choice but to try."

Maybe I've been spared the hell that was corporate life, but I also know very well how exhausting it is to have to try when giving up seems the most appealing. I tug on her hand and hold it close. There are some faint scars here, too, eyelash pinpricks along her veins. "I guess... well... one way to look at it is it's a new beginning. Only up from here."

She snorts. "You don't believe that."

"Well, maybe I do."

She's silent for a moment, her face crimping further. "Where do... we fall into that? You said you weren't going back overseas. Did you mean it?"

I swallow and feel more acutely the sweat gathering under my arms. The knot in my stomach still won't ease up. "Yeah. I did. Do, I mean. I... I want to figure out *us*." A few itchy, achy heartbeats. "But, shit, Amanda, that's probably really going to suck for you."

"For *me*?"

"I'm not used to being with someone... *kind*." I have to look away from her, out at the puffy clouds in the sky. "I'm basically going to be like the equivalent of a nervous shelter dog until I get it together."

"Maybe I don't care." She hesitates, then, "Well, I do care. Yes, it *does* suck. But you can't control your trauma any more than I can control my shitty boss or having gotten cancer. I don't *know* what exactly things will look like. I-I... I think it's worth it to at least try."

My throat is full of cotton. "Yeah. Yeah, it is."

***

We get to the farm without further incident. Greta isn't there to welcome us; instead Bill, the farmhand, takes care of the purchase and loads the car. She did leave a card for Amanda, though, on what looked to be homemade paper, that Amanda quickly skims, blushes, and stows away in the pocket of her leggings. She refuses to elaborate on the matter when prodded.

We have a nice, quiet lunch at a little local place that could've fit in on the seaside, the heaviness of the morning dissipating at last. I'm starting to feel more hopeful, even if the fish and chips feel leaden in my gullet.

Back in Poughkeepsie, the sun now cresting down towards the horizon and hinting at fall, Amanda guides me back down side streets to the pitiful entrance that served as their "loading dock." My hands are somewhat numb as I pass her the crates, herbs tickling my skin in a way that is at first pleasant, but then very quickly is nauseating.

Leah comes down the basement stairs and starts inventorying what we've brought. "How did it go?"

"Nothing really happened. Greta... Greta wanted me to pass this along to you." Amanda passes her the note, which Leah reads, then frowns.

I straighten, wincing at a crick in my back. The knives-in-stomach feeling has not much gone away; last thing I needed is another bloody flare. My vision swims. "What does it say?"

Amanda and Leah look at each other for a moment.

The sudden surge of nerves gives me another unpleasant cardio-vascular flutter. It would be downright stupid to assume the note was about me. Wouldn't it?

Leah stares at me a long time. She considers, then considers again. "It's about you."

I can still feel the rosemary and thyme oil on my arms. It itches. My mouth is watering in that pre-vomit way. I swear I feel the plants crawling up my arms. I look at my forearms; sweaty but devoid of plant matter.

Leah, her brows drawn tight with concern, takes another small step towards me. "Aaron. Are you–"

The urge passes from "urgent but manageable" to "should've dealt with it earlier, 5head." Before I can even think about finding a bathroom or trashcan, I puke onto the concrete basement floor. My mouth is flooded with copper and acid and a scratching horror, and when I open my eyes, a perfectly formed hydrangea petal is sitting in what looks like a pool of red coffee grounds. "I'm sorry... I'll clean it up... I–"

The itching in my arms crawls up across my back and settles in my chest, my already rebellious heart choosing that moment precisely to squeeze hard in a single, unending moment of agony.

Leah's arm is around my shoulder. Everything is both so numb and blisteringly painful, the vines finding new places to burrow deep–my right thigh, the space behind my eyes. I can't bring air into my lungs. She spits at Amanda– "get the emergency kit. Go!" My vision renders down into blurs. I remember this, I know how this feels, the dull prelude to death.

Leah eases me down onto the ground. The scratching, gnawing sensation is only getting worse.

"Leah–" It's not even a whimper, a squeak. "Leah, what's–"

She reaches for something tucked in her blouse; a small phial with clear liquid. She rubs some onto her fingertip and then across my forehead. "Aaron..."

I want to tear my skin off, and yet a numbness is replacing the pain, fuller, more complete than before. The thorns have wrapped around all my organs and bitten in. I can't even scream. Can't gasp.

Thunking footsteps, Amanda's face in hazy basement light. "What's happening?"

"He hasn't dealt with the attachment. Too much contact with the sacrament advanced the process–"

"What are you–"

"Call 911. I'm not sure what they could do, but–" Leah jabs a needle into my numb arm, rubs furiously. "Aaron. Stay."

All the efforts I took to bind to myself are failing. The vines, as they bite, are freeing me. I don't remember this. I don't remember it hurting so much. I thought–

The world turns inside out. I die, again.

***

My spirit is heavy, like concrete. You lift me up, arm around my chest, my head flopping against your shoulder. "Aaron. Wake *up.*"

Sharp flashing forces my eyes open all the way. The *colors*–this must be–

"Focus. We're running out of time."

You weave your fingers through my hair and force me to look through the

Shimmering great chasm gap stardust too much too much too–

"Dmitri–"

You huff. "You had to do it your way, didn't you? Look. Look at it."

Everything is white-hot. I can see, see through the chasm, the horrible puppet of my body, the brilliance of Amanda's and Leah's spirits. Amanda compresses my chest, once, again, again. I think she's begging. "...No..."

"We have to go *now,*" you say. "If there's any hope–"

"Why am I so dizzy?" I stutter. "Oh, god..."

"Because you're trying to be in two places at once. I should've known–all those fucking herbs–" You huff. Your face won't come fully into focus. "Aaron."

That's me. That's my name. Two syllables accounting for whatever I could hope to be. "Why is it scary?"

"Are you even *listening?*" you ask. "Aaron. Come on."

The shimmering/glowing/all-encompassing veil finely parts, sparkles of light lining a corridor for us. For me.

You squeeze my arm, and a shudder passes through what remains of me. "Go. Aaron. Go, now."

I glance through the dancing veil. I see Amanda, working over my body; Leah, hands clasped, maybe praying. "I'm so sorry," I murmur. And I start down the diamond-glimmering path.

HERE AND NOW

"**D**o you believe in God?"

We've been walking what feels like ages. Being dead and all, I can move without much trouble. I forgot how it feels to move without effort, without calculating the cost of every step. It occurs to me more than once that you're leading me off the path, off of where I am "meant" to go. "What do you mean?" I ask.

All around us, more pieces, memories, chains, flicker up in crystalline bursts. I barely bother to look at them. They align and realign themselves in my memory.

"You've seen all this. Do you still believe in God?"

I glance off the path, which I've only done in gasps. There's more out there, more burning spirits lingering in the ether, separated only by the sticky, gleaming barrier. "Well, there's something after this, isn't there?"

"...So I've been told."

"So I don't *really* know what happens after people die. It could be–anything."

"That's not really an answer."

I am weirdly above feeling, the rampant terror having faded with each step. I wonder if this is the sense of "empty, at peace" Fitzl always tried to instill in me. "Something has to have made all this. It's too horrifying to imagine *this* just happened randomly. Do I believe in a Christian God? Not really."

You snort. "Ain't nothing less Christian than a true believer."

"What do *you* believe?"

This pulls you up short. "I think I'm going to hell," you say, matter of factly. "If you survive this and return topside, well, that's the end of my road. I've got to pay for what I've done. I have to believe that karma evens out. Especially here."

"You think an eternity of torment is worth what you did to me?"

"I have to hope it's not *for eternity*," you tell me. "But yeah, a little, you know, spiders-in-the-eyes is a low price. I tried to kill you."

There's a weird pulse, in the path, like we've stepped on live wires. The path begins to widen, give way, shards of grass forming from the weird not-quite-matter we've been walking on.

I know this grass, know how it felt under my hands, because there was no snow, *there was never any snow*—

"Aaron," you say. I feel more acutely the weight of the binding between us, suffocating. "Aaron, you have to."

I have my incomplete, inaccurate account of events. I can wax poetic about that day, how I knew you were going to do it, how I made it through the snow and bound the first wound you gave yourself and you shot me in a fit of hypoxia because I ruined your plans. That's even mostly true.

But it is not *fully* the truth.

The light weaves and bends into approximations of that day. It hangs a scarf around my neck and fills my mouth with the scent of gasoline.

You stand in front of me, your eye missing, your jacket spattered with spectral gore. "So what happened?"

Clarity should be an incredible relief. To have all that uncertainty being washed away should be a vindicating experience. But when the worst day of my life cracks open, leaking its viscera across my bony palms, all I feel is guilt.

I didn't kill you.

I didn't put the gun in your hand and pull the trigger once, twice, three times.

But I did let you die.

THE LAST PIECE

Heavy, leaden, humid air split the insides of my lungs. At the time you'd indicated, I got out of the car. Despite always being late yourself, you hated tardiness.

Brown, mouldering leaves left from the hot winter covered the path. I waded through them. You'd made your preludes to me ever since last March; as far as I knew, this was another pitiful attempt to mend what was so horribly broken, to save face. That was exactly what I thought, at least, until I heard the first gunshot.

I did not tie the action to you, not at first; I assumed it was an irresponsible hunter and froze, my heart slippery in my chest. "--Hello?"

Through the dry and musty grass, I heard a plaintive wail. "*Aaron.*"

My veins geysered with panic, smooth and smarting. I dashed up the path towards the barn, my mind already cutting the scene into pieces, the whole already too much to handle at once–

Charcoal remnants of a fire;

The shiny silver revolver, still smoking a little, the rest of its clip still pregnant with violence;

Blood smeared across your face, with yet more blood pouring from a wound on your side. Your left hand cradled it awkwardly.

"Who did this?" I gasped. "Where did—" My eyes, not quite working right from the shock, catch the revolver again, not far from your right hand, the same one I've seen mounted on the wall in your house.

I stumbled back, the animal need to *run* almost taking over entirely. "H-How?"

You coughed, your chest heaving. "Has a hell of a kick."

I couldn't catch my breath either. I swore I felt each capillary as my heart thrummed *danger*. "You brought me here–to–*watch?*" Fury. Fury was easier than fear; I grappled for it, not quite reaching it.

"I brought you here... you..." Another, wetter cough. "I don't know. You weren't–I wasn't supposed to *miss–*"

I was still at least ten feet away from you. Before I could fully comprehend what I was doing, I surged towards it, to kick it further away, but you seemed to intuit what I was trying to do and seized it with your free hand. "You can't be *fucking* serious right now."

You held it there, trembling, not quite aiming it at either of us.

"Put it down."

Sweat gathered along your brow, making the blood on your face misty and pink.

"Dmitri." I could taste the inside of my throat. "Put it down."

There was a decision in your eyes. Hot.

You raised the pistol–

I froze, waiting for the bite, the punch, of pain, my muscles screwed up tight.

In the dull light, your fingers shook, half on the trigger. "You... you really thought... I was going to..."

"W-weren't you?"

"I don't *know*," you moaned, and before I could unravel myself enough to move, you brought it level to your temple and fired.

It wasn't enough to kill you. I came to understand what the inside of a skull looked like. "Dmitri..." Over the harsh ringing in my ears, our voices were warbled and alien.

Your hand was still shaking. Your other eye could still focus on me. "Don't," you gasped in this horrible, crawling voice. "Don't... save me."

There were two possible interpretations of that phrase. "Don't save me." "Don't, save me."

My system was so boggled with adrenaline that it took sincere effort to unwrap my scarf, cross those few final feet, and wrap it around your bleeding head. "We can—we can fix this—"

"Please. Please." Your skin was becoming horribly ashen.

"Hold on. Just... a little while longer, please—"

Hot metal rested on my thigh. I reached for my phone—

The thing about sudden, extreme pain is that your body can't quite comprehend it. Our minds aren't meant to take in that many stimuli all at once. At first, the novel ripping of muscle and sinew and bone felt no worse than tearing a piece of fabric. I watched it happen more than I felt it, temporary deafness redoubled.

And a wave of heat, wetness; I thought I'd pissed myself until I looked down and saw my lap covered in red.

Weirdly enough, there was still some small cognizant part of me that found the situation interesting, that I might *use it as a reference for art*—

My nerves twisted, burned, dissolved. The pain was so intense I couldn't even scream, but sort of fell back and writhed there for a second or two, head spinning. This wasn't happening. Isn't. I was at home and alive and *this is how it happened*—

Except my recollection of events has me crawl away and call 911 and make myself a tourniquet. I'm just *lying* there. Why am I just *lying* there?

"Oh, shit," you hiss, at my side.

We watch ourselves begin to bleed out.

"You have to help him," you spit. "He can't—he needs you—"

Dizziness rattles me. My past self. My present self. I don't remember this—

I crouch over myself. Eighteen. So young.

I could let it end right now. None of this will ever happen.

I grasp my shoulder and shake. The body stirred, hesitant, so *cold*. "It's not time yet."

For the first time I understand the weight of the debt. You tied us together so you could bring me here, now, so I could save myself, *then*.

Then-Me coughs. Hacks. Trembles from shock. We watch as your spirit claws its way out of your body. Then-You appraised me. "Oh *shit*. Did I—"

I feel all the bindings in and around us, squeezing me like corset strings. Then-Me wastes precious seconds staring at him. "You have to leave him," I tell me. "You have to go. You have to call for help."

"But he—"

"It's too late."

"I was too late."

"No. No, this is not your fault. It was never our fault." I can't quite feel our skin. "Go. Get help."

Half-spun with shock, I watch myself call for help, watch myself bind up my wounds. Watch myself bleed anyway. My child self lays trembling and delirious and thinking of dolls.

My heart doesn't stop until the paramedics arrive on site. As I wasn't conscious the first time it happened, I don't know what they look like, what they did, how they reacted. All I know is that I die, and when I die, you—it was always one you—takes my younger self's hand.

"Aaron," you say. "Aaron, it's going to be okay."

Then-me's eyes flitter around. "What's *happening?*"

Are those tears, on your face? "I need you to promise me something."

He looks at his hands, our bloody bodies. "Are we—did we—"

"This is important. I need you not to forgive me."

"*What?*"

"I did this to you. I meant it." You squeeze harder. "*Don't* let me off easy."

"*You* did this?"

"I'll take the pain—I'll take everything—and by god this time I will do it right. *Promise* me."

His eyes are so shiny. So young. "You killed me?"

"Oh, love. This was only ever going to end one way."

A cool wind stirs the hair across his face.

"Promise me." It's almost beseeching, almost prayer. "You still have to live. You have to try to go back."

He looks to me. We stare at each other.

He wants my permission.

"You have to," I whisper.

He swallows. "Okay. I promise."

The moment slows. Coalesces. The barn begins to fade from view, and with it, my younger self.

I hold the bindings between my fingers like a cat's cradle.

We're not quite anywhere now, you and I. This place is half-night, half-nowhere. What it does feel is peaceful.

"Play a game with me," I tell you.

In your true form, you let me wrap the yarn around your fingers. It is soft. Light. Pliable.

Your voice is gruff when you say, "You see why I couldn't tell you?"

"I gotta say I wasn't expecting *that*." Knots slip away. "Is that–technically–time travel?"

"God, no." Your fingers are callused, soft. They feel real to me. "No, I can't say there's any science behind any of this. But there's one thing you didn't understand yet."

I pause. "Of course there is."

"Not like *that,* dummy. You saved yourself then."

"So?"

"And you just did it now."

"Okay?"

"So there's something for you to return to," he says slowly. "A sort of loophole."

The yarn glows softly. What it must be like to crochet with this.

"You did it." The knots dissipate, slacken, and I'm left with one closed loop, knotted at one end.

I don't feel as though I've won. This is not something to win.

You're starting to dull, fade, at the edges. "Ah. There's my cue."

"This is just it?" I ask. "You go, I go back? That's it?"

You laugh a little. "What were you expecting?" With your fading hands, you close my fingers around the loop. "Don't let this go to waste, Aaron. I... you don't know how sorry I am."

"You're right. I don't."

Your fingers brush my cheek. They have the weight of tears. "No. No, don't cry."

This is it. This is the moment I walk away.

"Maybe... maybe someday I'll see you again, and this will all just be a sad story," you say.

"No," I say. "For me, this is it. That's all, Dmitri. That's all you get."

You look almost proud. "Okay."

It still hurts. Part of this will always still hurt.

You are starting to melt away, beyond the void and the thin web of memory that has rebuilt. "Buck up, buttercup. It's going to be a beautiful day."

My fingers fold around the knot, and pull.

***

Back through the sticky membrane, I return to my body alone. Leah sees me emerge first. "So you did it, then?"

I nod, brusquely. "Is my body alive?"

"We're working on it," Leah says. "Remind me to lecture you when this *isn't* a medical emergency."

Amanda, still in the midst of compressions, hears Leah's half of the conversation, and looks up.

This is the part I was dreading.

Her hands freeze for a moment, but she resumes her work, her eyes glimmering. "So. That's it?"

"That's it. I'm... I'm sorry."

Her lips twitch. "Is it really you?"

"It's really me."

I lean forward enough to touch her face. I feel the skin, it feels warm, alive. A sensation like gravity is starting to overtake me. For a moment she wraps her arms around what she can see of my spirit. "I have to, um, I have to go."

Returning to my body feels like falling asleep. Dreamless.

AFTER

This is what they don't tell us about CPR on TV—doing it *right* usually means breaking a few ribs. Amanda fractured three while saving my life. Unexplained cardiac arrest, attributed to a severe lack of potassium, a possible genetic component, aggravated by POTS. Et cetera. Check in with a cardiologist, if you can find one. That'll be $10,000.

I have to say that between the two, fractured ribs are a whole lot more annoying than a gaping hole in my leg. I can barely lift my arms high enough to put on a T-shirt. I'm still shimmying one arm into it when Amanda comes back into the hospital room with a tray of coffees (decaf for me for the foreseeable future, RIP).

She exhales heavily. "I should've known you would do that the second I left the room."

"I can dress myself." Through the sleeve; a dull slash of pain. "See?"

Amanda sets down the coffee and touches my face. "You're pale as fuck and shaking."

"But I did it. Didn't I?"

Amanda purses her lips. Her undereyes are swollen with exhaustion. As much as I pleaded with her to go home and sleep, she stuck by my side. TV says you need to be a spouse or relative to stay with someone in the hospital, but this place didn't really seem to care. "You have to *rest*," she stresses. "Button-ups, nothing more than ten pounds. And actually go see the orthopedist about your ribs."

"…If I can find one."

Her gaze kisses mine, then stares out the open door at all the newness she must be seeing. Spirits.

I stroke her forearms. "You need sleep."

"I'm not sure I can," she confesses. "Aaron, you never said it's *so much*–"

Guilt sticks in my throat. "I'm so sorry." I can't cry. Crying will make my ribs spasm. "Amanda. I really didn't think–"

She presses her finger against my lips. "I still haven't forgiven you for not telling me. But… Aaron, I don't blame you for *this*." She looks away from the hallway. "I guess at some point, be careful what you wish for."

I take both her hands in mine. "You'll get to it. You just need to take the medicine as it comes."

She sniffles, her facade cracking a little. "I held your spirit in my arms," she whispers. "I… I *saw* you."

Another sliver of pain in my chest. "I know."

"I saw you, and you were so beautiful, and it was so–*fucked* up."

Oh. So that's how it will end. Understandable. "I'm sorry."

Tears stream down her face. "You have to trust me," she says thickly. "I… I really care for you. I might even love you. But that can't happen if you don't *trust me*. I need to know these big things. I need you to be here with me."

She loves me. That dulls the pain in my chest. "Will you let me?" I whisper. "Will you let me, after I get better?"

Amanda hugs me, gently this time. "Only if you help me... understand this."

I take her hand and hold it tight, tight. "I will."

She kisses me once, softly. I taste the salt of our tears.

"I'm sorry." I'll never really know how much this hurt her. Even if I've been forgiven to a degree, guilt nearly makes me sick. "I'll... I'll... do better next time."

His words in my mouth. I mean them. I mean them so much it hurts. I *will* do better.

I have to.

***

The doctors don't want to stay home alone. No Jenna, no Matt, Amanda slots herself into the role. Claimed she needed space from her aunt. I told her to take either of the mattresses still left–Jenna's or the guest room's–but that first night she folds herself into my bed, careful not to jostle my injuries.

"There's no one here," she whispers. We watch a tree wave in the moonlight.

"I warded it, but there's not really anyone anyway."

"Do you feel watched?"

"I never really saw it that way outside of him," I admit. "Spirits are just people. Why would they care, usually?"

"My eyes hurt."

"You haven't slept." Just having her near is a comfort. "Relax, Amanda. I'll wake you if anything happens."

The doctors didn't give me any opioids, and my ribs flare with pain a bit. I adjust the ice packs, swallow tylenol, ibuprofen.

I am alone, yet not. Alive, so alive. I burn.

It feels good.

***

The couple who buys my house is only a few years older than me, yuppiesh Brooklyn media types who are very eager to "start their life in the country." They have twin girls with auburn curls and a goldendoodle that takes an immediate shine to me– "A good omen. She usually hates men."

I won't be there when they sign with the realtor. She'll pass them the keys, she'll walk away. But the mother takes a few moments to chat one afternoon before I move out, having come to measure for drapes and furniture. They've all been living on top of each other in a rental, she says. They're looking forward to the space. A real chance to be a family, with the yellow schoolbuses and all.

"I've been really hoping to get into sourdough, now that I'll have a real oven." She has her daughters' curls and big, round glasses on a face that can only be described as twee.

"I have a starter. I can leave you some," I tell her.

I may as well have offered her gold. "What–really? One you made in this house?"

"Oh, yeah."

"Mature?"

"Almost ten years old."

"See–that's how you know this was all meant to be." She looks around, beaming, but then becomes pensive. "You grew up here. Will my kids be happy?"

What a question to ask. "They'll be happy so long as you're happy."

She nods very seriously. "So, where are you going?"

To be determined, really. Charlie said I could stay on his and Nellie's couch until the rest of my money came through and I could afford a room or apartment of my own. It's more than most people are lucky to get. I can't find it in me to be stressed about it. Ever since Dmitri left me–since I've been freed–I feel a sense of peace so deep I can't help but distrust it. At least my way forward is my own.

***

I have no choice but to put Dad in a shopping bag. I wrap him in a blanket. I don't trust putting him into a box. He will not sit in a storage unit, I've decided.

As I'm playing tetris with the stuff in the Honda, I find the rose-gold frame, the wrapping paper torn slightly at the edges.

Amanda calls me from the front door. "I think that's everything. You might want to check, though."

I bring it over to her. "Here. It's for you."

There's a smudge of dust on her nose. "For me?"

"It was your birthday present," I say sheepishly. "Before, uh–"

"You were too busy dying," she says. "Let me guess–a drawing of peonies?"

"How'd you–"

She crosses her arms. "It was on Greta's card. Peonies would signify the beginning of your end. I wonder..." She trails off.

"...What?"

"All these things Greta can sense... I wonder if I could do that, too."

"What, like, see the future?"

She taps the side of her face near her eye. "Put these bad boys to good use."

"I'm sure you *could*. You could do anything."

Amanda looks down. "I kind of wish I had gotten to speak to him."

A warm breeze stirs from up the driveway. "He... he found some sense of resolution," I tell her. "But I'm... I'm so relieved. I can't lie about it." I squeeze the frame a little tighter. "So... this is trash, then?"

"Putting an Aaron Bateson original in the trash? Over my dead body." She takes it from me, and starts laughing. "Sorry."

"No. That was a good one."

Her palm lingers against mine. "I'll meet you at the motel."

My home for the next three days, while Charlie and Nellie were away at their LARP event. They forgot to leave me a key. I could use the peace and quiet. "You're coming with me?"

She shrugs. Not quite blushing. "Do you not want me to?"

"No, I... I do. I think. I'm pretty sure."

Amanda kisses me on my cheek. "Did you... want me to wait for you?"

"I have to do this myself."

She nods. Winks. Then, "I'll miss this place."

"Me too." I touch the banister of the porch. "There will be others."

I wait until she gets into her car and drives off. The doctor, understandably, said no more cigarettes, something I've *mostly* managed to set aside, dealing with sticky nicotine patches and headaches worse than the chest pain ever was. One more, a stale Marlboro I found among the rest of Dad's things, won't kill me.

The smoke flutters on the early fall air, delicate, like filigree.

I look around my blue room one last time, the bone-white stain on the carpet. The empty rooms, echoing with memory, waiting for someone else. I set the small jar of starter on the kitchen counter, breathe deeply, once, and put the keys in the small lockbox out front for the realtor.

And then I walk away.

***

I bring the ashes of my father and my allotted array of things—two suitcases, a backpack, and a carry on—to the local Quality Inn. It occurs to me when I park that I should probably have gotten condoms, and I sit for a minute leaning against the steering wheel and feeling like I've swallowed a bunch of tiny knives.

Before I can make any further decisions, though, I'm startled by a gentle knock on the passenger side window. Amanda, in a honey-suckle-yellow sundress, a bottle of what appears to be champagne in one hand. I'm not really supposed to drink, either; both the meds and possible cardiac complications this early in the game. My ribs are mostly healed. I will probably only always be *mostly* okay.

And then I see the label; sparkling apple juice. She remembered.

I wonder at what point I will get over being treated well. "What's that for?"

"Celebrating." She smiles. "I'm owed a birthday, I think."

I grab the carry on that I will be living out of for the next few days and go to check in. I've never had reason to stay in a motel in my hometown, and the Quality Inn is about as much as you could expect; outdated, unfussy, but clean, with heavy carpeted hallways. Not much different than Dad's facility. My window overlooks the parking lot.

Next to the dingy, single-use coffee machine are two glasses wrapped in paper. Amanda frees them both and pours us both juice, tapping her glass softly against mine. For a moment, we both watch the traffic on the main road pass, a few spirits walking along the sidewalk.

"How do you feel?" she asks me.

"You would think I'd be—sadder." Something about never going home again. "I'm mostly just glad to be over all the paperwork. At least until I have to deal with more estate bullshit."

"Must have felt like a long time coming."

"Not... not quite. I'm unemployed, legally homeless... you think I'd be freaking out."

She rests her head on my shoulder. I catch the jasmine and white tea of her perfume; she must've reapplied. "I can help you. Just like you can help me. I feel... so many things, that aren't mine. Is that normal?"

I only ever felt the gut-punch of other spirits' emotions at really highly charged events—like Jenna's graduation, or concerts, or during certain times of the year like Christmas. "I don't think it's *ab*normal, per se. I... I don't know. I never really got to spend an extended amount of time with someone who also has it."

"Leah said something about everyone's sight having its own nuance," she murmurs. "And I was like, what the absolute fuck does that mean?"

"Maybe there's more magic to it than Leah likes to pretend. You've been part of this community. Maybe it's time to start tapping into it."

"What, like make a support group? "Mediums Anonymous"?" She raises an eyebrow.

"I don't know. I just know that without people like Greta and Leah I'd still be up shit's creek. Worth thinking about. We could at least make a Facebook group or a Discord or something."

She softens. "Yeah. Yeah, I kind of like that."

We sip our juice in a companionable silence, watching all the people go by. When the cups are empty, we sort of lean against each other. My skin feels like it's buzzing where it touches hers.

"I... I didn't come here with any expectations," she murmurs. "I wanted to... to spend time with you. That's all."

I brush my fingers against her face, feel her shudder. "I know. But what if–"

And then we're kissing, the sort of kiss that feels like fire, like unravelling, and I learn that with her, it's safe to let go.

***

The day and night unfold; we have to stop, often, so I can rest, my heart still trying to figure out how to work properly. To her credit, she doesn't make me feel bad or even embarrassed.

She shows me the scar on her abdomen, the one that wasn't there the last time we made love. Narrow, white with age, just below her navel. "They scooped me out," she says. "They had to take the bad ovary, and because leaving one meant possible recurrence, I had them take the other. And I figured, while they were in there, and I couldn't use it now *anyway*, I had them take the whole thing."

What did that feel like, to have that possibility–or perhaps the fear of the unwanted–taken away?

"They let me keep it all except the bad ovary, because it went to pathology. I have it in a jar in my room," she tells me. "I'll show you sometime. It's cool." She holds up a fist. "The source of all my problems was like this big."

"That's pretty hardcore," I tell her. "But weren't you... wasn't that hard?"

"Not really. I never wanted to be a mom. I think my mom took it harder than I did." She shrugs. "Honestly, I'm surprised your first thought wasn't, "sweet, she can't get pregnant.""

That honestly didn't even occur to me. Her not mentioning anything about protection should have been a giveaway, if I was thinking at all. "Oh, uh, well, I mean that's a good thing, at least." I considered how *I* would feel if any sense of theoretical fertility was stripped away. My issues are largely genetic; passing that on to a child would simply be cruel. To *know* something like that would not survive me would be a relief. So I could understand to a degree why she wasn't so cut up about it. "You've mentioned a few times... stuff that makes me feel like it was really serious."

Her eyes slip from mine. "Cancer isn't serious enough?"

I level my gaze. "What happened to no more "half-truths"?"

Amanda takes a deep breath; I watch the scar rise and fall on her belly. "*Fine.*" She knots her hands, primly, and traces the ceiling light with her eyes. "I told you how Gina died. That infection..."

I prop myself up on my elbow.

"She *did* die that way, you know. Ended up being pneumonia, her body couldn't fight it. And so on." Her voice catches. "But I got sick in treatment too. My aunt got COVID when she was down in the city. She was always *careful.* Masked, sometimes two–always got the most recent shot. She even said she would forgo seeing her boyfriend while I was in treatment, if that's what it took. She... it made her so sad, to miss him, I said fine, go, just this once."

"That's all it takes," I murmur. "That's how I ended up with POTS."

She blinks quickly. "Well. My body didn't really like *that.* It settled in my lungs. They had to... intubate me, and everything. I wasn't... I wasn't close enough. To get the sight, I mean."

The added context made her obsession with ghosts clearer.

Her eyes flick back and forth, watering. "They told me I wouldn't remember anything, but a few times I... swore I cut through the sedation, or else I maybe *was* leaving my body... And my aunt had left her phone open, this open-ended call with my mom... they kept telling me it was okay to let go. I didn't–*want*–to let go. I know they only meant it because they didn't want me to suffer..."

I take her hand and rub small circles into her wrist.

"I never wanted anything so much as to be alive," she says. "Don't you–don't you think?"

I pull her close to me, breathe in her shampoo and perfume. She clings back almost too hard given my ribs, but I let her. "Yes. I do."

IT'S JUST A BURNING MEMORY

September brings with it an uncharacteristic coolness. That morning, I have one of my father's sweaters wrapped around me. Sometimes the grief is weirdly purifying, like peroxide on a cut; others, it stings so badly I can barely move. It's hard to *accept* depression after fighting it so much. I call my sister at least twice a week, and we talk about him.

I am going somewhere else today. Among the things I found when going through all my old stuff were an old scarf and shirt of Dmitri's, soft with age. Anyone with sense would warn me that going here would only further complicate matters, but Dmitri's gone, and he left me a fail-safe. I made him a promise.

Divorced from memory, the trail and the barn are a quaint curiosity. Fragments of yellow vinyl police tape can still be seen clinging to branches at the head of the path, long torn away by hikers and wildlife. I take a moment to pull free what I can reach.

In typical Dad style, there were two copies of the police file hidden in the bowels of his filing cabinet. One I will hold on to–I'm not sure yet for what–but the other is deceptively thick in the manila folder in my hands. Transcripts of police interviews, photos of the evidence; in a cooler, more interesting story somewhere, maybe they would've thought me a suspect. Hard to suspect me when I never touched the gun. This sort of file is not even uncommon. Someone gets gun, has a crisis, fires. A dime a dozen. Nothing worth legislating about.

The fire pit is still here, and looks relatively recently used. They even left a few logs big enough to sit on. Setting my load down, I gather some twigs and dried grass and tent them in the old ashes, crumpling up bits of the police report to help as tinder. I take the lighter from my pocket, and the 100ml plastic bottle of vodka, and spill it in an arc in the pit. It lights easily.

No; I will not mourn you. I will not forgive you. You will not be some sadly misunderstood woobie. You understood your own lack of redemption. Some things cannot be taken back.

But some things cannot be held on to, either.

When the fire is burning good and hot, I place the remains–the scraps of tape, the scarf and shirt, and the police report–in the center. They fade slowly into the ether. At least you made good on your many, many promises. This time *was* different.

I watch the fire until it burns to ash, then cover the embers with dirt. I look around this place, slowly, the moldering barn, the silvery shards of memory buried here. I already know I will not be coming back.

In the distance, through a copse of trees, an old, fuzzy spirit watches me. I want to say something, to acknowledge them; to ask what holds them here, as well. And then I think I understand. "He's not here anymore."

The spirit pauses, and dissolves into wisps.

Maybe there is something to this, this idea that Amanda had. All I know is that I've been adrift these past four years, carrying a ticking time bomb. If I had someone like this, if I just *understood*, maybe things would've been easier. It could've saved me so much grief. I'm still not good at this–I'm not even fully sure what *this* is.

But I will find out. *We* will find out.

This is how we begin.

CONTENT WARNINGS

This Time Will be Different is the first book in a series about death. Coverage of serious topics is to be expected. Specific content warnings can be found on the next page, which contain some spoilers.

General Content Warnings

Grief, healing from trauma, portrayal of traumatizing experiences, domestic abuse, chronic illness portrayal/exploration, abandonment

Specific Content Warnings

Domestic Abuse

Controlling behavior, up to and including isolation of a partner; partner threatening to kill or otherwise harm themselves, shown on page; physical violence (including hands-on contact and gun violence, both of which are portrayed on page); coming to terms with abuse without forgiving the abuser.

Grief

Loss of a parent, shown on page; loss of an abuser, shown on page; loss of bodily autonomy, shown on page

Abandonment

Parental abandonment, explored and discussed on page

Chronic Illness Portrayal

Aaron has POTS (Postural Orthostatic Tachycardia Syndrome). This permeates every aspect of his life and is shown and discussed in-universe.

Amanda is a cancer survivor. To a lesser degree, this is discussed.

Acknowledgements

Veilside has been a passion project of mine for many years, through many (many, many) iterations.

Firstly, I would like to again thank Indie Author Revolution for their continual advocacy for indie authors, which allow works like this to be published more easily than they might have.

Secondly, I would like to thank my sensitivity readers, Eloise and Brooke, for their careful eyes regarding Aaron's POTS and the nuances of his relationship with Dmitri. Any mistakes I made with those topics are my own.

The cover of this novel was created by Bretnie Shepherd, an incredible artist. You can follow her online on Instagram at @book_smlut and on TikTok at @idgafbitemexoxo.

I owe a debt of gratitude to Michelle, who has read too many versions of this story to count—thanks for not giving up on me.

And as always to Killian, for never giving up on me.

About the Author

Rachel E. Wilder (they/them) is an indie author based in upstate New York. *This Time Will be Different* is their second novel.

Rachel has been writing for nearly twenty years across all genres: literary, fantasy, horror, sci-fi, and more. When not working on writing or promotion, Rachel likes to crochet, bake, hike, and create scripts for very niche video essays that they hope someday to film.

Rachel has a degree in creative writing and a Master's in Library Science, both from public universities.

To connect with the author, follow them on TikTok at @rachel.e.wilder, on Bluesky at @rachel-e-wilder.bsky.social, on Instagram at @rachelewilder, and online at rachelewilder.com.

Other Novels

Heartlines (2025)

www.ingramcontent.com/pod-product-compliance
Lightning Source LLC
Chambersburg PA
CBHW071302140726
47996CB00005B/1601